IS THAT ALL THERE IS?

By the same author:
The Strangled Impulse (1997)
Swansong (2001)
Leaving Ardglass (2008)

Is That All There Is?

WILLIAM KING

THE LILLIPUT PRESS
DUBLIN

ISBN: 978 1 84351 3940

A CIP record for this title is available from The British Library.

10 9 8 7 6 5 4 3 2 1

Typeset by Linden Publishing Services in 11 on 13 point Bembo
Designed by Susan Waine
Printed in Spain by GraphyCems

To Liz M.

'What then?' sang Plato's ghost. 'What then?'
W.B. YEATS

I

AUBURN STANDS on the side of Cooper's Hill and breathes a sense of privilege and old money. Set among trees, the free-standing houses of red brick or granite, with the odd cottage thrown in, compose a picture of comfort and good fortune.

At least that is the impression from high up on Beresford Road. From that vantage-point, the tall chimneys and slated roofs look snug amid beeches, maples and willows that line the sweeping avenues to these fine houses. On a summer's day, a tremulous gleam glides along the tops of the trees and leads the eye to what generations of children have named The Sleeping Giant: a rocky island out in the bay, with an expanse of sloping green sward running towards the village. The trees were planted in the late nineteenth century when Auburn was home to merchants, bankers and a sprinkling of doctors and Protestant civil servants who remained after Ireland had won its independence.

Beresford Road dips down to the village, where once the houses along the harbour, in some cases neglected, snuggled close for protection against the rough seas of winter and the rain that frequently lashed the grey pier. In those days, a few boats reeking of mackerel rose and fell with the sway, while the fishermen drank in the pubs.

Now, the same houses form a row of fashionable restaurants and boutiques facing a forest of yachting masts glistening and bobbing with *attitude* in the marina.

The trees and the long avenues ensure that Sunday strollers on their way around the Head are kept at a distance from Auburn, and, in this way, Auburn people can continue to enjoy the privacy in which they and their ancestors have taken comfort for over a century and a half.

A narrow path, known as The Nuns' Walk, leading towards the Head from Beresford Road by way of a turnstile, borders the gardens on the south side of Auburn, and continues on its winding way upwards. In late spring the hill on each side of the path is a glorious patchwork of yellow gorse; in May the hedges, laden with the white froth of hawthorn, give off a perfume of summer promise, especially after a shower of rain. The path eventually climbs to the summit of Cooper's Hill and opens to the wide vista of Dublin Bay and the Irish Sea beyond. Here the newly rich now live: television personalities, rock stars and lawyers, who have made fortunes out of the inquiries and tribunals that have been a feature of life in the country for the past number of years.

In summer The Nuns' Walk is lush with fuchsia, meadow-sweet and honeysuckle. It has always been a favourite with young people in love for the first time, and with couples and their children from the cottages and the squat bungalows of the late 1950s that stretch away towards Dublin airport. The builder of that ribbon development, a member of the Knights of St Columbanus, named the estates after Popes – Roncalli, Pacelli and Sarto – and used street names that denoted a deeply Catholic culture: Lourdes, Ave Maria, Assisi.

Then a new generation of residents came together at the time when the same culture began to unravel, and renamed the streets, The Downs, The Elms, and Estuary Boulevard. They wanted, they said, to make a small contribution towards harmony with the Unionist population in the North. 'Show them that we're not a priest-ridden country any longer. Enough trouble up there without adding to it.'

Sometimes the Sunday strollers stop and gape at the tranquil grandeur: the houses with their valleys of slated roofs, and the self-assured chimneystacks looking secure under the protection of the elegant trees. The afternoon quiet, too, suggests that families are out sailing around the Head, perhaps away in France having cheese and wine in a garden where the air is warm and laden with the scent of lavender.

The strollers wallow in the dream of having the whole bouquet: the children attending the convent school, playing hockey and off on skiing holidays during the Easter break. Many of their own parents, by scrimping and saving, had made it to the bungalows from tenement houses deep in the bowels of the city. The strollers themselves have secure jobs: in the city corporation, in teaching or in the civil service. Now they dream of going one better, to a place like Auburn, but they know in their heart and soul they never will.

That was all before the dream became a possibility, before American software giants and pharmaceutical companies arrived in the country. All boats began to rise. Money from Europe provided an open sesame to the bank manager's office: tradesmen became golf-playing developers and left far behind the old order of doctors, dentists and civil engineers.

More restaurants with French and Italian names open up in the village; young women with university degrees come from Poland and Romania to serve those who pull up on the seafront in Mercedes, a concertina of credit cards in their wallets.

Loud money shatters the composure of Auburn. The invaders are loud also on Saturday nights when they break bread into their soup and boast of being 'in the right place at the right time'.

Old Auburn residents retreat behind their curtains, and take some comfort in past glories; they cling to family stories of grandfathers whose draper shops in North Earl Street had been ransacked in the looting after the 1916 Rising. Over afternoon tea, when they glance out with rheumy eyes at The Sleeping Giant – a sight dear to them for generations – they recall great-uncles who had fallen in Flanders Fields, or who had dodged bullets in order to render medical aid to dying British soldiers during the Easter Week attack on the Dublin South Union. One frail woman's father, a coroner, had been compelled to have the baths in Belfast converted into a morgue when the city was bombed in 1941.

Some – those who are growing feeble, who are suffering from macular degeneration, or who have had stents implanted – are ready to loosen their hold, even if they shake their heads at the disruption. Of late they have been anxious. One elderly couple had been tied up and their silver and jewellery taken. Another couple went out one morning to find that their beehives had been destroyed and their herb garden trampled on. So, many of the older generation moved to more secure apartments in Malahide to be near a son or daughter. This, along with a greatly enhanced bank account, was some consolation for leaving their beloved Auburn.

Down near the village, Les Sœurs du Perpétuel-Secours à Lyon, a teaching order of nuns, also sell up: they shuffle into the mini-bus that takes the girls to hockey matches, and retreat to the motherhouse in Rathgar. The house they leave behind was once the home of Jamesy Lennon, the famous Dublin surgeon, who had given the property to the nuns when his only child had taken the veil. Notre Dame du Bois goes to the highest bidder: a television chat show host, who moves in with his boyfriend and two cats.

As soon as the furniture removal vans trundle down the avenues laden with roped mahogany, silver – polished for generations by women from the cottages – and genteel china, the Jeeps, Pajeros and Range Rovers ride in, and join the fever of buying and selling houses. Hot on their heels come men in high visibility jackets and tool belts, pencils perched over their ears. They buy the *Mirror* and the *Star* and twenty Johnny Blue in the village Mace, and line up at the delicatessen counter for baguettes filled with deep-fried everything. The light from a bain-marie reflects their laughing faces as they swap jokes in Polish and Cork accents about conquests the previous night at some bar or nightclub.

In a country now on a merry-go-round, a few of the buyers come from the ribbon developments: men who had worked on the construction of the glass temples along the Liffey quays, close to where their fathers had rolled barrels onto Guinness boats fifty years before.

Following the builders' instructions, the men with the tool belts work long hours and well into the weekends, for which they are highly paid; they install wet rooms, Shaker kitchens, cupboards in sage or cream, kitchen islands of polished granite, and Richmond duel fuel ranges. Some of those who move in have made a killing in computers, security alarms or conveyancing, and are passing each other at the revolving doors of banks with smiles and signed-off loans. Carpets are pulled up and thrown on top of skips where radiators and parts of window frames surface among the fragments of plaster and bricks. Bare floors are sanded and polished until they shine like a convent corridor. When it rains, mud drips from the slow-moving wheels of trucks, leaving behind parallel tracks on Beresford Road.

Older residents in tweeds and box-pleated skirts watch with scorn as their world crumbles about them. When they meet in the Marine Hotel for afternoon tea, they hanker for *the good old days*, like when Maurice Nugent brought home the cup after winning the Irish Open at Fitzwilliam, and Captain St Lawrence kindly made the Castle ballroom available for a celebration.

Nevertheless, once they have exhausted past glories, they turn to the latest mouth-watering house prices from the Property Sections of the newspapers. And those who haven't bequeathed their property to their children pay close attention to the rocketing prices: they have grown weary of rattling around houses too big to manage even with the help of Polish cleaners. So, from time to time, estate agents' signs appear on Beresford Road, and nobody is greatly surprised when one appears advertising the auction of La Salle, a Georgian house, owned by the San Christophe Brothers.

With the collapse in vocations and the loss of others through death or retirement, the Brothers departed, one by one. They handed over their school on the Dublin Road to a board of management who appointed a lay principal. Those Brothers who needed special care were taken to a nursing home.

2

THE APPALLING ACCOUNTS of stabbings and suicides he reads about nearly every day in the newspapers must have worked themselves into Doc Clifford's sleeping life, because he wakes one morning from a strange dream and, staring into the darkness, tries to understand the language of the night.

Over forty years before, Clifford, a medical doctor, moved into Auburn, along with his wife, who was expecting their first child; they lived next door to La Salle and became familiar with the Brothers' comings and goings. At Christmas they exchanged gifts of brandy or whiskey.

Gradually, when the fog in his head clears, his dream takes shape. He is at his old university before it became the National Concert Hall, strolling by the stalls during Freshers' Week, when a weird sight stops him in his tracks. In one of the stalls, black plastic cutouts of human shapes are swinging from a clothesline. He calls to one of the students, hooked up to an iPod; the student is wiggling and rocking in his private world.

'What are they?' Clifford asks.

'What?' the student snaps, removing an earpiece. Frowning, he looks up to where Clifford is pointing. 'Oh,' he shrugs, 'they're just guys who topped themselves this year. And I'll be with them soon.' He replaces the earpiece.

Clifford grabs the student's arm: 'No, you mustn't. Talk to me.' The student breaks loose and runs away, leaving Doc Clifford holding the student's detached arm in the jacket sleeve. 'What's the point?' the student calls back.

Clifford reaches out and presses the light button on the bedside clock. Six-thirty. Another half-hour to doze. Banishing the frightening images, he is drifting off again when he is surprised by a sound like thunder, and shouting that comes crashing in on his drowsy state. His two cocker spaniels are yelping in their kennel. At first he thinks it's another dream until he sits up in the bed and switches on the lamp.

The rattle of gears reverberates in a powerful engine; a throttle is opening up, followed by the crack and crush of foliage, so close it could knock the house down. By force of habit he glances across at his dead wife's bed, empty except for his dressing gown where he'd thrown it the night before, as he always does. Through a chink in the heavy curtains he can make out the bulk of a JCB reversing and turning, causing powerful headlights to sweep over the grounds and the gable wall of La Salle, with its long lunette window.

Wide awake now, he recalls a chance meeting at the auction with the new owners of La Salle, Philip Lalor and his wife, Samantha, who, she tells Clifford, since her college days has never been known as anything else but Sam. With bird-like movements of her head, she was alert to every shade of change in the room, so that their conversation seemed a distraction to her. When the sale began, she was the one – not Philip – who kept outbidding the others, although, he – head and shoulders above her – whispered now and again in her ear.

A few evenings later, while calling in to say goodbye to the Brothers, Clifford stood back when a shining black SUV pulled into the grounds. 'Here come your new neighbours,' the Brother said while Sam, Ray-Bans perched on her blonde hair, was parking beside the flowerbed of Celtic Cross design. Philip, lean as a greyhound, stepped out on the passenger side and, with an open stride, came around to introduce himself. He had an eager handshake.

Their chat was fitful: the difficulties of moving house, parting with neighbours, and getting used to new surroundings. Their teenagers, Dylan and Zara, hop down from the car along with two golden labradors who bound ahead of them. As the kids are making for the front of the house, Philip calls them back, smiling an apology for their lack of courtesy. They endure an introduction – Zara showing her mouth brace when she grins; Dylan in black, with a mop of hair that hangs over his sulky looks.

After a while, Sam begins to fiddle with a measuring tape: a plain signal for Clifford to renew his good wishes, and start to move off just as her BlackBerry rings. She dives into her handbag.

'No!' she flares up. 'No, I will not settle for that, and if you can't do it, then I'll instruct my architect to look elsewhere.'

'Ned,' the Brother calls to Clifford, 'let me walk with you to the gate … No shortage here,' he says out of the side of his mouth; 'they haven't sold their house in Raheny yet. Of course, he's getting plenty of cheap money. A banker – lending managers, they're called – and herself is in advertising.' He chuckles. 'They're doing all right. Still what – mid-forties?'

'In or around.'

Clifford switches off the bedside lamp and opens the curtains. The JCB is shunting and jerking – the headlights sweeping through the bare branches of the trees that line the party hedge, catching the sheen on the ruthless teeth of the digger as they sink into the spot where the Brothers had nursed colour out of the earth each spring.

Just as he is about to disconnect the alarm system under the stairs, his eye falls on his stethoscope and blood pressure sphyg on the wide hall stand where he had left them after returning from his day's work in the clinic. 'Gets me out of the house,' he jokes to his golfing friends at Robin Hill. The clinic in the village had been his until one of his sons took it over, extended the bungalow out into the back garden, and engaged two other doctors – a physiotherapist and a part-time dietician. It suits him to do one day a week: he can keep in contact with patients he has looked after for donkey's years.

After retirement he planned to go on a world tour: a dream shared with his wife. Then she discovered a lump under her arm one morning in the shower, and dismissed it as a cyst. So, apart from the visits of his sons and their families, and golf at Robin Hill, he is alone for the first time in his life. And fearing that he might go to seed – like some of his patients have done after such an upset – he came out of retirement to do locum two days a week: one for his son in the village, the other down in Greystones.

The rising smell of the coffee he has left to brew and the bread he has popped in the toaster revive him while he is stirring porridge. And, following the habit of a lifetime, he lays his diary on the table as he sits down to breakfast. Routine complaints of the previous day cross the screen of his memory: an ingrown toenail, children with coughs, a student worried about a sexually transmitted disease, a young woman looking for the morning-after pill. And the dreaded blood test that might show a positive reading.

While having breakfast, the sharp teeth sinking into the ground take over Clifford's head. In his mind's eye, he pictures one of the Brothers, through the hedge, putting all his bulk on the spade, bending, then raising and shaking out the brittle earth: a ritual that begins each year after St Patrick's Day.

As dawn is breaking over The Sleeping Giant, he takes a cup of coffee to his study and looks across at La Salle. Seagulls are dipping and diving around the JCB in search of an early break-fast. The practised hands of the digger operator work the levers; the bucket rises into the air with a scoop of earth, shunting out of the way the statue of the Virgin Mary and causing it to tilt forward. The next time the teeth don't miss: the statue is hoisted in the metal bucket and is dumped with a thud on the lorry parked alongside. One arm has broken off, leaving a bare rod reaching out for deliverance. With a tip of his shovel against the side of the lorry, a man, trampling all over the Celtic Cross flowerbed, signals to the driver, and the lorry moves off slowly towards the avenue. The statue sways like a drunk as it disappears around the curve of the driveway.

For generations, the Virgin Mary had become the landmark Auburn people gave to their visitors: 'When you see the statue at the front of a big old Georgian house, you're nearly there; we're just around the corner.'

Clifford's wife, while giving directions to house guests over the phone, might say, in a moment of mischief: 'We're next door to the monks' goddess.' Though a lukewarm Catholic – a pavilion member, as she used to describe herself – ever since a priest refused her absolution because she was on the birth control pill – she would have been sorry to see the goddess destroyed.

Thoughts of his wife bring back a memory that has been haunting him since she passed away – the evening he returned from his practice to find her asleep in an armchair with an empty bottle on the low table, and a broken wine glass on the carpet. When he woke her with an offer of coffee, she rounded on him: 'You've a brass neck to lecture me about my drinking habits after you fucking that nurse. Get away from me!'

Over the past two years since her death, he has been holding fast to a routine: locum days, golf days, and visits from his two sons and their families at the weekend. But at times such as this when they would rake over the latest news, he catches himself planning a blow-by-blow account for when she returns to the house, or when they next drive down to the Marine Hotel for a coffee.

He closes his diary and sets off on his morning walk which begins on the path around the side of the house, along The Nuns' Walk, then up to the summit of Cooper's Hill, and finally around to the village for the newspaper.

The JCB engine is idling as he hurries by the back of La Salle. A man in a hard hat is shouting into a mobile phone.

'I need them two fuckers down at the convent in Carlow bright and early tomorrow, to clear out the place. Do you get me, boss?'

Clifford slows his steps.

'No, I'm tellin you, I need that chapel cleared out by Wednesday. We're convertin it into a restaurant. The chippies are after me, so move your arse.'

Raindrops cling to the fuchsia branches; across the bay, The Sleeping Giant is shrouded in mist, but the dogs are delighted with themselves – running ahead and sniffing interesting nooks in the hedgerows.

As he drives to Greystones, his mind wanders from one

patient to the next: those who cannot sleep, or who want something to calm their nerves. The women cry and tell him their deepest fears: 'Do you think, doctor, that our savings will be lost? Or the house?'

'Ah well, it's not that bad.'

'But they're saying that those banks – Fannie Mae and the other one – ours could go the same way in a year or two.'

'As far as I know, that's a problem that's confined to America, those sub-prime loans.'

'I hope you're right. So will you give me something to help – you know – with the sleeping.'

Right through the spring, the Polish workers arrive before dawn at La Salle. Then, all day, until after dark, they shatter the well-bred air of Auburn with the grating sound of concrete saws and the pounding of hammers; pick-up trucks, encrusted with dried cement, are pulling in with fresh lengths of timber, double-glazed windows or Valentia slate. Filling the air with the acrid smell of diesel, the trucks carry off the wooden panels that were used to divide bedrooms when the Brothers were at full strength. The builders winkle out the crest of the Blessed Jean Christophe, founder of La Compagnie de Jésus from over the door, and fill the imprint with plaster, so that by Easter no trace is left, apart from the name of the house, which Sam and Philip consider sufficiently European to retain.

As soon as the Poles have laid cobblestone paving at the front of the house, and built a fountain with a copper statue of Aphrodite where the Virgin Mary once stood, the Lalors move in. Now and again they come across Clifford when they too are walking their dogs up Cooper's Hill, or pacing the harbour wall of a Sunday morning. And they fit into the habit of Auburn where people weave their own social network around one of the schools or the sailing or golf clubs. On weekdays, the newcomers rarely lay eyes on one another except to pass by in their suvs with darkened windows, or soft top Mercs, and when they meet at parties or at the tennis club, they are 'busy, busy, busy', and carry their BlackBerrys everywhere. In addition, the women are run off their feet helping Belvedere College or Goldsmith Park with the latest African project.

On one such walk around the Head when the gorse was saffron, and the coconut-scented air had well and truly broken the back of winter, Clifford runs into Philip and Sam as he is emerging from Moss Lane. Sam is excited about the house-warming they are planning for June, 'but we're not in barbecue weather yet'.

'No. Not for another while. Still a bit of frost at night.'

Their dogs are exploring each other and trotting on ahead. As on previous occasions, Sam is openly demonstrative with her husband: idly picking petals off the gorse and holding up a handful for him to inhale the perfume, and full of enthusiasm about inviting the neighbours over for a barbecue.

When Clifford continues on his way, however, Sam picks at an old sore. Will the women of Auburn, who have had fountains in the back garden since they were children and grandfathers who had clothing shops in North Earl Street, detect that she is not really one of them?

3

WHEN HE ARRIVES into Nat Am on the Monday morning after his chance meeting with Doc Clifford in Moss Lane, Philip spots some of his colleagues having a cup of coffee in the Plaza before the day's business commences. The Plaza is a bright concourse with high palms in terracotta pots and glass panels in the roof. Situated in the middle of the six-storey building, it serves as a meeting place and coffee dock. Among those at the table is Kevin Egan, Philip's best friend since schooldays; best man at his wedding.

'The bubble could burst,' Egan is saying in his teasing way, when Philip brings a cup of coffee and pulls up a chair beside them.

'Oh, come on, Kevin. Don't tell me you've joined the scare-mongerers,' says a woman from HR. 'The Minister put paid to that last year, didn't he? Told them, if that's their attitude, they should get lost or leave the country.'

'So are we learning anything from Northern Rock about reckless lending?' Egan holds out. Thus far the conversation is relaxed and playful until Wheeler, an acolyte of Aengus Sharkey, the bank's CEO, says: 'Nonsense. Our banks are well-financed, and to imply otherwise is downright irresponsible, and it could adversely affect our standing in world markets and with foreign investors.'

Lisa from Customer Service has news that Merrill Lynch is in trouble.

'Merrill Lynch. Jesus!' One of the junior bankers is shocked. 'Can't be.'

'No, it's true.' She had heard it on the BBC that morning. 'And not only that: one or two of the big hitters – AIB, for one – have sold off some of the family silver already, including their headquarters down the road.'

'What?' the junior banker is disbelieving.

'Our neighbours. Sold off their trophy, and laid down a condition that they would have first option on leasing rights. Quite obviously they're afraid of a nose-dive in the market. So they have six hundred million in the sack for lending,' Egan says. 'When the big hitters are doing that, it's time to sit up and take notice.' One of the others adds that an office block out in Santry has been empty for the past two months.

The cold wind of change is the talking point over lunch at Katie's, and in coffee shops on Merrion Road; anxiety is spreading and affecting bank employees, despite the assurances from government ministers about 'the fundamentals being sound'.

Sharkey too had read the newspapers and subsequently talked to his directors; he had overheard words like 'sub-prime' and 'toxic loans' in the mouths of those who wouldn't know one end of a balance sheet from the other. These words now are being tossed around on chat shows, and on the way into work on the DART.

To restore confidence, he calls the section heads to an ad hoc meeting in one of the smaller conference rooms, and brings in Breffni St John Dunleavy, the bank chairman, to address them. The conference room is on the executive floor, where some of the top developers in the country, hoteliers and shopping mall owners are treated to *cordon bleu* cooking, and Domaine Paul Pernot Meursault.

From an old land-owning family in Waterford, proud of its Catholic heritage, St John Dunleavy has a high profile around the Shelbourne Hotel, and the RDS where his family has won many prizes for pedigree cattle. He appears on television, and, from time to time, is featured in the business sections of the national dailies; some had bought his carefully orchestrated spin that he was largely responsible for building up Nat Am from the time when it was a 'basket case'. In truth, Sharkey had done the donkey work, like knocking on debtors' doors and showing no mercy to defaulters. By dint of his headlong determination, Amalgamated, a small merchant bank, became National Amalgamated, and eventually Nat Am.

In his perennial tan, St John Dunleavy is ebullient. He talks up the healthy state of Irish banks. Yes, he had seen the television programmes. 'Nothing more than that little pipsqueak economist has been trotting out for the past couple of years now. Look, my friends, it's as plain as day. We have access to European money – the supply is virtually unlimited. Secondly, the Yanks are here to stay; the pharmaceutical and the computer industries are in good health, and all that guff about bubbles bursting is only another example of the national propensity for pessimism.' And regarding the fact that AIB was selling its headquarters? Well, he explains, that's good business sense. Pure and simple. 'Ladies and gentlemen, many thanks for your time.' He rests his hands on the desk, leans towards them, and in his West British accent endorses 'the lending policy this bank has pursued, which is the envy of other institutions. A policy that is good for the business community, good for our country and good for Nat Am.'

'Hear, hear!' Conrad Brennan, another one of Sharkey's yesman, calls out.

But St John Dunleavy isn't quite finished. 'As a matter of interest,' he says, as if imparting a secret, 'if push comes to shove – I can reveal this to you, since you've been loyal to Nat Am – we on the board are in accord with granting another eight percent in the case of domestic loans, if, say, a couple needs a boost with their mortgage repayments. And, incidentally, give the begrudgers a wide berth. Nat Am will continue to be fitter, leaner and more competitive than our rivals. So my advice to you all is this: keep the naysayers at arm's length, ladies and gentlemen. As the bishop once said on television – "We've become a nation of knockers."' Another round of applause follows.

When Dunleavy leaves the room, Sharkey gives them a pep talk about lending, and finishes by saying: 'And to translate

Breffni into plain speaking: fuck the begrudgers.' Sharkey is well known for his foul language; some, especially those seeking promotion, link it with strength and control, and ape him whenever they can get away with it.

Sitting beside Philip towards the front, Egan joins the applause, but doesn't share their confidence in the market as they chat in groups over coffee served by staff wearing white jackets. Privately, he has fears about the Celtic Tiger, especially when he glances at the property sections and sees that one can buy a villa in France with a tennis court for the same as a house in one of the corporation estates in Dublin. He can see sense in the perky economist's warnings.

Nat Am, however, is not the place to voice such doubts; Egan has seen how Sharkey puts under pressure those who hint at caution, and eventually wedges them out. And, after all, he too has benefited from the bank's low interest loan to buy a fine house on Sandymount Strand. Like the majority of Nat Am personnel, he has availed of the bank's share options, and loans to invest in the Dublin Docklands Development. One day when the price is right, he vows, he will sell his shares and make a killing and, like they do in the City, take early retirement.

Sharkey holds an impromptu meeting of the lending managers in the conference room. 'No need to sit, guys,' he says. 'No matter what rumours you hear, continue to lend.' He pauses and, over his half-lenses, scans the room with a twinkle in his eye. 'Continue to lend. It's as simple as this: if we don't lend, the other fuckers will lend. Our investment portfolio is sound, so gun to tape, guys.' Then, like a football coach, he draws them into a huddle, his arms around the two men who flank him. 'Lookit, guys: sell. Sell everywhere. Rugby clubs, golf clubs, move your asses.' He is getting louder. 'Move your asses, because other fuckers like Anglo, AIB, Bank of Ireland, and Ulster Bank have cottoned on to what we have done for the lending market, and are on our heels. Take your clients to Lansdowne, Croker, Shanahan's. Take them on the fucking Orient Express if you want. If golf is their thing, take them to St Andrews. If they get off on tennis, take them to Wimbledon. No prob about tickets. Uni pals, friends: network, guys, Get out there and fucking network. Continue to hook them in.'

The whole manic performance is troublesome for Egan. Afterwards, he voices his concerns to Philip.

'You're a worrier, Kev' is Philip's response. 'Behind the jokes, you always were. You see dangers that are only in your head. Remember when you were up the creek before exams and you always came out first or thereabouts. Nothing that eighteen holes shouldn't fix. Let's get down to Mount Juliet or the Glen on Saturday.'

'But Bear Stearns – one of the giants in the US. What next?'

'That's America. Europe is still sound.'

Behind his buoyant mood, however, Philip sleeps badly that night. He recalls the early days when Sharkey held a credit committee meeting every Friday at Icarus Hall, a Nat Am mansion in Dawson Street, and tore strips off anyone who couldn't show proof that a loan application was backed by security, cash flow and personal assets. 'On your head be it, if this loan goes belly up,' he used to shout at junior members of the lending teams. 'And check the fucking net worth of every client.' Now the credit committee is being ignored: no talk of net worth or of audited financial statements – the client's word is sufficient.

So, to calm the ferment in his brain, Philip gets in his car the following day at lunch-time and drives to the National Gallery, where his father used to take him and his brother, when they were children. 'This is my oxygen, lads,' his father, a primary teacher, would say when they were going through the front door. His face seemed to look younger. 'Food for the soul.'

In a low voice he would set them a test: 'What do you feel – not think – when you look at that painting? Heart – not head, lads.' After a while he would point out things they had missed, like where the light is shining, the look on certain faces, *why is the beach deserted?* and so on. Why did Hopper paint that woman sitting on her own in the hotel bedroom? Notice the suitcase. *What's he trying to tell us about ourselves?*

It was there too that Philip went with Ellen on a couple of occasions, while the affair had them in its grip. 'This is one place you won't find bankers' was her joke. She had studied at the National College of Art and Design before she joined the bank.

'Why?' he had asked when they were sitting at a table in a dim corner of the coffee dock.

'Why what?'

'Why did you … well … art to banking?'

'Simple. On an art teacher's salary, you can't do Chamonix in January, and you'll have to think twice about getting a bridge done if you lose a tooth.'

That day he has lunch alone in the sunlit restaurant, surrounded by chatter, the rattle of cups, and the grating sound of chairs being pulled up to tables.

While he eats, he scans a gallery brochure, and becomes aware of the rise and fall of conversations. A young woman at the next table is telling a civil-service type about her new Bose home entertainment system. 'Eighteen grand. You should hear the sound from the fucking eight speakers.'

The civil servant nods.

Despite St John Dunleavy's bluster on television, and Sharkey's boasting around town that the bank's loan book is healthy, and that share prices are holding up, the forecasts, like clouds looming over a garden fête, are threatening to call their bluff. With worried looks, bank staff sit at the round tables near the palm trees in the plaza, and exchange pieces of information. Someone's sister, along with her partner, has moved into an estate in Athlone, and half the houses there are still empty after ten months. Someone else, on her way into work, is keeping tabs on an empty office block – which has been like that for ages now. The colours on the estate agent's sign are fading in the sun. She knows of an estate agent who had to close down the Rathmines and Finglas offices.

The News Roundup team, armed with microphones and cameras, is loitering around Nat Am and other banks for a sound bite. Sharkey decides on a pre-emptive strike. 'I'm going to invite them into the foyer before lunch some day. I've talked it over with Breffni,' he tells his cronies. 'I'll be prepared, so they can't ambush me. A few minutes in the foyer. I'll need you guys close by. Looks good. Team-thing, get it?'

The reporter – a woman with thin lips – fires the questions: 'Many say that our banks are lending recklessly.' She thrusts a microphone in front of his face.

'I can tell you categorically: Nat Am does not take risks – absolutely not – and, though I've no right to say this, a similar policy obtains in the other financial institutions in this country. In Nat Am our policy is, and always has been: unless we have assurances of security and cash flow for our loans – and indeed personal assets – no deal. No, Emma,' he beams to the camera, 'we are in robust health, and continue to outperform other banks in this country and abroad. No problem whatever with capitalization, or liquidity. Take it from me, and I've been in the business for longer than I care to remember: the probity of our bank is above question. Hand on heart, I can say that, in general, our bank is serving the Irish people in a responsible manner, and we intend to continue to do that.' He gathers his trench coat about him and smiles. 'Now if you'll excuse me, I've business to attend to.' Afraid to let a big fish get away, the reporter's voice grows shrill; a vein is swelling in her neck: 'Reckless lending, Mr Sharkey, for the Galway Races brigade.'

For a split second, Sharkey loses control, a flash of anger in his beady eyes. He wags his finger in the reporter's face.

'No. Not reckless, but a willingness to support those who are enterprising, who have the courage to launch out. Our bank has been the catalyst for the prosperity that Irish business is now enjoying. We have a policy of responsible lending to those who are the backbone of this country. The fundamentals are sound.'

He composes himself; the Sharkey grin returns. 'We need *can-do* people to drive our economy; we don't need hurlers on the ditch. We need *chutzpah*.'

'Sorry,' he turns again to the camera, 'have to go, Emma. Meeting with a senior member of my staff. He's spearheading a project to help the less fortunate people of Tanzania. *Noblesse oblige*, right?'

When the camera is turned off, and the television crew has left, Brennan and Wheeler applaud. 'Game, set and match, Aengus,' says Wheeler. The three men are laughing as they go through the revolving door.

Sharkey had built up a reputation for helping worthy causes, one of which is Philip's project to provide education for children in Tanzania. Every May, Sharkey organizes a golf classic at Druid's Glen. 'After all, guys – it's only fair to help out a colleague. I mean bloody decent of Philip to put in the time,' he announces in the club one Friday evening while a few of them are planning the event. Those eager to move up the ladder know that by supporting Sharkey's projects, they are showing loyalty – a virtue he prizes above all others.

But 'money down the toilet' is the way he describes helping Africa when he and some of his kitchen cabinet are on their own in the washroom. 'Corrupt bastards out there hijack most of it,' he says while drying his hands. 'Lazy fuckers who won't do an honest day's work. No time for that shit. But, lookit – good optics for Nat Am.' Under strip lighting, he examines his reflection in the mirror and pats the few strands of hair across his scalp. 'No. Give me the American way any time: get off your arse and earn your crust, or else suffer the consequences. For the life of me I can't figure out why Philip would be so naïve. Who does he think he is? Mahatma fucking Gandhi?'

'Seems a favourite uncle, a missionary, was out there for years. Philip used to visit during holidays.'

When they have finished planning the golf classic, like racing punters discussing form they exchange pieces of information on the state of the financial institutions, share prices, and the mood of the market. Sharkey delights in telling stories about those who had started from scratch and now have apartments along the Golden Mile in Marbella, next door to the sheikhs. Men like Flannery, the chief of L&K Merchant Bank, who had begun trading at his own kitchen table. 'Can you get your head around that?' He looks at the others, and opens wide his hands. 'The kitchen table for God's sake. Just the two of them: Jones and himself. *Chutzpah*. Balls to approach the banks for a few million; they lend to farmers and small companies for starters. And give the best rates in town.'

With dancing eyes, he raises his tomato juice in a salute to his heroes: 'Balls of brass. And believe you me,' he adds, rising from the table, 'that's what made the Irish economy in the past ten years. And Flannery has that in spades.' He leans towards them and lowers his voice: 'Get it into your heads: we're the money-makers and fuck those in their ivory towers that give out about us.' He removes a cigar case from his inside pocket, 'Excuse me now while I enjoy one of life's little pleasures.' Chuckling, he holds up a Cuban cigar: 'Even though it was made by the Commies.'

Philip decides to drive home rather than take a taxi like most of the others, so, apart from a glass of wine earlier, he stays with mineral water. He has been keeping an eye on Egan, who, with the passing years, had begun to drink more, and who is sailing close to the wind by venting his own life's frustrations on Sharkey.

Philip had warned him: 'Kev, listen to me. Sharkey is a ruthless bastard. We've both seen how he kicks ass: he'd have no hesitation in giving you the same treatment. This isn't the Bank of Ireland or AIB.'

Sharkey is at peace with the world when he returns. 'And, guys,' he says before he sits down, 'would you believe this? In the early days, it wasn't unusual for him to call a meeting on Christmas Day.' Some bloke objected, saying that this was a day for the family.

'"Right, my man," said Flannery. "You can have all the time you like with your family, because now you are going to go and clean out your desk and fuck off out of here. As far as L&K is concerned, you're history."'

Sharkey circles the group with a shifty eye, and picks up hostile vibes from Egan, who, earlier in the night, had been finding every comment hilarious.

'Has to be done, Kevin; that's business. Shareholders breathing down our necks.'

'An exercise in bullying – that's what it is.'

The temperature drops. Philip begins to stretch. 'Time we were all abed, Kev,' he said. 'C'mon, I'll drop you off on my way back.'

'Unfortunately, that's the way things are, Kevin. In the Piranah pool, the weakest is swallowed up. That's life, guys.' In front of the others, Sharkey affects moderation.

'My arse,' Egan snorts. 'Jumped-up pricks ready to trample on anyone for the sake of their own glory.'

The party talk freezes. Some look away, or drop their heads. Philip can see that Egan is signing his own death warrant.

Suddenly a drunken smile appears on Egan's flushed face; he reaches over to Sharkey and pats him on the back: 'Only having you on, Aengus; no offence. What'll it be?' And with that, he raises his hand and calls over one of the servers.

They stay for one more: Sharkey hardly touching the glass of Ballygowan. The lights have gone out with Egan's salvo, and they are scrambling to effect small talk. 'Right then,' says Sharkey, taking a sip from the glass. 'Thanks for that, Kevin.' He turns to Philip: 'Looking forward to seeing you in action with this new barbecue. Next week?'

'Next Friday.'

When Sharkey stands to go, all follow.

4

Sam's fear that she won't be acceptable to the Auburn women lessens as soon as she begins to throw herself into the house-warming. This she does with the same enthusiasm that is making her career such a success with the advertising company, High Resolution.

Philip has no such baggage, although his father, Seamus, had come from a haberdashery in Killenaule, and had little to recommend him, except being described around the village as 'Killenaule's Tyrone Power'. Philip's mother, a school principal, had nurtured in him and his brother a relaxed sense of coming from good stock. He had heard her stories of her two uncles – the war heroes – who had fought 'for the rights of poor little Catholic Belgium'. Both army captains, they had been assigned to the Connaught Rangers: one was killed in action, the other taken prisoner at Augustabad. Her stories too, of the prize-winning cattle her father reared in his lush fields outside Roscrea had engendered in Philip's mind a relaxed confidence that he was among his own sort at Blackrock College.

For him, the house-warming might serve to advance his position with Nat Am since a few of the guests would come from his banking colleagues, including the chief executive, Sharkey. Despite the boom, the banking world had become a bear pit; no one was secure – especially at Nat Am, where Sharkey was an exception to the banking culture of finding a quiet corner for someone who was not shaping up. 'Keep them on their toes: that's my motto,' Sharkey reminds his staff constantly at the bank. 'Shape up or ship out. In this fucking world, guys, you're only as good as the last loan you nailed down.'

When the guests arrive on the evening of the barbecue, Sam and Philip are out at the front of the house to greet them. In the spacious hall, with its curved stairway, and balcony, are glasses, bottles of wine, whiskey and minerals on small tables. Women from The Auburn Society – as they call themselves – help to serve the drinks. Since their foundation they have devoted themselves to fund-raising for worthy causes, such as drought in Ethiopia, and now Philip's education project in Tanzania. They are also alert to any rezoning in the area, and badgered the city council when they got wind of plans to build low-budget houses in the land vacated by the nuns.

As the guests stand around with glasses in their hands, the spell of exceptionally fine weather and the lovely job Philip and Sam have done to the house serve as openers for their party talk. 'Let's hope,' they say, 'we're not getting our summer this week and then wall-to-wall downpours when the children are on their holidays!'

In a cream linen suit, Sharkey parks his Bentley Continental halfway down the avenue. With him are his 'Eyes and Ears' as they were known around the bank: Wheeler, and Brennan. Of the two, Wheeler is the more junior at Nat Am. He is the son of an insurance broker with whom Sharkey has had the occasional game of golf while they discussed investments in Nat Am. Wheeler's chief desire in life had been to gain a tennis scholar-ship and then go on the circuit. A self-made man, his father wouldn't hear of it, and contrived to meet Sharkey. 'All that seems to be in that young man's head right now are tennis courts and young ladies,' he said over lunch. 'But I've no intention of seeing him become a tennis bum. He has already fathered a child and won't go next or near mother or child.'

Never happier than on a tennis court, Wheeler still nibbles at the dream of winning one of the regional tournaments, even if he is now well into his thirties.

Very soon, BMWs and Volvos, as well as a few Mercs and SUVs, which seem straight out of the showroom, line the avenue. One man, small and stocky, his Leinster rugby shirt stretched across his barrel chest, tells Clifford and the others in the circle about his collision of the previous week. 'A gobshite from Eastern Europe smashed into me. Broadside. Lucky thing my Merc has a side impact protection system, and excellent road-holding.' His listeners nod in sympathy. The gobshite of course had no insurance. Lucky thing he himself had comprehensive. '25k the damage. Keep a whole village in his fucking country for ten years.'

The attention he gains from the side-impact protection system and road-holding of his Kompressor sets him up for a lecture on its overall performance.

'Jeremy Clarkson drove the shit out of it. You know Jeremy,' he laughs. 'Gave it the thumbs up. I went out the day after and traded in.'

In the kitchen, steam is rising from the big cauldrons on the Richmond duel fuel range; the air is filled with the aroma of spices. The Auburn women help Sam to look after her guests: they trip out onto the patio offering titbits, nuts and canapés. The warm sun shines through the beech trees and casts dappled shades on the women's linen dresses. They compliment Sam on her new hairstyle.

Very Hillary.

Very Sam.

One of the women has breaking news: 'Yes, she's back. Got rid of Fergus and looking fabulous – can you believe it? Wearing Paul Costelloe. And guess what? She's been asked to go on *The Restaurant* later in the summer.' She turns to include Philip's mother, Una, who is sitting on one of the wicker chairs. 'You know – the one with Tom Doorley. Great fun.'

'Oh,' says Una, for politeness' sake. 'Yes, I understand. Great.'

More guests arrive with hugs, air-kisses and bottles of champagne. The hallway echoes to the sound of loud conversations spilling out into the kitchen and the lounge. The bright sunshine on the kitchen cupboards and the living room furniture gives the house an air of unreality, as if it is the setting for a play, and the guests and their conversations are characters with a prepared script. The connecting doors are all open, affording free movement: people are chatting in the living room and in the kitchen, and out at the back by the French windows, so that the selection of popular classics and jazz pieces that Sam had programmed in the Bose Sound System goes unheard.

When Sam is satisfied that everything is under control, she leads the Auburns on a grand tour of La Salle. 'Needed a relationship with the garden.' She indicates the double-glazed patio doors, and shows how she has opened up the back of the house to the light.

'Absolutely, it *really, really* works,' says one of the women.

'Well done, Sam.'

'Oh my God. Yes, that works.'

'Now,' says one of Sam's school friends, 'you have to see a lunette window to die for.' She strides ahead to the east side of the house. '*Voilà!*' she says, and waits for the effect to sink in.

'Yes, gosh. Awesome.'

They move on. The lights are Danish; Sam spotted them in a shop during an idle hour in Copenhagen. *Had* to have them.

She takes them right through the upper storey and back downstairs to the dining room. 'House of Ireland,' she says with a sweep of her hand over the dining room suite. 'At a snip.' The tour ends at the spacious kitchen with its ivory oak-painted cupboards, the breakfast room, the white walls and marble floors. 'Natural light,' says Sam, 'only penetrates for six metres, so bright-coloured walls and floors make the light reflect, and give a great sense,' she makes a curving gesture as if her two hands are holding a precious vase. 'Connectedness and positive karma.'

'Yes,' one of the women reflects, 'you know what the house does also? I've just discovered.' They turn towards her. 'It goes out there to the garden, grabs the landscape and brings it right back into the house.'

'What an achievement. Good for you, Sam.' Sam's school friend gives her blessing to the finished product.

'Yeah,' Sam leans smartly on the basalt stone top of the kitchen island, and declares: 'We are now masters of our own destiny.'

Out on the garden, where Philip is busy with the barbecue,

a group of men – mostly Nat Am colleagues – are standing around having a beer. Sharkey is holding forth on a solution to the shootings and stabbings, now a weekly reality in Dublin and provincial towns. 'Social welfare should have been cut for these parasites – long ago. And I'm talking back in the eighties. They've been laughing up their sleeves at us paying for their savagery. I used to see them going into boozers in broad daylight and then next door to Paddy Power's. Goddamn layabouts who spawned these savages.'

'Should've been castrated, Aengus,' says Wheeler.

They chortle.

'Surely at this stage the death penalty has to be considered,' says one of the men who had read in the paper about an attack on an Australian couple at five in the evening. 'A hundred yards from the Gresham. Can you believe it?'

But as they draw on their cigars and sip their drinks, they move on to more pleasant subjects: they are full of praise for the enlightened way the banks are being allowed to get on with their work without interference.

'Say what you like about her, Maggie Thatcher freed up initiative. A lot to be said for the free market.' The stocky bloke in the rugby shirt gives himself space to sum it all up. When he inserts his finger into the ringpull of a beer can, he releases a swoosh of trapped air; foam rushes to the top and spits in his face.

'Yes,' says Sharkey, 'this country is really on the march. No reason why anyone shouldn't be on the property ladder. Get on the ladder, guys, or it'll be too late.' He has a few apartments in Galway and Limerick, the country house and stud outside Gorey, but the villa at Cap Ferrat is strictly family. He avoids telling them about the millions he has invested in the Dublin Docklands Development and in a Canadian mining company. 'The apartments are a welcome source of revenue. The students are fine, but one has to keep an eye on these goddamn non-nationals. They'd fuck off without paying.' Cigar smoke and the scent of freshly cut grass idle in the still air.

'Best thing that ever happened to this country were the tax

breaks for urban renewal; opened up the economy,' says a Nat Am client. All the while, Philip, who has a mound of spare ribs, burgers and steaks on a tray beside him, is throwing in the odd word about apartments and generous loans while he works.

A woman, crammed into a black dress, arrives alone. She laughs a lot and is loud in her explanation that her boyfriend is running late: 'You know boys and their football.' One of the caterers hands her a glass of wine. She summons up a wide grin for the women out on the patio, most of whom she doesn't know. Nevertheless, living up to her reputation as the hilarious one in Sam's office, she does a routine of the latest jokes, some self-deprecating about her size. When she has exhausted the list, she goes back into the house to refill her glass, and runs into Sam in one of the hallways. She is gushing in her praise of Sam's figure and chiffon dress. 'Picked it off the rack in Barcelona,' Sam says, admiring herself in a baroque wall mirror.

'Oh, it's *so* you. For that figure, I would kill ze bull.'

'By the way, Barcelona was a hoot.' Sam is still preening. 'You've simply *got* to come with us the next time.'

'Next time. Most definitely next time.'

Alone in the corridor, Sam looks in the mirror; her party smile collapses and a lost-looking forty-three-year-old child stares out at her. In her heart, she is jaded, and wishes she could go upstairs, slip between the cool sheets and sleep for a week. But the house, resounding with the buzz of party-talk, reminds her to replace her mask: she strides out towards the French windows. Once again, she is Sam, who keeps all the plates spinning.

Already some of the guests are forming a line that leads to the kitchen where two or three Auburn women are at the ready behind plates of smoked salmon, cold cuts of meat, shrimp bought that day from the fish shop in the village, and bowls of tossed salad.

Gradually, they return to the patio with their plates, and become animated about the Finnish lake experience at some hotel in Wexford. One of the women interrupts them, picks up her glass of wine as Sam is passing by. 'C'mon, Sam,' she says, 'this is your evening. Where do you see yourself in five years' time?'

Sam tilts her head in a girlish way. 'You've got me there.' She thinks for a moment and then smiles broadly: 'With my finger in many pies. And still top of my game.'

'Awesome,' says a woman, standing with her legs apart. 'We know what we want and we're not afraid to ask for it – right, girls?'

They raise their glasses.

'What I want to know,' says one of the tennis players from the local club, 'is where do you get your energy?'

'Positive karma,' Sam beams, and rests her plate on a low table.

All the while Doc Clifford is immersed in the rhythm of the evening. This is his scene: the laughter, the mouth-watering smell drifting from the barbecue, and the conversations. Evenings he and his wife hosted when he played the piano until late come winging back to him. As soon as he steps onto the patio, the big woman comes over and says: 'Isn't Sam unbelievable?'

'And throws a great party.'

Gradually the women who had opted for Philip's steaks return; they place serviettes on their laps and continue their chat while they eat. One of them has a newsflash: the Le Masneys have sold 'Shangri-La' in Suffolk Downs. 'Wait for it, girls – for €2.4 million.' Her sister is great friends with them – Mal and Grace – she's devastated that they're leaving.

They look at her with blank expressions.

'Don't you know?' she explains. 'The Le Masneys – the crystal glass people. I hope,' she continues, 'it's not one of those country fellows – a Johnny-come-lately – who's moving in. The Le Masneys were good fun. Never met anyone who can work a room like Grace.'

While she is holding forth on Mal and Grace, the spare figure of Father Tom McKeever appears from around a corner of the house. A priest who returned to Ireland, having contracted malaria in Kenya, he came across Philip and Sam while he was a tutor in UCD, and a part-time chaplain there.

Sam rushes to greet him with an embrace. She calls to Philip and the three of them go on about how it's a shame that it's been so long since they've met, and how quickly time passes. Sam describes him to her women friends as 'our bolt-hole from college days; almost succeeded in leading us to the far Left.' She recalls the times they crashed out in his St Stephen's Green presbytery, the stacks of sleeping bags lying around, and the many cups of coffee they drank coming up to exams. 'We'll catch up later, Tom,' she says. 'So glad you could come.' Then, after getting him drink and food, she is off again.

While scrutinizing the circle of chiffons and linens from Barcelona, McKeever listens to a woman beside him announcing that her son, who is at King's Inns, is off to South Africa in the summer to build houses for the coloured people. McKeever indulges her with broad smiles and nods of approval.

The main group has recovered from the interruption, and continues to talk about the K Club and to praise Russell, who has a couple of the Ladycastle apartments overlooking the eighteenth hole.

'A gentleman,' says one of the Auburns. 'No time whatever for those who try to put him down. He's a downright decent man, and not a bit pretentious. Great fun, and a panic when he does his Monty piece.'

'What's that?' a woman asks.

'He puts on his Field Marshal Montgomery uniform – his Monty bit. Just for a laugh. He'd have you in stitches. We played golf with him down at the K Club.' She and her husband have been to his house in Barbados – 'And he's so good to charities.'

'Yeah, smart fellow, alright.' McKeever chuckles while chewing his food.

They had forgotten him, and, now surprised, turn in his direction. The golfing wife continues to talk about Barbados, but McKeever says almost to himself: 'They tell me his pot of gold is abroad. Clever man. Mr Collector General will never get near *that* little piggy bank.'

She frowns. 'With due respect, you're conveniently ignoring the fact that, through his initiative, he's giving work to hundreds who contribute to the economy.'

'Oh, yes, I'd forgotten. Yes, they certainly contribute to the economy. You're right there. When you think about it,' he looks away towards The Sleeping Giant. 'That American woman – oh, her name escapes me now. She was right: *only the little people pay taxes*. Ah, such is life.'

In deference to the occasion, they suppress their irritation, and resume their small talk. The priest once more becomes invisible. While he eats, he scans the terraced garden: men in chinos and sports shirts are laughing loudly and opening beer cans. One of them is doing air swings with an imaginary golf club. Some are standing in groups near the barbecue where Philip is in his element. The big woman is taking photographs of a group lazing around where the Brothers used to play croquet. Above the trees, and way out on the bay, yachts are heading for the harbour.

McKeever sighs: 'Well now, isn't this great? What a lovely place.'

He spots a cricket bat lying on the patio, puts aside his plate, and stands to show the women how a batsman readies himself for the bowler. He had been dipping in and out of their conversation on the latest self-development course: Inner Harmony. Gives a total balance of yin and yang. It's amazing. Total relaxation.

'Interesting what you were saying there about that ... what did you call it? Interior?'

'Inner Harmony.' The golfing wife stands tall at the patio doors. 'I don't suppose that would be part of your agenda,' adding with a sneer, 'Father.'

McKeever runs his hand through his mop of silver hair and smiles. 'Makes us happy – is that the idea? Sure, aren't we all for that?'

'Yes,' she snaps. 'Happy and free of baggage.'

'That's why we must be the happiest people ... is it in Europe, or in the world?' He knows that she is staring at him but he starts to do a short backward swing with the cricket bat. 'Willow, that's what cricket bats are made of, and then they treat them with linseed oil.' He holds up the cricket bat. 'Linseed oil – makes them more resistant to shock, wear and tear.' He grins: 'Might try some myself.'

Una finds the quip very funny.

The golfing wife, however, is not finished with him. 'Shrewd business sense and can-do is what has dragged this country out of the dark ages. That's why we're the happiest.'

'Yeah, you could be right there.' McKeever feels along the smooth surface of the cricket bat. 'Happiest,' he says. 'Well, I don't know. I was speaking to the city coroner recently. He was telling me that six young men … God help us … gave in to the dark in the last year. One or two claimed to be accidents, but … he has a theory about that too.'

'So?' a woman asks.

'Six young men in the past year. Young people binge-drinking like there's no tomorrow. Happy, are we?'

'We're the envy of Europe.'

As if to himself, McKeever says: 'Envy of Europe. Hah.'

He leans on the cricket bat. 'I love those old folk tales; you know – the ones about fairies.'

One of the older women smiles: 'My father used tell us those, God rest him. Used to scare the life out of us.'

'Well maybe you've heard this already. It's about the man who in the dead of night plays beautiful fiddle music for the fairies. The best you've ever heard in your whole life. Anyway, doesn't your man get a whole pot of gold from the fairies because they delight in his music. He goes home happy, sleeps like a baby. The first thing he does in the morning is to look into the pot of gold. But sure, all that's in the pot are dried up leaves.'

He lays the cricket bat against the wall. 'I don't know,' he says as he begins to saunter off. 'Maybe there's something in us Irish always looking for the pot of gold. Hah? Sure we can always blame the Brits, and what they did to us, if things go wrong. *Go bhfoire Dia orainn*. I enjoyed our chat.'

When he is strolling away towards the barbecue, a woman turns to the one beside her.

'What's he on about?'

Holding two bottles of chablis to charge their glasses, Sam joins them for a minute; they explain what had happened. She looks down the garden where McKeever is now hovering around the barbecue. 'He was never like that. Full of life. It could be the malaria, or maybe it's Africa. He did a stint there.' She lowers her voice: 'Someone said he got a breakdown.'

The stars are out when the guests are drifting off. A faint smell of cooked meat lingers around the barbecue where Philip has lit the patio heater for the few men, including Clifford, who are having a last drink and draining the evening of its remaining pleasures. Egan is giving Ponies and Yankees for Ascot and the Curragh.

Just as when they arrived, Sharkey and his disciples make a noisy departure, and are full of praise for what Sam and Philip have done for La Salle. 'You've opened the season in great style,' he commends them at the front door. Others are getting into their Mercs and SUVs, so that a red stream of brake lights is lighting up the driveway, and powerful engines are purring in the balmy night.

'The American Evening is only what … a few weeks away,' Sharkey remarks to Philip. 'Your twist, Philip; but if you want to pass on it this time …'

'No prob. Booking all done for Robin Hill.' Philip had no intention of passing over a glorious opportunity to network with major clients and useful contacts from other banks.

'I'd like to run something by you,' says Sharkey. 'Lunch next Thursday? Let's do La Mer.' They chat for another while and again praise the weather and the success of the barbecue. A full moon is shining on the cobbleblocking, and the sultry breeze coming up from the bay bears a promise of long days ahead.

'Sharkey wants to *run something by me*,' Philip tells Egan as he walks with him to his car.

'When Sharkey wants to run something by you, he's already made up his mind,' says Egan before he steps in.

'We both know that.' Philip taps the roof of the car. 'See you tomorrow.'

5

J UST DOWN THE ROAD from the RDS, La Méridienne, like
other wine bars and restaurants in the area, has become a
favourite watering-hole after rugby internationals, concerts and
for dinner, especially on Thursday and Friday evenings. Along
this stretch of road, too, when summer makes an appearance, the
trendy set from the nearby financial institutions congregates
outside the pubs on Friday evenings: they sit beneath the awnings
or spill on to the footpath in front of Paddy Cullen's or Crowes.

When Sharkey with his disciples, Brennan and Wheeler, steps
through the front door of La Méridienne on the Thursday after
the house-warming in Lalors, and makes his way between chairs
and around tanned legs, all eyes in the bar are riveted on Tiger
Woods, who is lining up his shot for a birdie at the eighteenth.
The hushed voice of the commentator is clear in the anxious
silence. 'Do or die now,' he says in reverential tones.

Knees bent, Tiger Woods does a take-back, looks at the hole
a couple of times, and steadies himself again. At first the ball looks
like veering away, but then it curves, and disappears into the
green sward. The bar explodes with cheering and high-fives. 'In
the bag' they call out to each other. 'No one can touch him now.'

One man leans across and kisses a woman right on the lips.
Her head tilts back; they are both laughing and he has to hold her
so that she doesn't topple off the barstool.

Philip has found a spot at a bend in the counter. 'Behind for
seventeen holes. What an escape out of jail. Sheer genius,' the

kisser tells the woman; their craving for each other is crystal-clear.

Though he has been taking his time, Philip has half his pint drunk when Sharkey beckons from the other end of the bar, and squeezes his way towards him.

Since childhood, when he had played around the roads in Marino, Sharkey had learnt that control meant having a coterie of camp followers: this he has always managed to do, even in college. He plays golf and goes to the races with his henchmen, and after his divorce, has been seen more often in their company in Toner's or Doheny & Nesbitt's. He would nurse a Ballygowan or two, while they reviewed the week's work, until he'd get in his car and drive to Delgany.

So for Sharkey, Wheeler and Brennan were a godsend. As he said to a few golfing friends one night in Druid's Glen: 'Give me guys who are streetwise, practical and loyal. You can keep your eggheads; they know fuck all about the cut and thrust of banking. I need idealists like a hole in the head.'

In tricky situations the disciples are Sharkey's shield and a formidable cohort at meetings; when he wants to get rid of someone, they spread malicious rumours, making life impossible for the victim. When they go for a pint after work, Wheeler and Brennan look an odd pair: Wheeler well over six feet, and Brennan, hardly up to his shoulder, trotting along beside him to keep up.

Though he is the chief executive officer and radiates confidence, Sharkey has a recurring dream which surfaces after an especially trying day. In the dream, he himself, his younger brother, two sisters and the baby are squatting in a house off Fairview Strand; they have no heat, and no running water. A lighted candle on a kitchen chair reflects their frightened looks. The January damp rises from the cold floor, causing them to shiver, while his father, unable to sit still, tramps up and down on the bare boards, smoking cigarette butts, and waiting for the Saint Vincent de Paul men to arrive.

The dream is close to reality. When his father had lost his job in Brooks Thomas, the builders' providers, the family had to squat to force Dublin Corporation to house them in Marino. And, like they did with some of their promising pupils, the Christian Brothers in Fairview took a special interest in Sharkey's father, and got him into Lemon's sweet factory on the Drumcondra Road. But in Sharkey's nightmare they are doomed to remain squatters for the rest of their lives.

He himself fears being toppled and this fear and suspicion hindered him for a long time from getting the top job at Nat Am, even though he was the most suitable candidate, being the one who had built up the bank from the time it was just a small office in Andrew Street, and when the equity was just over a million and a half pounds.

Sharkey was getting results, so St John Dunleavy and the other directors gave him his head, though they intervened when he offered to hire debt collectors; not office workers with brief-cases and umbrellas, but hustlers with bulging muscles in suits, who were prepared to twist arms unless the debtors coughed up.

The energy that drives Sharkey to put daylight between him and the frightening smell of poverty comes from the same region of his brain that fostered fear and suspicion. St John Dunleavy relies on him, but he will never be the Fitzwilliam Tennis Club type.

Without a word of apology for being nearly a half-hour late, Sharkey announces to Philip that they will go straight to their table; he clicks his fingers at a waiter.

'Follow me, gentlemen,' says the young man with a foreign accent who leads them along a corridor to their table in the restaurant. As the waiter is turning to get the wine list and the menu chart off a sideboard, Sharkey calls to him: 'Where are you from, bud? Poland?' Dropping peanuts from a bowl into his mouth.

'No, sir. Romania.'

'Right, bud.' He waves him away with his hand, turns to his companions and says out of the side of his mouth: 'Probably one of Ceauşescu's indiscretions.'

Brennan laughs as if it's the funniest quip he's heard in ages.

During the meal, Sharkey reveals the purpose of their

meeting: he is on a cost-cutting rampage at Nat Am, and he wants Philip on his side. 'Too much fatty tissue, guys; time for invasive surgery. We've no option; we can no longer be nursemaid to lame ducks. Look at what happened to Northern Rock. None of us is safe.'

He starts with women who are away on maternity leave. 'I want to put you in the frame.' He fixes on some point above their heads. 'We were always generous with them; loads of time off to have their babies. Take Sorcha – expecting a fourth in two months' time. Told her she may have a future somewhere else, but not with Nat Am.' He affects a look of hurt and leans in as if to impart a secret. 'What does she think – that we're the Vincent de Paul? I mean a fourth for God's sake. Goddamn walking incubator.'

'Bunny rabbits,' says Brennan; 'herself and that teacher guy.' He glances at Sharkey for approval.

Sharkey leans forward again. 'Heard today she's talking Labour Court.'

'Silly bitch,' says Wheeler. 'With Labour Court history on her CV, no one will give her a second thought. That's a no-brainer for a start off.'

'Absolutely,' Brennan echoes. 'Branded as a trouble-maker.'

While she was having her third baby, Sorcha's work had been farmed out to others who were junior and willing to work for less to get on to the ladder. She returned to be told that the 'Red Braces' gave orders to rationalize. Her desk had been removed from the open plan office and she found herself among the most junior staff at Customer Service.

'Take it or leave it, Sorcha,' Sharkey had told her. 'Out of my hands.'

Ten years before, when Sorcha had joined the bank, Sharkey had got a picture in the business section of the *Irish Independent* – he at the centre, Sorcha at his side and then others from the corporate section, all smiling with perfect teeth showing. Sharkey had insisted they take the photograph at one of the doorways of Nat Am where he could stand on a step.

Philip glances at Brennan, who is expatiating on how women

can be ever so moody after child-birth. A lot he knows about women, Philip thinks. With his hair gel, must think he's one of those chaps you see with leggy blondes in the glossy section of the Sunday papers. The bald patch on his own head is getting bigger, despite that hair-restorer promising a full head of hair like the smiling bloke on the packet.

Brennan moves on to rugby, and how he hopes to keep his place on the thirds next season. 'But you have to work your ass off,' he informs them. Two nights on the back pitch, and two more nights pumping iron.

Sharkey chuckles: 'I envy Conrad's youth – and energy. Don't you, Philip?'

'Yes, indeed.' Philip manages a smile. *Creep. I wonder will he be so cocksure of himself when he's another twenty years on: a marriage going dead in the water, and a son who glares at him over the breakfast table.*

Brennan is excited about the progress his son is making on the under-tens team at Willow Park School. 'In fact, as recently as this February, Father Keane, who has been there for yonks, says to me at the touchline: "I've seen that scrum-half style somewhere before. The apple never falls far from the tree."' He goes into more details about his sporting career. 'Couldn't make the tag rugby practice at Donnybrook yesterday evening. A mob of crazies had caused a traffic build-up outside Merrion Road Church.'

'What?' Sharkey asks.

'Loonies. Following the bones of some saint or other.'

'Yes, I saw a picture in the paper of the coffin being taken into the church. Philip adds his tuppenceworth. 'I thought that day had gone.'

'Well, I never. Bones in a coffin.' says Sharkey. 'Do they actually still believe that rubbish? '

'Apparently so. Look at the crowds that turn up for that prayer gig over in Galway.' Though he has no great issue with a saint's bones in a coffin or the Galway novena, Philip doesn't want to appear out of kilter.

'For the life of me, I can't understand these zany bastards who make a nuisance of themselves, causing needless traffic delays.' As if someone is going to take his plate away, Sharkey, as ever, has one hand hovering around the edge of it while eating.

'What's as bad, Aengus,' says Brennan, 'are those idiots who hold up work on major road-building. A guy I used to know in college was telling me – he's a civil engineer on the Tara bypass – his company had to down tools for weeks and meet challenges in the High Court. A shower of morons who claimed that the settlement was part of the country's heritage. Who cares what went on in old God's time? High Kings of Ireland, my arse, when we're trying to build a solid infrastructure to get the country on the move.' He checks his watch. 'Sorry,' he says with a look of surprise. 'Duty, you know.' He casts the crumpled napkin on the table, 'Sandyford – the transport guy looking for the guts of ten mill. Meeting him at the Radisson. Wants to climb the greasy pole. I've vetted his file; he's low risk. Net worth is healthy.' He looks at Sharkey. 'Ticks all the boxes. Cash flow and securities and personal assets. Used be Sorcha's client, but while our baby-maker was having her last one, I had to step up to the plate. I'll keep you posted, Aengus. See you, guys.'

Like a proud father, Sharkey looks at him as he stands, then rests back in the chair. 'Great to have young blood on board, Philip.'

'Great.'

Philip manages to steer the conversation away from banking: experience had told him that Sharkey would very likely mis-quote him to his own benefit. So, over coffee, they return to the sheer genius of Tiger Woods and Sharkey's next sailing trip to Scotland. When the bill arrives, Sharkey looks at it, and then pushes it across the table to Philip.

'You know what, Philip. You take care of that and I'll sign off when you present it for payment.'

'Sure.' Philip takes a credit card from his wallet. *Yes, got me again – he'll sign off on the expense and I'll be in his debt.*

'Isn't he something else?' Sharkey is saying, while the card is being processed.

'Sorry.'

'Conrad.'

'Oh isn't he?' *Yes, something else alright.* Philip keys in his PIN. *A little bollix who will bide his time on less pay while he climbs the ladder, and then some other ambitious git will take his place. And Sharkey will be commended and given a bigger bonus at Christmas for getting rid of someone who has spent years with the bank.*

Sharkey turns to Wheeler. 'I've to admit I envy you guys; you've got it all ahead of you. Philip and I, well, we're not as agile as we used be. Mileage on the clock. Don't know about you, but I aim to retire at fifty-six, which – I hate to admit – is only a few years away. Then I'll be hoisting *Gatsby's* sails.'

'I'm still a few years behind you, Aengus, and I can do a steady 60k on the bike nearly every Sunday morning.' Philip winks at Wheeler.

Sharkey begins to rise from the table: 'Ah, Philip, you and I are only trying to deny the inevitable.'

They laugh it off as the three of them stroll out into the evening sun.

6

WHENEVER he is introducing a guest speaker in the assembly room or at a conference, Sharkey makes sure to slip in some reference to his Alma Mater. Debating a point of minor importance, he might laugh and say: 'Well, you'll understand, if I seem picky: Harvard does leave its mark.' At other times when he wants to put down recruits, straight out of the Smurfit School of Business and oozing self-confidence, he might comment in a throwaway manner: 'Of course, the Smurfit is fine so far as it goes, but it's not ... well, we had a different perspective in Harvard. Best brains in the world.'

This exaggerated claim is at variance with the reality: soon after graduating from Trinity, he had completed a three-month course at the Harvard Business School. 'My research thesis', as he refers to it, was a booklet he brought out during that period of study.

One of his American ideas, relatively new to Dublin, is to introduce a chill-out day. It means wearing casuals, such as sports shirts, on the last Friday of the month. 'You guys,' Sharkey says in his email, 'might find this somewhat OTT. Not in Cambridge, Mass.'

The day after the meal in La Méridienne is 'chill-out day'. Apart from the odd exception – a country chap new to Nat Am who had turned up in the red of the Cork Gaelic football team – all wear rugby shirts. And even though the only game some of them would have played was soccer in the nearest green space to the swathes of semi-detached houses in which they grew up, they learned quickly that the rugby shirt, like the Merc, was a statement.

Unless he had meetings with developers, Sharkey appeared in the colours of his old school, Belvedere College. Step by step, he had made it to the Jesuit school through the persistence of a mother, full of country ambition, who had badgered her husband to get weekend work in The Cat and Cage pub, even though he was jaded from working long hours in Lemon's sweet factory. The added income enabled her to put a down payment on a house off Griffith Avenue: here she was relieved to be away from 'the riff-raff of the city' and among 'people who are making something of themselves' – Guards, shop-owners and teachers.

Although he now joins the chorus that condemns the Christian Brothers as sadists, he had done well in the Brothers' school. For months before the examinations, Sharkey, along with other clever boys, was given free tuition each Saturday; then, after the Intermediate Certificate, in which he got third place, his mother went straight to the Rector of Belvedere.

That chill-out Friday evening, Philip decides against going with the others to Doheny & Nesbitt's; instead, he would take the DART to Auburn, and maybe get Sam to join him for drinks and a bite to eat at one of the restaurants in the village or at Robin Hill. And while there, he would confirm arrangements for the American Evening. But as he is lifting his briefcase off the desk, he realizes that it is her Spa weekend with the girls.

Thoughts of being on his own dishearten him. So, instead of going to catch the train for Howth, he decides to make the most of the fine evening, get a taxi into town, stroll along the quays and then grab a burger in Temple Bar.

The weekend crowd of younger bankers has already gathered outside pubs in Ballsbridge. Froth from their half-drunk pints clings to the glass; cigarette smoke carries in the light breeze. A man calls out to a woman passing by on the footpath: 'Krystle later? Save the slow ones for me, babes.'

She releases a high-pitch laugh, and slackens her pace.

Playing with a set of keys, the man is on a roll and he knows it. 'Got my new Harley. Some power there. You should try it some time. I've got an extra helmet.'

'I'll take you up on that.'

At Tara Street, Philip gets out of the taxi, crosses Butt Bridge and saunters along Custom House Quay. Reflection from the glass towers by the quays is casting a sickly shade on the slow-moving waters of the Liffey. With time on his hands, he intends to take a look around the International Financial Services Centre, but the stark figures of the Famine Memorial stop him in his tracks. They stand out against the glass and chrome cathedrals, as if a rogue artist had planked them there to challenge the gods of pride and money.

Images from his student days flood his mind. He is back a quarter of a century to nights when old men were clasping ragged bundles and shuffling out of dark alleys to the white van parked near Baggot Street Hospital.

With Father Tom, he is distributing soup in paper cups while Sam and other students give out slices of buttered bread. Steam from the cups rises in the night air; the men wolf down the bread and, crouched against the hospital wall, nurse the soup with both hands buried in their tattered coats.

Joey's comical grin takes shape in his head: Joey who was found frozen to death one January morning outside Haddington Road Church. They skipped lectures at Belfield, packed into the same white van and travelled with Father Tom to the Paupers' Grave in Glasnevin.

A cloud descends upon Philip, something to do with the memory of a time when he would improve the lot of misfits and no-hopers, *make a difference* – McKeever's motto. *We pass this way but once*. But he scolds himself for his gloomy thoughts: many have genuine cause to be low-spirited – cancer patients, those like Joey, those in dead-end jobs. Even if the light is going out in his marriage, he has had a good education, lives in a splendid house, and has a well-paid job. He doesn't suffer from the depressions you hear so much about nowadays. A school friend, who had a thriving medical practice in Terenure, went off down to Ennis one Friday evening. In a hotel room, he wrote out directions for his funeral, swallowed a bottle of pills, and lay on the bed waiting for his appointment with oblivion.

Despite an appeal to reason, Philip fails to banish the albatross that has perched on his shoulder. He thinks about phoning Ellen, and searches for his mobile. 'No one knows, so we're hurting no one' had been her argument that last night in a Bayswater pub. *Why is it so good with her, but not with Sam? Can't remember the last time …* He runs his eye down along the jaundiced Liffey waters, avoids the Famine Memorial and turns his steps towards the centre of town.

'*No terms and conditions need apply,*' Ellen had joked soon after their affair had flared up.

But the tide turned, as they both knew it would: terms and conditions slowly but surely crept in. 'I'm just your piece on the side. For fucking. Wham bam, thank you, Ma'am,' she had said when they'd been drinking and she wanted to meet more often. 'I go back to an empty apartment; you return to the bosom of your family.'

'We both agreed: no strings attached.'

'Don't be ridiculous – people always expect.'

He puts away his mobile.

Set free from drudgery, the city is teeming with weekend promise: trolley cases rattle on the pavement, as girls rush to Connolly railway station. Others are absorbed in the world of their mobile phones. With paint stains on their jeans, men with broad Slavic features and sallow complexions are hopping onto buses. A pink stretch limousine pulls up while Philip is waiting at the junction of D'Olier Street and Fleet Street. Young women have their heads out the car windows and are screaming. 'Shag, shag, shag' in a mindless sing-song way until the lights turn green. 'Shag, shag, shag.'

One of them, with heavy mascara and dark eyeshadow, and wearing a bridal veil, eyeballs him as the limousine is moving off. 'Hey, Mr Hot Shot Businessman, want to come to a party?'

Another one of them cuts in: 'Briefcase, do you want to fuck?'

Crossing D'Olier Street, he can still hear the shouts, 'Shag,

shag, shag' fading in the distance. A little woman, with a small white terrier looks up at him, smiles and puts her hands up to her ears. Two hefty female Gardaí are having a great time, getting their photograph taken with a group of American tourists.

A waitress finds Philip a table in The Elephant & Castle and, while waiting to be served, he glances through the window. Across the way in a lane, a young man, unsteady on his feet, is leaning against one of the walls; suddenly, a rope of green vomit erupts from his mouth and slides down the wall to the cobblestones. When he is finished, he wipes his mouth with his sleeve, shuffles out to the street and disappears from view. The waitress, who has returned with Philip's burger, follows his gaze.

'Is it always like this?' he asks her.

'Oh, all times.' She forces a smile. 'And later, many later, oh, yes, and very noise.'

The evening rush for home is well over when he arrives at Tara Street DART station where his train is almost empty. A teenage boy and girl enter, and as soon as they settle themselves in the seat facing the few passengers, they start necking and making wet sounds with their open mouths: their smacking lips and giggles are loud in the silence of the carriage.

When the carriage shunts and the train moves off, the young woman begins to stroke the back of the lad's head, and then straddles him, causing her summer dress to slide up her rounded thigh. His tongue searches for the inside of her mouth; they exchange teasing smiles, whispers, and laugh at some shared secret.

At Fairview, a priest with severe eyes and a tracery of veins on his nose and cheeks enters. Dressed all in black and carrying a breviary, he removes his hat to show a head of dyed brown hair that stands out against the deathly pallor of his neck.

When the train is moving out of the station, the couple start up again, now more eager than ever. The priest glances at them, and clears his throat; throwing him a look of contempt, the young woman whispers in the lad's ear. They laugh.

Apart from seagulls on a food mission to the fishing boats and declaring war on each other, the road up from the station is deserted: everyone is at a party, raising their glasses, laughing and playing music. Pewter clouds hang over The Sleeping Giant. Remnants of the evening lodge in Philip's head as he climbs the hill: the couple in the train, the green vomit, and the screaming girls in the garish limo.

He needs to talk, at least, to clear his head, and considers the golf club, but Friday night is music night, to entice members to the bar: the last thing he wants is the blare of loud music.

As he told Clifford later, he was on the point of phoning him to chat over a shot or two of whiskey that might take him away from derivatives, share prices, net worth and the bond market. And leverage – always leverage.

But no sooner has he turned the key of his front door than he hears loud sobbing coming from the den. He drops his brief-case by the hallstand and treads lightly to the open door to see his daughter Zara curled up on the couch before the home cinema screen, her feet drawn up beneath her, her head sunk into her chest. She remains like that when he walks slowly into the room and sits beside her.

After a while she looks up at him, then her head sinks again; she starts to rock herself. Over the years he has grown well used to her fits of crying: whenever she didn't do well in an exami-nation, or when someone else in the class is the teacher's current pet, or she has been excluded from a game in the school yard. Experience tells him he will have to be patient until she is ready to talk.

After a lengthy silence, broken only by her sobbing, he ventures: 'Zara, what is it?'

'I'm *so* dead.' Her cheeks are smeared with eyeshadow.

'How, love? Tell me.'

She turns away.

'It often helps to talk,' he says in a low voice.

'Please, Dad; please don't ask me.'

'You might feel better.'

'No, I wouldn't.'

He waits for her to recover, and, eventually, she sits up, reaches for a tissue on the low table, and blows her nose.

After some time, when she has stopped sobbing, he happens on an idea. 'Let's go for a walk around the Head with the dogs. We can treat ourselves to a Beshoff's, and pick up a DVD. How about that?'

She brightens and, once again, he is seeing his ten-year-old driving back in the car after they had been tapping a ball over the net at the tennis club. She is going to be Sharapova, and he will be her coach when she takes the women's singles title at Wimbledon for the third year in a row.

Disappearing now and again into the heather, the dogs run along ahead of them. The stroll is reviving Zara, and when she and Philip have gone through the turnstile at The Nuns' Walk and climbed the hill away from the houses, she stops and holds fuchsia petals in her cupped hands as if protecting them in case they fall and get crushed by passers-by. 'Dad,' she says. 'Some girls in school are … they put things on Facebook that are *so* mean.'

'That is not nice, love.' He watches her admiring the fuchsia. 'People can be very unkind to one another, but we must remember there are good people also – it's what keeps us going.'

'Dad?' she walks ahead of him. 'Am I, like … fat.'

'No. Of course not.' He looks at the rope of black hair falling on her back. 'Why do you ask me that?'

'You don't think so?'

'No. Most certainly not. Did anyone – ?'

'No. No, it's OK, Dad.' She links him, and rattles on about how she can't wait for the family holiday in August and, this year she'd like to bring Chloë and Michaela.

'Do that, love.' But his thoughts are not on the August holiday – he and Sam have short-changed their two children. Too taken up with themselves and their preoccupations – positive karma and the Christmas bonus.

'Let's do this more often,' he calls to her while putting the fish and chips to reheat in the microwave, and she is plugging in the DVD.

'Cool. Yeah. I'd really love that, Dad.'

'Once a week around the Head. A family thing.' Or stay in. He could count in one hand the number of times they stayed in to watch the home cinema together.

'Brill, Dad.'

His BlackBerry rings. He takes the call out on the patio. Sharkey has sent him an email with details of some clients who are in default: would he ever run his eye over them and phone him in the morning?

'With you in a minute, Zara,' he calls out as he opens his laptop in the living room.

He has over thirty new emails on his computer. All are urgent.

7

AFTER THE FALL of Northern Rock, when word from America is that the giants – Merrill Lynch and Goldman Sachs – are in trouble, academics are ringing alarm bells for all they are worth. Ireland, however, is on a carousel, and doesn't want the fairground music to stop. That is, until they notice that some of the cranes over Dublin have now come to a standstill, and estate agents' signs are fading in their windows. Moreover, the line of men waiting for the breakfast roll at the village Mace is shrinking by the day.

In the pubs and cafés along Merrion Road, however, they cling to the stock answer: 'Our banks are well capitalized.' Sharkey, however, doesn't like one bit what his 'Eyes and Ears' bring back from rounds of golf, and what he himself knows anyway. So after consulting with St John Dunleavy, he wastes no time in calling a meeting.

In his shirtsleeves, he stands beside a PowerPoint and begins with what he calls his golden rule: consultation, co-operation and collegiality. 'That was, and is, and always will be my motto, and that's why Nat Am is such a driving force in international banking. My colleagues, no matter who is or who isn't, Nat Am will always make the cut.'

He is in speech-making mode. 'We live in a pool infested by piranhas, guys,' he says, 'and our share prices have taken a slight dip.' He runs his hand along his pink tie: a sign for those who know him that he is about to spin a web of lies. 'Nothing to be concerned about; no need for a flap. But,' he cocks his finger at them, 'it's action stations. Guys, we've got to pull up our socks. We give good interest rates, better than the rest; now they're getting in on the act, and Nat Am is slipping.' To add drama to his pep talk, he speaks in a hushed tone, for their ears only: 'Listen up, folks – Nat Am doesn't do slipping.'

Turning to Karen, his personal assistant, he asks her to display the progress report; then, with a rod, he points to the tables, the dips, the share prices.

'Upstairs,' he jabs the rod towards the ceiling, 'the Braces don't do slackening.' He nods to Karen to close down the screen, and says that he will be looking forward to hearing a full and frank discussion about all this at next month's conference at Windermere Hall. 'My main objective is to have my team with me.' Now he is thumping the floor: 'We're only as strong as the weakest link.' Sitting near the front, Brennan is nodding and looking around for agreement.

'So, my friends,' Sharkey pauses for effect, and rakes the gathering, 'I plan to bring in our trusted friend TOM.' He chuckles. 'Many of you here are well acquainted with TOM. I refer, of course, to the Target Operating Model, which has served us well in the past. Those of you who came on board in the last two years or so won't have met TOM – fine chap is TOM.' The disciples chuckle with him.

From experience, the assembled staff knows that TOM is always a pretext for cutbacks and redundancies. And unlike other banks which take pride in breeding and refinement, and which always look after their own, Sharkey has no hesitation in firing personnel. 'If they bring home the bacon, if their numbers are good, they will be rewarded at Nat Am. If they fuck up, then I shoot them. Simple as that,' he reminds the disciples over coffee in the plaza. 'I can get loads of young guns from the Smurfit; only waiting on the touchline to race onto the pitch.'

To the novices whom he brings into the circle of collaborators, he explains the Sharkey Treatment for getting rid of dead wood. First you farm out their portfolios. Tell them that in these dodgy times we need all hands to the pumps to expedite the work. 'Move their desk into some fucking quiet corner, and if they don't like that, dangle the carrot. A handshake, and fuck them out. Younger guys like yourselves, loaded with testosterone, will now be called on to keep this ship afloat.'

The seasoned ones, like Philip, can read his mind by now, but they too have to endure his cant. Encouraged by Sharkey and St John Dunleavy, they have taken out loans to invest in the bank, and in student apartment blocks in Waterford, Limerick and Dundalk; in holiday homes in Connemara and in France. The robust health of Nat Am determines their ability to live in places like Auburn, or across in Dalkey.

While Sharkey is talking about TOM, Philip remembers the whispered confidence of a former colleague at Ipswich & General. 'He may be wearing Armani, but he's still the ruffian who frightened the shite out of other kids around Marino – he and his gang. Wouldn't believe him if he swore on the Bible.'

The following Monday, the TOM men and a woman arrive, like school inspectors, with cold looks and self-important brief-cases. Sharkey takes them for coffee to the executive floor restaurant to meet St John Dunleavy and other directors.

Later that day, he calls a meeting of his team. 'More a brain-storm, guys. Our friends from TOM will sit in.'

The afternoon is sunny, so they have to close the blinds for a clearer definition of the material on the PowerPoint screen. Sitting to the side, the men from TOM have a commanding view of the assembly, although they spend most of the time poker-faced, staring across the room, or concentrating on their computers. In that respect the whole setting evokes memories of the classroom; the dormant pranksters watch for an opening to make the odd joke, while the responsible children who sit at the front and who have morphed into ambitious bankers take notes whenever the TOM people intervene.

At the end of the week, when the auditors have submitted their report, Sharkey calls a meeting of managers, including Philip, to discuss the results. They sit around his desk.

'You see from TOM, guys,' Sharkey says, looking out over his half-lenses, 'the hard facts we must square up to.' While he glances at the report, the managers scrutinize the pages. 'We have to do some root canal. No other option.' The rustle of pages fills the silence.

He turns to Brennan. 'Conrad, you've come up with facts and figures.'

'Yes. Some costings that may help.' Brennan takes over the presentation. He shows how they can farm out more back office work.

When he is finished, Sharkey turns to the managers. 'Conrad has already opened up a conversation with the Pakis.'

One manager keeps flicking through the pages before he speaks: 'So, redundancies, Aengus. The bottom line?'

Sharkey removes the half-lenses, sinks back into the comfort of his plush chair, and works an arm of his glasses around in his mouth before he speaks. 'No other option. As simple as that.' Beneath the few remaining strands of hair, the light catches the shininess of his bald head. He leans over the desk towards the managers: ' "Cometh the hour, cometh the man", guys. It's your asses too, when the heat is turned up.'

More creaking of leather, while he gives time for his warning to sink in.

'Well said, Aengus,' says Wheeler. 'Well said.'

'Last in, first out' becomes the guiding principle at Nat Am when the directors decide to outsource to Pakistan. One by one those for the chop are called in to Sharkey's office like fractious children to the headmaster. They return to clear out their desks and leave by the forecourt where, at the entrance, a large framed display board shows two hard-hats taking levels at a building site, a happy-looking college graduate with gown and mortar board, and a smiling man and woman with two children in front of their dream house. And beneath the slogan: 'We care about your future at Nat Am.'

The women cry and are hugged by those who are glad the axe hasn't fallen on them; the men put on a shoulder-shrugging act and go to Bellamy's pub or Crowes with their colleagues, although some – even those with whom they used to play tag rugby – stay well away, as if they might become infected by the spreading virus.

Insisting on paying for a round, the fallen soldiers joke and make a T sign like referees at rugby internationals: *time out to smell the roses, guys*. They raise pints of Heineken to their lips and then trudge back to apartments around Ballsbridge, some of which are owned by clients of Nat Am who are now failing to honour their loans. And, long before dawn, the fallen soldiers who hadn't slept a wink are listening to the troubled pulse of the night city.

Over the following weeks, others are let go, including some of Philip's staff, so that soon Nat Am is in the grip of anxiety. Excited chatter about upcoming city breaks to London or Amsterdam, or the week in Andorra with all the family, fades; instead, those who want to hold their jobs, and repay huge mortgages, show the vicious side of human nature when survival is the goal.

During lunch in the plaza, those in Finance, Treasury and Lending believe that the layoffs in the back office sector should have been greater. After all, they themselves are the money-makers – the sloggers who spend boring afternoons at Croke Park with culchie clients who shout like savages and stuff their faces with burgers at half-time.

If possible, Philip arranges to meet any of his team who has received the bad news, like Gavin, who had to undergo the dreaded visit to Sharkey's office, and is told that this is 'a learning curve' for him and that he has a bright future.

A couple of weeks after Gavin's being let go, Philip takes him to a restaurant on Ranelagh Road where they can talk without the risk of running into someone from the bank. Unlike the crop of brash young men who are loud in Paddy Cullen's, and who have bought cars more expensive than they can afford, Gavin has remained at the edge of their conversations. Despite a good academic career at UCD, and a Master's from the Smurfit Business School, he blushes frequently and avoids eye contact.

They are given a booth which grants them privacy. Gavin picks at his meal, while he recounts his meeting with Sharkey. The chips on his plate grow cold. 'And then he says, "a chance to use your excellent skills elsewhere: call it a career change, Gavin." ' He is looking away in the direction of an old John Player sign on the wall. 'Haven't slept since God knows when.'

'How is Claire taking it?'

'I try to hide it from her. Things look much more frightening at four in the morning when you're staring at the street light through the curtain.' Some nights, he goes downstairs and flicks from one channel to the next. Re-runs of soaps and quiz programmes, and reality TV. 'How anyone can watch that shit beats me: *X Factor, Big Brother, The Apprentice*. Jesus! They must be getting off seeing some bully on the panel embarrass the crap out of the morons who put themselves through it.'

'It's the times we live in, Gav. People are desperate to be noticed.'

Gavin grows silent. 'I can't tell Claire. I go out before she gets back from the hospital – don't want to worry her. She has exams coming up.'

Just before he showed him the door, Sharkey read out a letter, carefully composed by the bank's lawyer. It is the standard issue for all who are being sacked – 'economic downturn'; 'responsibility to the banks and the shareholders'.

'I tried to bring up projects I'd worked on, and how successful they were. He just kept pointing at the letter.'

A weak smile appears on his pale face. 'Played my last card then: the mortgage and my engagement.'

'"With your ability," Sharkey says, "this is a glorious opportunity to move on, further your career. I know for certain, I'd love the chance to get working on my golf." ' And all the time, the fucker is rearranging the pad on his desk and looking at his watch. I know his game, Philip: it's all about ego, and making big investments. And golf with the Barbados set.'

While Gavin is letting off steam, Philip glances at him. His sensitive face is strained and white, and for some strange reason puts him in mind of his own father.

'You have to keep trying, Gav. My dad was like that for most of a year. Backed the car out of the driveway, waved to me as I was getting my bike out of the shed. Then he drove out to

Bullock Harbour, read the paper, or books from the library, couldn't tell my mother.'

'What … was he long out?'

'He went back and studied to be a teacher – not easy at thirty-four – but he held in there.'

Gavin isn't listening. 'What makes it worse, I'm getting married in September, and now I feel I'm letting everyone down, Claire most of all.' After a while he raises his head. 'Got part-time work.'

'Oh. I'm glad.'

'Mickey Mouse fucking job. Phoning people and knocking on doors when they are about to sit down to dinner. "We are upgrading the service in your road and we would like you – our valued customer – to be one of the first to avail of the special facilities we have on offer." Crap.'

'Well, it's something.'

'Yesterday evening I knocked on a door. Identity tag around my neck, like a labrador. A poor old dear answered. Thought I was her grandson. Her husband had died that morning, and she was making arrangements for his burial. *Jeesus.* Then she asks me to go down to the Mace corner shop for milk and bread. I'm up shit creek, Philip.'

Philip is being dragged into the other man's desolation, but, for his sake, he maintains an upbeat manner: 'Don't let it get to you, Gav.'

The two men grow silent; Gavin sinks into the seat, and allows his thoughts to wander. 'The other evening at the platform in Sydney Parade … thinking, wouldn't it be …' He looks at some point above Philip's head, and after an awkward silence, rushes in with: 'Ah no. That's not me.' He shifts uneasily, and is saved by his mobile ringing.

'Grand,' he says into the phone, 'grand, yeah.' He listens. 'Absolutely, and with my qualifications, especially with the Smurfit under my belt.' He laughs: 'Yeah, getting there. A chance to look at other options. Onwards and upwards. What's the crack?' After a moment's silence, he works up a hearty laugh. 'Sure. Count me in, Ro. Have to talk to Claire, not single any more like you guys. The Playwright. Cool. I'll be running late. Busy-busy. You know yourself. Hold a seat.' He folds the mobile. 'Good liar, aren't I?'

'You should be on the stage.'

And, as if the phone call has given him new heart, Gavin affects a breezy manner about meeting the guys at the weekend in the pub; about Limerick's chances in the hurling championship, and the fortunes of his own club.

Philip studies his face while he is wriggling out of his embarrassment. He is right. It's to do with share prices and the stock exchange, and Sharkey taking out more loans from Nat Am that only a few of them know about – not even the board whose heads are up their arses anyway. Sharkey showing off: photos of himself on the fucking Onassis yacht for that celebrity wedding. And playing golf with M.J. and Dermod in Barbados – 'real down to earth blokes'.

As they are leaving the restaurant, he tries one last time to offer advice. 'No need to suffer alone in this, Gav. If ever you want to talk, you have my number.'

'No worries, Philip. This won't get me down. Gav is made of stronger stuff than that.'

8

Though she hadn't slept until well after midnight, Sam is up at four o'clock to check everything for her meeting in New York. A light sleeper at the best of times, she is anxious about her presentation to the board of Arrow, the new car manufacturers, who are breaking into the American market. Howard MacKinley in New York, who acts as agent for High Res, had organized the meeting.

'Mega bucks here for High Res,' Ciara, Sam's boss, had said when she assigned her to the job of devising a television advertisement for Arrow. 'American company but the money is coming from China.'

'Like everything else these days.'

'The Chinese want to make it the new Toyota. Seems one of the top brass of Arrow was staying in the Four Seasons last summer and happened to see a High Res advertisement on the television – yours – and wants you for the job. So it's the Rockefeller Center. Break a leg.'

To steady her nerves, Sam invokes her therapist's formula. Rubbing her enamel ring she had brought from her time in New Mexico, the ex-nun's coping device made them both laugh: 'Think of them in the restroom, Samantha: trouser legs down around their ankles – little boys wiping their arses.'

The kitchen still holds the sour taste of the previous night's scene with Philip: they had both been bickering until he eventually declared he was off to bed. Her trolley case and laptop stand waiting on the gleaming tiles. After her cleaning woman's work of the previous day, the recessed lights on the ceiling catch the shine on the chrome trim of the high chairs, and the copper pots and pans (rarely used) hanging above the Richmond range. Steam rises from her mug of coffee on the kitchen island.

As soon as she hears the taxi at the front door, she takes a last sip from the coffee mug and empties the remainder down the sink, making sure to scour the mug and the sink before reaching for her bags. Passport, computer, hard copies of her proposal for the directors, she has already checked a couple of times. She gathers her handbag, BlackBerry and laptop, starts to wheel her trolley case, and switches off the lights. Over the spire of St Killian's Catholic Church, the flashing lights of a plane are dipping towards the airport.

Instead of Dave, her usual driver, the taxi company has sent along a man who knows about everything: the weather, where the health service has gone wrong, and the shower in Leinster House – wasters. Dave had to go with the missus; she's having some hospital tests done. His own missus never wants to talk about sickness or doctors, and won't go near a graveyard.

'What do you make a that?'

'Yes, I suppose people differ about these things.' She takes out her BlackBerry, but the previous night's stand-off with Philip comes between her and the lit-up screen. Philip too hadn't slept: tossing and turning, and sighing deeply as if trying to rid his heart of some burden.

'Them preservatives,' the taxi driver is saying as they join the traffic at Sutton Cross.

'Excuse me.'

'What's causin all the cancer. We never had that before. Them preservatives. An all the pressures on people today.'

'You're right.'

'Like a dog chasin its tail.'

'Excuse me.'

'Puttin ourselves under too much strain. Never satisfied.'

'Right.'

She endures his prattle as a way of escaping the guilt that is rising within, and the echo of her mother's recriminations.

'You're a cheeky bitch who wants her own way. I gave in to your father most of the time. See how well we got on.'

The driver launches into the surgical operations that go wrong – he saw it on the telly the other night: he even had the percentages. She dials her own number and holds a business conversation about deadlines and projects.

'I gave up the smokes meself about ten years ago, and, I'm not jokin you, I never looked back.'

'Really.'

At the set-down in front of the main terminal, brake lights glow as cars and coaches pull up. The morning air is filled with the smell of aircraft fuel.

Sam tips the driver, releases the handle of her trolley case and hurries towards the entrance where young men in a huddle are smoking outside the automatic doors. Beside them is a stack of golf clubs on a trolley.

'I guarantee you won't make the cut this time, Anto,' says one with a shaven head.

'I won't like fuck.' While he speaks, Anto's head keeps darting from side to side. 'I'll wipe the fuckin course with you. Come on or we'll miss our poxy flight.'

They fling their lighted cigarettes on the concrete and barge ahead of her, leaving a jet stream of stale beer when the automatic doors open.

Inside she joins the airport fever, and has to sidestep to avoid the trolley cases. A group of people are gathered beneath a flight information board; others are rushing to join long lines in front of the check-in desks. Stewardesses are parading their figures and flirting with cockpit crews; their high heels beat a come-hither on the floor. A voice-over issuing a warning: mind your property, because unattended bags will be confiscated immediately. She is glad to see only two men in front of her at the priority check-in desk: some recompense, at least, for the red-eye tedium.

Inside the security area there are checks, scans, and the clatter of trays on the conveyor belts as they rumble through the scanner. His belly hanging over the waistband of his trousers, an agent is ambling up and down in one of the bays issuing orders, quoting regulations: if someone has liquids in a bag, remove them please. Place all belts, coins and any metal object in the tray. His arms hang loose from his body as if he's ready to whip a six-gun from a holster. Signals bleep in the personal scanner; he orders one of the passengers to go back and take off his shoes.

The big bloke is now bragging to a blonde agent about a bargain he bought off the plans in Spain, while behind his back, the blonde woman glances at a colleague and rolls her eyes. Sam is put in mind of her father, Ollie – God's gift to women – who even tried to charm Sister Marie Bernadette, the school principal, at a Christmas concert. 'Your dad is a very funny man, Samantha,' the nun said the following day as she tripped along the corridor.

Rising at an ungodly hour, lining up at the security check and waiting at the gate is getting in on her, but this is what she has to go through to afford La Salle, the Iranian cats-eye marble floors, meals with the girls at Hugo's wine bar, and being able to send her children to private schools. And she has no intention of going back to pebble-dashed Raheny. She puts her computer into its case, and resumes her *attitude*.

Yet, something deep inside seems to be loosening, or not quite under control, despite the mantra to which she clings – *modern woman is keeping all the plates spinning*. Not even the move to La Salle is having the desired effect. The invisible curtain is always there between herself and Zara. Dylan is becoming ever so ready to argue. Only a short while ago, when they were in Raheny, he was snuggling up to her as they watched *The Simpsons*.

And Philip. The last time they made love must have been that night when they returned from the Four Seasons after the Christmas party, and even then, she was faking it, in an attempt to recover the rich space they had once shared. Like the night in UCD when the examinations were over and they got a sudden wild notion to leave the student bar, run across to one of the rooms and give full rein to their craving for each other on top of the lecturer's desk in an empty and darkened theatre.

She passes by a row of brightly lit shops, and stops at the

Dolce & Gabbana counter: the thought of buying perfume gives her some respite. While she examines the shelves, her thoughts are racing. She has made it to the captain's table, and she isn't going to let that slip. But four hours' sleep and being dictated to by a bloated security agent is not exactly what she anticipated when High Res made her the senior creative director of the Irish operation. Then her head was turned by the glamour: giving presentations in London or New York, and being whisked away from Kennedy in a limousine. She would be the woman who had it all: a planet away from the empty life her mother led, whose days were circumscribed by *Coronation Street*, and going out with himself, Gorgeous George, to show off their Boston Two-Step.

To calm the dissident voices from within, she steers towards the Jo Malone counter. There she buys Sweet Lime & Cedar Cologne from a Paris Hilton lookalike, who, while wrapping the cologne, tries to tout other products in the range. 'This is our new iconic cream-coloured box, black tissue and grosgrain ribbon,' robot Paris Hilton says. She glances at Sam's MasterCard, and wants to know if Samantha would like to look over their selected gift ideas?

'Another time.' On her way to the gate, she buys a latte and a copy of *Hello!* The three fat women who had spilled out of a taxi ahead of her at the set-down point are now tucking in to the Full Irish. With a tissue in her plump fist, one of them is wiping perspiration from her forehead. Sam despises them. Probably in some dead end job – Saturday night in the local, and then to the Chinese for a curry, two weeks in Costa bloody del Sol.

Out on the apron, men in overalls are refuelling a plane; others in the next bay are casting bags on to a trolley. Pink streaks are showing on the horizon.

Already passengers are gathering at the gate. Among them, a stout man with a boozy face is pacing up and down as he talks into his mobile. 'The quantity surveyor,' he bellows. 'That's what I'm paying the fucker for.' Adjacent passengers affect a deep interest in their newspapers. He closes down the mobile, and continues to mutter.

Sam catches herself gazing into the distance, but childlike wonder is not allowed for the modern woman who is expected to be indifferent to everyone except her private concerns, so she checks her BlackBerry. 'Sorry about that, Mum. Won't happen again. Love you, Zara' is the only message, sent at 4.56 AM. Images of the row with Zara over her refusal to eat her dinner seep through Sam's defensive wall. Her competent mask is inclined to sag, but she suppresses her tears and tries to concentrate on her New York meeting.

Why does life have to be so fucking repetitive? Her own days at university come winging back. Checking her weight a couple of times a day. Worried to death in case she had put on a pound, and yet, striking a pose among the group when they gathered at the main hall of the Arts Block, where she had to be the centre of attention. Someone was talking about a new band called U2. Father Tom was rushing by with flyers: rehearsal for the charismatic Mass on the Friday. Her private hell now bequeathed to her daughter.

To appease her rising guilt, she hits on an idea, and rushes back to House of Ireland where she has seen very smart pendants in Celtic design. She will have it engraved when she gets back to Dublin. Zara will love it.

The strap of her laptop is cutting in to her shoulder; she uses the handle, and leaves the shop, striding towards the gate, her high heels sharp on the concourse floor. Hughes & Hughes is displaying the number one bestseller, *I Never Loved Him Anyway*. A cardboard cut-out of the author with glittering stars on her blonde hair stands at the entrance to the shop. Sam picks up a copy along with a tabloid version of the *Irish Independent,* and joins the queue for the cash register.

The crowd at the gate has got bigger: they are leafing through newspapers; the builder is still pacing, still giving out on the mobile, one chubby hand covering the other ear. Sam takes her personal diary from her bag, and shuts out the world. Her therapist had introduced her to dreams: *the royal road to the unconscious, Samantha.* She reads over the one she had had the other night.

In the dream, she is driving into town in her SUV. Peggy Lee comes on the radio singing: 'Is That All There Is?' – a song she hates; she grabs the tuner to turn down the sound, but the knob falls off; the music blares. Anderson's Crêperie was playing it one afternoon when she was having a latte with the girls. She wanted to get away from the clang of the coffee-maker, the crying of young children, and Peggy Lee's plaintive voice.

She woke with a start, causing Philip to wake also. He touched her arm: 'What? What's wrong?'

'Nothing.'

He turns away on his side: 'You were shouting, something about music, "stop the music".'

'Oh just a silly … you know … dream.'

'OK.' In a minute he is breathing evenly, and she is left staring at the ornamental ceiling rose, and the set of special lights she had to have after seeing them in Interior Décor.

Only a few seats in the business class are occupied. Across the aisle, and a couple of rows to the front, a stout bloke is removing his jacket when a stewardess comes hurrying to him and offers to hang it in the clothes rack. His wide bulk strains the crisp white shirt. He throws a sly glance in her direction, and busies himself taking pillows from the overhead locker. On another flight she had to endure his bombast about the government ministers he knows, and their party pieces at Christmas socials in The Shelbourne. He knows Charlie well: been to The Curragh and Punchestown with him – great party man.

When he started on the different contracts his firm had in hand, she took out her laptop and made some excuse about being under pressure to check over details for a meeting that day in Manhattan. His face fell into a childish pout; he emptied two baby Jameson into a glass, tossed off the whiskey and fell asleep, now and again waking himself with his deep snoring, and then smacking his lips and settling once more into the pillow.

He had been featured in the Business Section of one of the papers: 'Son of Irish navvy a major player in the construction industry'. Another success story, like Quinlan, who is flying the Tricolour over Claridge's. *The Paddys have arrived.*

As soon as breakfast has been served and others are pulling down blinds and turning to sleep, Sam takes out her laptop and reviews her progress report for the six directors who will be seated around a table scrutinizing her presentation. She is anxious. What if they don't like it, or fire questions she hasn't thought through? Will it fall asunder? After an hour or so, she closes down and checks the flight path on her monitor.

The flight attendant is at her elbow with a coffee pot, and when he has sashayed to the galley, she sits back, catches her reflection on the vacant monitor and is surprised by the tight set of her mouth.

She rubs the diamond stone of her earring: Philip's present. He had bought the pair in Nice while she was having a facial. Then when they were celebrating her birthday with lunch at Peploes Wine Bistro, he slipped them under her napkin. She looks through the window at the pale abyss. He'll be going over his fifty or sixty emails now, making sure his clients are kept sweet. 'If your clients are happy, and your numbers are good, the Red Braces can't throw you over the cliff' has been his golden rule over the years.

Even moving to La Salle was only a temporary lull. *A fresh start* was their agreed pact. *Let's put all this hassle behind us.* They were both tired of squabbling anyway, so they sealed the pact with a meal out: a sacramental set piece to celebrate a new beginning. From now on they would reserve one night a week for themselves. *Philip 'n Sam quality time. Let's drink to that.* They had raised their champagne glasses.

Jesus! The chocolate wrappers of last night – did she bin them? Yes. Or did … ? In her mind's eye, she sees herself taking good care to wrap them in a plastic bag, and pop them in the bin at the side of the house. Or is she just imagining it? A relapse after her set-to with Zara: the old flaw lurking in some dark corner and ready to ambush her, despite years of therapy.

She had a minor relapse when they moved to La Salle. 'Moving house is big in the stress scale, Samantha. Right up there with divorce and bereavement,' her therapist had calmed her once again. That time Philip found an empty chocolate box under their bed, and had held it up in front of her. 'What's … ? Don't tell me, Sammy.'

With a brave effort to be casual, she had continued to do her eyeshadow at the dressing table. 'Oh, you know Zara and her friends. They had a sleep-over on Friday night.'

'You're not…'

'Me?' She returned to the eyeshadow, and smiled to the mirror: 'That day is gone, thank goodness.'

Philip had been her anchor during their college days when she was bingeing and then running off to the nearest toilet to vomit. They had sat on the low wall beside the campus lake, surrounded by the high fever of last-minute revision, students lying on the grass, shading their eyes and clutching textbooks, others gearing up for free-wheeling days of filling pints in Shepherd's Bush, or waiting on tables in Cape Cod.

'Why?' he had asked. 'I want to understand.'

'Something to do with my mother. So pretty, and slim …'

She had opened up to him in a way that she'd never done with anyone. Told him about her father too, and the evening she was going up through Raheny village with her friends, and was about to wave when she saw him in a car with Denise, the bookkeeper in his used car business. The two were taken up with each other: she laughing and her head inclined towards him. It all locked into one sickening eye-opener. The photos he had taken of the Christmas parties – Denise in every single one.

Searching for a clue, she had watched every gesture her father made that evening in the kitchen. The look of contentment on his flushed face deepened her suspicion. The boys were arguing: the same argument – Liverpool are better than Manchester United any day. No, they're not; Liverpool are poxy.

'How many times did I tell you not to use that word?' Her mother in her Costa del Sol apron is draining vegetables.

'Well, Sammy.' He notices her downturned head, and tries to tease her about Dara, who wants to take her to the hop in The Grove.

'Where did you get the sunburn?' her mother snaps at him.

'Who? Me?' the broad smile is fading on his fat face. He turns to the boys: 'Boys, have I a colour?'

They continued to race their cars over the linoleum and, without glancing up, they chorus: 'Yeah, Dad, you've a colour.'

'The heat of the kitchen.' He glances at his wife, and tries the Ollie charm: 'OK, I give up. Crowley rang.' He throws up his arms in playful surrender. 'Kept at me until I gave in. Went for nine holes to Portmarnock.'

'I knew it,' said Myra. 'I knew it. You liar,' breaking into a smile, and throwing a tea towel at him. 'And I wanted you to bring me shopping.'

'No bother, love. Take you tomorrow. Yeah, I'll get one of the lads to cover. We'll do Sutton and have ourselves a treat.'

Myra rises from the table and does a swingback of her arm as if to swipe at him; he joins in the play by ducking and raising his hands to protect himself.

'Liar, liar,' the boys laugh. 'Dad is a liar.' They all laugh except Samantha.

He is quick to notice her mood, and tries to charm her with their song:

> Mr Sandman, bring me a dream,
> Bung bung bung bung
> Make him the cutest that I've ever seen …

'Right, Sam. Ready,' he taps the table like a drummer.

> Give him two lips like sunrise and clover …

But instead of joining in, as she used to when tripping along beside him over the sand dunes at Dollymount, she bolts from the table and dashes to her room.

Too angry to cry, she lies on her bed staring at the ceiling; downstairs the boys are still arguing about their soccer teams. She loathes everything about him – the stupid shirt, open at the neck to display a fucking gold chain, the showy buckles on the patent shoes. And the way he tries to hide his Dublin accent and use words like 'observe' and 'as I recall' when talking to Sister Marie Bernadette.

He had crushed her dream: the two of them going to the fairground on the Whitehall Road – candyfloss and his arm around her when they went up on the Ferris wheel. 'You'll live in one of them big houses one day. As good as the best of them,' he had said, pointing across towards Auburn.

On the way back in the car, they sang at the top of their voices:

> *Sandman, I'm so alone*
> *Don't have nobody to call my own*
> *Please turn on your magic beam ...*

She hated her mother also for being such an airhead. The shame of having to watch them when they led the floor at fundraisers for the school, showing off their dance steps: he with his suntan, and she the sequined doll.

In the early years of her marriage, she could share these painful memories with Philip. Now she can talk only to her therapist. To admit her weakness would be giving him a hostage to fortune for the next row. 'You're still fighting Ollie,' he had thrown at her during their last blow-up, 'and I don't know what that therapist is doing with you, but I know one thing – I'm getting the brunt of it.'

'I wouldn't be going to a therapist at all if it hadn't been for you and your whore-banker.'

Having broken off with Ellen, he decided to admit his guilt – hide nothing, Sam would understand. He would then have wiped the slate clean, like when his mother brought him and Andy for Confession each First Saturday. Instead of granting him absolution, Sam had to go on sleeping tablets and she lost over a stone in two weeks.

'You're not available to me; you're somewhere else,' Philip had argued. 'You're stuck back there in your childhood. Jesus, I don't know ... And if it's of any interest to you – that's why I turned to someone else' had been his defence.

'Right! Fucking typical. Blame me.'

The rows usually end by either one storming out and getting

into their car and escaping to Dollymount, or taking the dogs around St Anne's Park.

With one hand resting on her hip, the hostess with the French plait is striking a relaxed pose while chatting to the successful navvy's son. He is in full flight: something about moving into Connecticut – a contract to build condos. She laughs in the right places; when she crouches to pick up a fallen serviette, her skirt slides up along the curve of her thigh.

Later, when Sam is waiting for the toilet to become free, she overhears the hostesses chatting in the galley. 'Loaded,' one is confiding to the other. 'Where does he want to take you, Audrey?'

'The Ice Bar, and then dinner.'

'Lucky you. Grab it, Audrey.'

The captain's update on the flight path and what to see to the left and right drowns out the rest of their conversation.

When Sam returns to her seat, Lucky Audrey is bringing her date a glass of wine.

Sam grows drowsy. Her grip on the BlackBerry slackens, like a child falling asleep and loosening its hold on a teddy bear.

As soon as she enters the conference room of the Rockefeller Center, and Howard MacKinley introduces her to the Chinese businessmen, Sam's anxiety falls away. This is her territory. Her work has brought these men halfway across the world.

She had already arranged her pictures on Kappa boards, and refers to them during the course of her address. 'You have invested billions in your concept: this advertising campaign alone is going to cost millions. It may decide the success or failure of your product. Here's the deal before we start designing an ad for television or the movies.'

They warm to her brisk manner. On her fingers, she lists the selling profile of the major car manufacturers. Volvo for safety. BMW – German engineering. VW – reliability and brilliant re-sale value. Mercedes – prestige and performance. Now I'm going to get you working.' She takes down the Kappa boards. The adren-alin is pumping; the Chinese are grinning and looking at one another behind dark-rimmed glasses.

'What's your strong selling point? What is different and better about your product? Think about it.' Sam explores every avenue. 'What is the American motorist concerned about today?'

'The price of gasoline,' one of the Chinese says with a broad smile.

'Correct. Americans drive long distances, gasoline prices are going up. Wars in the Middle East make the motorist nervous. Gasoline is one, comfort is another. You tell me you are targeting women drivers. Right. Here's another question …'

From then on she is freewheeling. The copywriter and assistant art director follow her keynote address with some technical points.

During a coffee break, the Chinese leave the room to confer; MacKinley goes with them. When they return, the look on Mac-Kinley's face is enough for Sam – High Res has it in the bag. Afterwards they go for drinks in one of the bars nearby. Mac-Kinley sidles up to her while one of the publicity team is trying to explain to the Chinese the rules of gridiron. 'Another five star, Sam.'

'Thanks.'

Without delay, he makes his pitch: 'If you are at a loose end, we could meet up for – '

'Thanks, Howard, but I could sleep for Ireland right now. Can't wait to get to the hotel and soak in a bubble bath. I've to be back in Dublin tomorrow evening. Two teenagers, ugh!' she gestures with her raised hands, simulating a woman going crazy. 'Doing my head in.'

'I know the feeling, but I'm not going to give up that easily. Just thought it would be a shame for an attractive woman to be alone in New York.'

'I'll have to pass up on that one.'

'Dinner, and then Central Park at this time of year – '

'Afraid not Howard.'

He had tried before, and she had to be wary then too; a blunt rejection could cause trouble for her – MacKinley had clout in advertising.

'With this in the bag, High Res may be on the phone for you to work here. Four times the salary.'

'Something to consider.'

'I'll be recommending you.'

'Thanks, Howard.'

'We could talk more over dinner.'

'Another time. I'm jaded. But thanks.'

While the bath is running, she switches on the music centre and selects Ella Fitzgerald from the jazz section. When the water is at the right temperature and a head of foam is rising to the top, she sinks in and lies there with a glass of chablis resting on the bath's rim. Gradually, the soft water and 'Summertime' loosen her residual guilt about deserting Zara, and muffles the blare of the street below her window.

She takes care with her make-up, changes into a lime green dress and brings her airport book down to the restaurant, where a waiter, with mannered smiles and gestures, escorts her to a corner table and hands her the menu.

After dinner, she considers sitting at the bar just to be near the sound of human voices, the casual comments between the barman and customers, and the pianist playing Scott Joplin and Dave Brubeck, but she had been pestered before by guys who were willing to 'show you a good time in the Big Apple'. She decides, instead, to take her book to her room, and asks the barman to have the wine brought up.

I Never Loved Him Anyway fails to hold her interest; she throws it on the bed, and saunters aimlessly around the room before she stands looking down at the street. Darkness is falling over the humid city. She is still a bit wound up from the presentation and the excitement of winning the contract; yet her success fails to raise the mood she's been in since the plane journey. She thinks about phoning one of the girls, but she's already texted two of her Pilates group. And she is supposed to be living in the fast lane, out celebrating – champagne in the ice bucket, and not mooching around a hotel room in New York, while her daughter is weighing herself back in Auburn.

Zara's is the only text on her BlackBerry. 'Have a good trip back, Mum. Luv you.'

'Luv you, Zara. Back 2moro.'

A yellow taxi pulls out from the kerb and brakes just in time to avoid a crash with an oncoming car. The driver hits the horn, brings the car to a sudden halt and shouts abuse through the open window at the taxi; a policeman's whistle cuts through the haze.

Her mind begins to flit from one thought to another. Peggy Lee. Is that all there is? A five-star hotel bedroom in New York on a summer's evening; meeting the girls at the Town Bar and Grill for lunch. One of them is shocked: her new neighbour in Abington is using cheap furniture polish on a dining-room table. *Oh my God can you believe it? Instead of beeswax* – she whose father traversed the men's clothing department at Clerys for forty-five years with a measuring tape around his neck.

With each glass of wine, Sam becomes more stirred up. Weekends with the girls in Barcelona where they overspent, one to be better than the other. Lladró figurines and ormolu ornaments on the mantelpiece. She picks up her sad reflection on the blank television screen, and the sense of being cut off causes her to reach for the zapper and flick to distraction. When she finds herself dozing off with the television at a low volume for company, she undresses and gets into bed, and is surprised when she is roused by her wake-up call at six o'clock.

9

THE DAY that Sam is meeting the Chinese businessmen, Philip is treating James Feeney and his daughter, Mary Pat, to lunch at the Merrion Hotel. Along with his two brothers, Feeney, as a nineteen-year-old, had left Mohill for London in the late nineteen fifties. By dint of hard work and, at times, a brutal treatment of workers – most of them Irish – the three brothers, raw-boned men, made millions clearing up the fallout of Hitler's visit. Then, with an army of Irishmen, they set about giving London a face-lift.

The last time Philip had met Feeney was at the funeral of the former Taoiseach, Charles J. Haughey. 'The end of an era' was his comment when they chatted just before the Requiem Mass began at Donnycarney Church. 'And the Irish people – all of us – owe The Boss a lot. God rest him,' he said, looking fondly at the coffin covered in a white pall and flanked by four tall candles in front of the altar. Keeping vigil are a couple of frail nuns bent over rosary beads. 'An old rogue, but he never let down the trade. Look,' he grinned, sweeping his hand over the front of the church where stooped men with weather-beaten faces were greeting one another. 'If the roof caved in, there wouldn't be a developer left in the country.'

Although well established as a builder in Dublin and the surrounding satellite towns, Feeney now wants a further piece of the action down in the Dublin Docklands. Philip checks with others in the department and makes a report to Sharkey.

'You could put your shirt on Feeney, Philip. No problem there.'

'But the rumours about unsold houses, empty office sites. Not good.'

'Philip, if Nat Am doesn't give him the loan, others will – only too delighted to. Now can we afford to suffer a drop in the market because we haven't got the balls? You were never like that. You always had balls of brass.'

'It's just what one hears, and then that Trinity economist ...'

'Fuck the Trinity economist! Doesn't know Jack shit about banking or the housing market. These arseholes have their heads stuck in books. They should get out a bit more often. But if that would ease your mind, I'll set up a meeting along with Kimberly and our legal team.'

'Don't you think we should put it to the credit committee, like we used do each Friday morning?' Egan argues. Philip had asked him to sit in on the meeting.

'No need, Kevin. Feeney has been a reliable client: he has ticked all the boxes – cash flow, security and we have recourse to his personal assets, so what more do we need? But if it will ease your minds, I'll inform the Regulator.' He winks. 'Meeting him Saturday at the Glen. You know by now, guys, business is done at the nineteenth.' He looks towards the display of pictures on the far wall. Among them is one of himself and other golfers, including a member of the Regulator's force taken in front of his villa at Cap Ferrat.

'This time last year ...' Egan begins to explain.

'Kevin, this-time-last-year, I'm sick of hearing the naysayers about the number of houses that were sold.' He is in a tidying mood, dropping pens into an earthenware holder, taking up a sheaf of pages and aligning the edges against the desk. 'Lookit, we're on a roll. Let's give a wide berth to the shitehawks. I never had much time for hurlers on the ditch. And these gobshites who like the sound of their own voices on the television.'

He swivels in his chair and takes in the wide view provided by the glass panels at his back and to his left. Looking away in the direction of Dun Laoghaire, he says: 'You know, if Desmond and his likes hadn't taken this country by the balls, we'd be in Queer Street. And if I – and I say this in all humility – hadn't gone after the big fish, we'd still be loaning peanuts to couples out in some fucking backwater – like the credit union does – and you guys, let me remind you, might still be listening to the fucking nightingale in Berkeley Square.' The famous Sharkey guffaw causes heads to rise, out in the open-plan office.

Sharkey takes pride in recalling how he door-stepped the debtors. No longer were they receiving polite letters dictated by St John Dunleavy on vanilla paper with the bank's crest. 'The gloves are off, guys.'

He wheels around again. 'Pay no attention to these economists. Eunuchs in a whorehouse: can't do it, only look on.' He laughs again and straightens his canary tie. 'When I urged Dunleavy to open branches in country towns, and proposed that we float on the market, these self-proclaimed gurus called us upstarts. But Nat Am shares rocketed in six months: everyone wanted to buy. We were the new kids on the block, but by heck we were wiping the eye of the top guns. This is only a seasonal blip.' He stands. 'Business as usual.'

Along with Mary Pat, his solicitor, and his accountant, Feeney arrives for a meeting in Philip's office on the Friday. With him also are his quantity surveyor and one of the directors. The terms had been already ironed out and agreed upon by both lawyers: all they need to do is to sign the contract. A lap of honour.

Giving off the scent of allure and Estée Lauder, Kimberley from the legal team takes a sheaf of documents from her attaché case. Within ten minutes a loan of forty million Euro is granted to Feeney Holdings for a larger investment in Dublin's Docklands. The mood is celebratory while they sign the documents, and when the deal is done, they relax. It is now time for Nat Am to show hospitality to a valued client and his entourage in the executive floor dining room. The following September the bank would indulge Feeney's love for Gaelic football by having Philip take him to Croke Park on All-Ireland day. First Nat Am would host a lunch at The Shelbourne, and then they would provide executive limousines for the journey across to the bank's corporate box in the stadium.

Sharkey joins them as they are about to travel up in the lift. The conversation is pure pleasure: Fairyhouse, Gowran Park and how Seánie hates to lose at golf. 'Seen him in a right state one evening at Mount Juliet,' says Sharkey. 'He wasn't making the cut, so what does the bastard do except put an extra bet on each hole.' Sharkey's bulky shoulders shake while gloating over Seánie's misfortune.

They have an aperitif in the lounge across from the dining room where the green walls, hung with Paul Henrys and le Brocquys, set off the dark mahogany chairs and table, and where sparkling crystal stands tall on a linen tablecloth. One of the Polish waiters brings in a bottle of champagne; he is followed by another with a tray of glasses. Philip pops the champagne and proposes the toast: may Feeney Holdings continue to flourish and always remain a valued client of Nat Am.

The team of waiters in black ties is fussing around to make sure everything is in order. Philip and his guests begin with smoked salmon and a delicate chardonnay and then attack the strip loin of tender beef, all the while putting away two bottles of Gevrey-Chambertin 1988.

Sharkey purrs. Nat Am is still bringing in the big fish. He becomes voluble, calling to mind his time in Harvard and, for Feeney's benefit, their first meeting at the pokey premises in Andrew Street. 'Ah sure, I remember it well. Mr Dunleavy had one of his gout attacks.'

At one point, during the dinner, when the others are making expert predictions on the England v. Sri Lanka cricket test match, Feeney loses interest; he leans over to Philip and thanks him for a good day's work. They do small talk for a while until Philip notices Feeney fidgeting with a teaspoon.

'So,' he asks him, 'how is your development in north County Dublin going?'

Like a hypnotist's subject coming out of a trance, Feeney springs back to life. 'Sure, I'll have it done in jigtime.' He places a huge fist on the tablecloth. 'Do you know one of the best lessons I've learnt in life?'

'What's that, James?'

'Every man has his price.'

He had run into snags in the north County building project, and the work was held up for a couple of weeks. Even though he had the councillors on his side, the school principal up there, a young man who had trained the winning team in the Cumann na mBunscoil for the previous two years, had got the parents to lodge a protest. He believed that apartment blocks close to the sports pitch would bring a lot of traffic around the place, and be a risk to children's safety.

'Rubbish,' says Feeney. 'Indoor basketball and changin rooms and a few thousand to the parish priest for the restoration of his church organ. Sure I had the board of management eatin out of my hand!' He suppresses his laughter, and says, out of the side of his mouth. 'And now the holy man has the best organ in Dublin.'

The meal over, they accompany him to his gleaming black Kompressor parked at the front, and exchange a few words before they part: glad to do business again; best bank in town; old friends are best. And Sharkey has every confidence in the market. They will talk soon.

Philip turns to Sharkey on their way up in the elevator. 'That's well and truly put to bed now. And we can bank on your man; he's got the connections.'

'Correct. No shortage of TDs with him at Croker last year.'

While they are waiting for the doors to open, Sharkey says above a whisper: 'Although he still hasn't quite learned how to use a nail brush.'

'Hah, we'll take his money, all the same.'

'Incidentally, Dunleavy is talking about lunch at Fitzwilliam on Friday. You should be getting an email today. Just a few of us. To close out a good week at the office you might say.'

'Fine. Never refuse a lunch with Breffni.'

The standing joke at Nat Am is: 'When Dunleavy invites you to his tennis club, open another loan account for investment.'

It being a Thursday evening, they can afford to relax, so they take another coffee in the lounge. Sharkey is jubilant, but because Philip has challenged his viewpoint on banking issues in the past couple of years, they are never fully at ease with each other; so Sharkey calls Brennan and Wheeler to join in the celebrations.

Across the corridor the Polish caterers are setting the table for the next show of hospitality to the Golden Circle. Down below on the street, people are hurrying by: a woman is pushing a buggy; an oil lorry has pulled in to the Maxol garage up the road and the driver is inserting a hose into an opening in the ground. Three schoolgirls in rust-coloured uniforms go by; two of them are on their mobiles.

'You see all of them, guys,' says Sharkey, turning round towards the glass panels, and pointing down to the street. 'They are the little people. And guess what? They will always be the little people. They will always be down there. *We*,' he spreads wide his arms like a priest inviting the congregation to join him in the prayers of the Mass. 'We belong up here. And once you're up here – make no mistake about it – you're untouchable. And you know something else – if we blow it, *they* will pay for our mistakes. And the pipsqueaks in the media can go and fuck themselves. That's the way of the world, guys. Has been since old God's time.'

Sharkey's guffaw causes the Polish caterers to steal a glance across the hallway.

Usually, when St John Dunleavy hosts lunches at Fitzwilliam, he makes much of greeting fellow members on the way in, and introducing his staff in the manner of a proud patron. In the wood-panelled foyer, he gives Sharkey, Philip and Kyran Wheeler a potted history of Ireland's premier club. Silver trophies in glass cabinets bathe in amber light.

The bankers happen on one of the club committee who is excited about the forthcoming Irish Open Tennis tournament. 'Some first-rate chaps from across the pond,' he announces. 'Needless to say, they have to be rewarded.' He rubs his thumb against his fingers. 'The days of playing for the love of the game are dead and buried.'

'Ah,' says Dunleavy, 'how one wishes for *les amateurs.*'

The committee man turns to Wheeler. 'Of course, Kyran is one of our esteemed members here, and he carried off the laurels on a couple of occasions if memory serves me right.'

'We too are very proud of Mr Wheeler's successes. By the by,' says St John Dunleavy, 'many thanks for the Wimbledon tickets: you always come up trumps. Good show. See you soon.'

As they climb the stairs, St John Dunleavy does a running commentary on the black and white photos that line the wall: Wimbledon champions who had played at the Irish Open and were part of the club's glorious past. Nearly everyone at Nat Am knows about his selection on the Leinster Schools Team, when wooden rackets in presses were still in use, and about the day when he was a line judge at the Open and he had put manners on Bob Hewitt, the South African, who had come straight from Wimbledon that year.

Twice Hewitt disputed St John Dunleavy's calls. 'But I held my ground, gentlemen.' Sharkey and Philip have been through the routine before, but they nod as if hearing it all for the first time. 'Had a drink afterwards with him. Capital fellow.'

'Laver,' Dunleavy beams, and points to one of the greats, 'look at him with J.D.'

In the dining room, Wheeler's phone goes off: he is profusely apologetic. He stands, excuses himself again, almost bowing to Dunleavy, and talks into his phone as he is walking towards the door. Sharkey leans over to St John Dunleavy: 'Kyran, he's really getting his teeth into his work now.'

'Seems well clued-in alright,' says Dunleavy.

'The two contracts he secured,' Sharkey is excited in the telling, 'they were clients he made in, *of all places*, the gym. Can you believe it? At the gym in Blackrock. Six o'clock in the morning!'

'My word!'

'And guess what? One of them he poached from Ulster, the other from Anglo. He reminds me of Philip when I rescued him from London,' Sharkey laughs. 'Same enthusiasm.'

'Imagine buttonholing a guy… my goodness, at six in the morning.' St John Dunleavy shakes his head. 'Hell's bells, probably in the shower.' He throws back his large head and mane of white hair, and laughs.

'Balls we call it, Breffni,' says Sharkey, leaning in so that he won't be heard by those at the surrounding tables.

'Hah, quite so, quite so.' St John Dunleavy chuckles. 'Yes, we have to concede: the future belongs to Mr Wheeler's generation.'

Wheeler returns with many apologies. A developer up in Newry, a client of one of the other banks, is being given the run-around and he wants to talk with Nat Am about equity support for a shopping mall.

'All in the line of duty, Mr Wheeler.' Dunleavy bestows one of his patrician smiles, and returns to his topic – how, from now on, they have to be lean and mean at Nat Am. 'Our competitors are chasing us now, gentlemen. Can't leave any stone unturned.'

Philip watches him: white gold ring, and matching cufflinks when he raises the wine glass to his lips. This is a warm-up; the bastard is on a pruning operation with Sharkey to get rid of those staff whom they regard as a drain on the purse, and replace them with lackeys such as Brennan and Wheeler who will tout for business in gyms and golf clubs, and work their arses off for much less than they have to pay someone in a senior position.

Philip himself has to tread warily or be shown the front door. Can't risk that – not with a mountain of a mortgage, and much more from a Nat Am loan to reinvest in bank shares.

'How long are you with us now?' St John Dunleavy asks Philip.

'Twenty-four in August, Breffni!'

'My goodness,' Dunleavy signs the bill and drops it on the silver tray, placed discreetly at his side by a waiter. 'Ah well, gentlemen, sooner or later we all have to face the passage of time. *Gather ye rosebuds.*' He bows his head, and intones: 'For all that we have received, may we be truly grateful. Amen.' They mutter 'Amen'. He stands – giving the cue to the others to do likewise. '*C'est la vie*, gentlemen. *C'est la vie.*'

On the way down the stairs, past Rod Laver whose left-hand racket wrist was two inches larger than his right, and Goolagong's curves, Dunleavy talks of his plans to do the Hebrides again in

September if the winds are fair. The crew is mostly Downside. 'A pact we made on our last night in the dear old Alma Mater, and we've honoured our pledge every year without fail. *Renovabitur ut aquilae iuventus tua.* The old school motto. Although, truth to tell, at this stage, little chance now of renewing ourselves like the eagle, gentlemen.' He gives a broad salute to fellow members as he leads his guests through the automatic doors.

Out in the car park, the amber tail lights of his Jaguar XJ wink when he presses his remote control.

'As a matter of interest,' he says, cocking the keys. 'Forget the claptrap about the limitations and the market in jeopardy. The market was never in better shape.'

'No risk?' Philip says. 'And those empty apartments we're hearing about. And what about the Regulator, what does he – ?'

'The Regulator can take a running jump,' Sharkey cuts in and, enjoying his own quip, looks at his boss for approval. St John Dunleavy is sinking into tan upholstery; he lowers the window and laughs. 'Hah, quite so, Aengus. Well you know, chaps, as the finance minister has put it – *light-touch* regulation is the way ahead for our banks.' The Jag purrs and begins to cruise. He calls through the open window: 'We'll have to do this more often. Yes, very soon.'

Wheeler had to get rackets restrung so Sharkey travels back with Philip. Waiting for the lights to change at Morehampton Road, Sharkey says: 'It's all bigger than any of us – share prices, bond-holders, we're fucking slaves to them.' He glances at Philip, who is about to make a comment when Sharkey's BlackBerry goes off. Conrad Brennan is making a progress report on a client. 'Wow,' says Sharkey, 'you jammy bastard. Philip and I are returning to the grindstone. '

'Oh, hi, Philip.' Brennan fails to hide the surprise in his voice.

'Hi, Conrad.'

'Well then, we'll talk later.'

Sharkey chuckles when he hangs up: 'Isn't he something else? Landed another big one. Remember the hotel guy. We took him to lunch in Roly's last May.'

'Hotel guy?'

'Don't you remember? Had been a teacher and got in on the act. Saw his pupils – chippies and bricklayers passing him out. Decided he'd get a bit of the action. Anyway, he wants to increase his property portfolio in his own town: shopping mall, hotel and apartment block – that sort of investment. His bank won't bite.'

'Yes, I remember.'

'I like the guy; he's got balls,' says Sharkey.

After a while, Philip says: 'If memory serves me right, aren't there two shopping centres there already? And the population can't be more than ten to fifteen thousand. What about the planners?'

'Come on, Philip,' Sharkey laughs deep in his throat. 'You've been around long enough to see how they operate. Dosh, Philip: the only show in town. Jaysus, must I draw pictures?'

Before getting out of the car, Sharkey asks about the American Evening.

'Yes, no worries on that score. All we need now is spot of luck with the weather.'

Philip is so absorbed in working out Sharkey's sly ways, he nearly reverses into a new Passat in the next bay. St John Dunleavy's hatchet man will make life impossible for those he wants to cull; he's seen him do it many times. Some he will call to his office to tell them they have to clean out their desks. With others, he will play a cruel game of cat and mouse, such as being excluded from meetings, or no longer being considered for promotion. Then he will play the hurt card: 'You're letting me down. I always thought I could rely on you.'

Some would hold out for as long as possible: those especially who might still have the youngest child in college, or have a loan on a holiday home. Eventually the strain would tell, the victim would crumble or else begin to drink too much.

When he returns to his desk, Philip opens his computer to find an email from Ellen. 'Coffee tomorrow at Katie's. Elevenish?' He stares at the screen: her first note since they had called it a day.

The rain is showing no sign of a let-up when Philip drives down Serpentine Avenue and turns right for Katie's.

He waits at a table near the open door, and sits staring out at the downpour bouncing off the metal chairs; the fringe of the awning is being tossed and turned in the wind. Katie has the lights on in the café; along with her staff, she is busy making sandwiches for the people who stand at the counter; others are sheltering their coffee and rolls before making a dash to their cars.

While she shakes pearls from her umbrella, Ellen stands beneath the awning and smiles through the glass door: the red lipstick she had freshly applied sets off her black coat, glazed with rain. The sight of her reminds Philip of the stock comment from men around Nat Am: 'Single! What a bloody waste.'

'Sorry for not getting in touch before now,' he says, as she sits opposite him.

'No apologies. Remember what we agreed? No strings attached. Anyway, this is business.' High above the counter, on the flat screen, Adam Boulton of Sky News is reporting in front of the House of Commons; the ticker tape, rolling at the bottom of the screen, announces *More headaches for financial institutions.*

She loses no time in telling him that Sharkey wants to sideline a few of the senior managers. 'He's grooming Brennan for Kevin's job. Not a word or I'm …' She does a throat-slitting gesture. 'And Karen is history also.'

Over afternoon tea in the Orangerie of the Radisson the previous Saturday, Karen had given her the low-down. 'By the way,' Ellen laughs, 'Sharkey thought that Conrad was one of *the* Brennans when he interviewed him. Can you believe it?'

'That was kept well under wraps.' Philip laughs with her.

'Conrad put out the word that he was one of them. And during the course of the interview, Sharkey says: "Of course finance is in the genes". Brennan kept shtum. Anyway, when Sharkey discovered the truth afterwards, surprisingly, he took it in good part. Apparently he sees some version of himself in that arse-licker.'

Ellen went on to tell Philip how the whispering campaign against Egan has already started; how his wife Gillian was out on the floor at the golf club dance the previous Saturday night with some chap, and the two of them sewn into each other while Egan sat at a table drinking himself into a stupor.

'They're making out he's her slave,' Ellen says.

'Tell me about it. Wasn't I there when he first clapped eyes on her in London? She was his perfect woman; I could see trouble from the word go. Tried to get him to wait before becoming engaged. No. Wouldn't hear of it.'

Ellen cites Sharkey: ' "Egan is past his sell by. Made a dog's dinner of a file recently; only for Conrad stepping in, we'd have lost millions." And Dunleavy, with his silverware manners, is only too willing for Sharkey to do his dirty work, of course.'

The rain has eased off when they step out of Katie's: ragged clouds are breaking up, revealing patches of blue over the RDS.

They walk slowly back to where Ellen has parked: green leaves from overhanging branches had been blown on to the roof of her Citroën. 'This isn't altogether about Egan slowing up,' says Philip after a while. 'This is about Egan refusing to lick. He wouldn't support Sharkey in his bid for the captaincy of Druid's Glen, and, instead backed a guy who was with us in 'Rock.'

She shakes her head. 'So Sharkey had it in for him. Jesus! You boys, when will you ever – ?'

'That's alpha male, Ellen. Remember the two captains of industry down at the K Club a couple of years ago.'

'What about them?'

'They locked horns over the same thing: each wanted to be captain as if their lives depended on it. Sharkey was sore that Egan had let him down. Then the Senior Lending job came up and Egan was passed over.'

Philip's glance falls on the curve of her neck and the dark hairs that had charmed him when they were meeting secretly, but he returns to business. 'They were great buddies at the beginning. Poker nearly every Tuesday night.'

She presses the button on her car key. 'He harps on about the bank being the fittest, the sharpest and the meanest, and how it's such a dogfight in the financial world. No mention of his fat salary and a bonus – 1.4 mill last Christmas.'

'That I know too well.'

She hesitates before sitting in; an awkward moment passes between them. 'You know I haven't forgotten you.' She tilts her head. 'No. Better leave it at that. Thanks for the coffee, Philip.'

'Another time.'

'Sure. Another time.'

When he is getting into the lift, others are returning from an early lunch in the plaza. The buzz of weekend excitement rises from their conversation: 'Yes,' says one of them, 'the thing about Seánie is he's got a conceptual framework. Seánie won't be caught.'

'Jammy bastard.'

For the following Friday evening's wrap-up on the executive floor lounge, Sharkey forgets to invite Egan and other lending managers whom he has earmarked for the scrapyard. Unlike the credit committee meetings on a Thursday morning at Icarus Hall, where each lending manager is expected to give a full account of the week's business, this is an opportunity to 'warm down', as Sharkey puts it: a show of goodwill and loyalty to Nat Am. The meeting is followed by finger food and drinks from the bar. When it happens two weeks in a row, Egan covers his hurt with a carefree throwaway: 'Couldn't be bothered. Only waffle, anyway, at these meetings.'

It all comes to a head, however, when Egan has just returned after two days' leave: he had been attending his brother's appointment to a chair at Cambridge University. Again, torrential rain is dancing off the concrete forecourt of Nat Am, causing women with umbrellas, whipped by the wind, to hurry around the bronze statue. Drops of rainwater are sliding down the ribs of the umbrellas and forming little pools on the floor of the crowded lift as Egan travels up.

Another dreadful summer.

Worst ever.

Must be.

He steps onto the expansive office floor: low partitions divide one cell from the next in the vast honeycomb. Computers are casting a sickly pallor on the faces of those at their desks; others are exchanging a few words at a water cooler.

Away in the distance, behind the venetian blinds of Sharkey's office, Brennan, Wheeler and Sharkey are laughing: Wheeler's arm is raised for a high-five. In the background Karen, Sharkey's personal assistant, is gathering up papers from the desk. The laughing meets a sudden death when they see Kevin Egan, yet they keep on talking, but now throw sly looks in his direction. Sharkey beckons him into the office. 'Kevin,' he calls, 'the very man. Come in for a minute – need your advice on something. And welcome back.'

They do small talk: golf, the weather, and how did Cambridge go? 'Of course, loads of brains in the family,' Wheeler says. He holds a bulky file in his hands.

'Weather atrocious. Must be this global warming thingummy.' Brennan is shifty.

Sharkey slips into business mode. 'We just want to update you. The guys here have been doing a spot of time-and-motion, and we've come up with a few suggestions. Nothing substantive. Just that Conrad here will lend a hand with some of your workload.' His stretching routine gives his voice a yawning tone. 'We're not getting any younger. The writing is on the wall for all of us. These young tigers here are now snapping at our heels: we have to bow to the inevitable.'

Reeling from the haymaker, Egan rushes in with 'A few years left in the old dog yet, Aengus.'

Sharkey ignores the comment. 'I've promised myself another five.' He holds up one hand, fingers splayed. 'Then it's wall to wall golf at the Glen, and to the open seas with *Gatsby.*' He throws a fond look at a silver-framed picture of his forty-foot yacht on his desk.

Egan is scared: he knows from experience how merciless Sharkey is. The thought of empty days on end are causing goose pimples to rise on the back of his neck. 'As simple as this, guys,' Sharkey had boasted one night during a poker game. 'To make an omelette, you gotta crack some eggs. If a guy crunches the numbers, he'll be rewarded; if not, I shoot him.' He had done a pistol-firing imitation with his hand.

The guff he is trotting out now about retiring is a smoke-screen, but Wheeler and Brennan are making sounds of agreement. 'Unfortunately,' Sharkey jabs his thumb towards the ceiling, 'you know yourself, Kevin, the Braces.'

'They take no prisoners,' Brennan echoes.

'Ruthless,' Wheeler shakes his head.

'Goddamn shareholders looking for a return on equity.'

'They call the shots.'

'But not going to happen today or tomorrow. Just marking your card, Kevin. See you later. Perhaps we'll have a fourball soon.' Sharkey stands again.

When Egan returns to his desk, he finds an email from Sharkey, sent the previous evening: 'Kevin. Forgot to tell you, management team have been doing a spot of benchmarking; your office will be shifted next week. Just a logistics thing.'

IO

THAT EVENING when Philip is driving home along the coast road, the sun has come out and is making the most of the Auburn houses that dot the hillside, but he hardly notices them. He is playing over in his mind the hangdog look on Egan's face while telling him he is being shafted.

A group of women jogging on the green strip between the road and the mudflats at Dollymount distract his train of thought: they are struggling to keep up with the bobbing ponytail of their blonde leader, whose firm body contrasts with the quivering rolls of flesh inside their tracksuits.

A voice on the radio grabs his attention. The words 'justice' and 'concern for human dignity' sweep him back a quarter of a century to raw nights in February when stray pages of the morning's newspaper are whipped off the pavement and sent floating across Baggot Street. As if someone has flicked a switch and an old black-and-white newsreel is before his eyes, he sees stubble-rough men lurching from doorways and from under the bridge, squinting and peering into the winter streets, while frisky nurses from St Vincent's are tripping down the steps from their flats in Waterloo Road. He, Sam and others from the Commerce Soc. are lifting the lids off soup cauldrons at the back of the Transit, and releasing clouds of steam into the frosty air.

The voice on the radio is as strong, and Donegal-determined, as ever. The message is the same: a government that grants privileges to the well-off, such as tax reductions for investing their thousands, and allows horse breeders go scot free and, at the same time, refuses to redress the condition of the homeless, is a disgrace. 'Thanks, Father Tom,' says the radio woman. 'Great work you're doing; no doubt we'll hear more about this. And now for the sports results. Here's Des.'

Eyes full of fear, and alcohol-induced tremors come back to him. 'Blessins a God on you,' when Sam filled their paper cups. Names and faces surface in his head: Smokey and Johnno. And Keaveney, who wore a tattered naval officer's tunic and believed he was an Admiral of the Fleet.

It was Philip who introduced her to the work, one evening after a lecture. She was reluctant at first, but threw herself into it, making up Christmas gifts of socks and underwear for the Admiral and others. Ponytail busy, she issued instructions as she ladled out the steaming soup. Philip, in his beard and torn jeans, handed around paper cups, and tidied up afterwards.

In corduroy trousers and sandals, Father Tom talked about 'Option for the Poor' at the prayer group in Newman House. And after singing hymns they headed for Kirwan's where they planned their manifesto, while being handed pints over the heads of other students looking for tickets to the Five Nations.

When Ronald Reagan arrived to trace his relatives, the Newman Group appeared in the newspapers picketing the American Embassy, Sam gripping her placard – *Justice for Nicaragua*; she went head to head with an amused Garda Inspector.

Instead of turning in for Auburn, Philip drives up Beresford Road and parks at the Summit. There he sits and scans the Dun Laoghaire coastline and the Three Rock in the background. A ferry is heading for Dublin Port, leaving a slipstream in the sparkling water.

One Holy Week, when other students were disappearing to Connemara and Dingle with rucksacks, they had done a forty-eight-hour fast outside the Bank of Ireland for Father Tom's homeless people. Then back through empty streets to Newman House on Holy Thursday: starving but high on self-sacrifice. For

Mass, they sat around on bean bags or with their backs propped against the wall, bright-eyed in the flicker of candlelight; grapes, loaves of bread and wine on a low table at the centre. A tweed Jesus from Nicaragua with arms outstretched hung from one of the walls. The air was filled with perfumed incense.

Squatting among them was Father Tom; over jumper and slacks he wore a stole – the only vestment that showed he was the celebrant. Guitars at the ready for the opening hymn: 'Give Me Joy in My Heart'. They shared in the homily: how they would live out the implications of their Christian commitment to the poor. Everyone received from the earthenware chalice.

For this and for 'a flagrant disregard for the rubrics of the liturgy, such as celebrating the Eucharist without being properly vested', the bishop withdrew faculties from Father Tom to offer a public Mass or hear confessions for six months, and directed him to go to a monastery in North Wales 'to reflect on your being a source of scandal for impressionable young Catholics'. Instead of North Wales, he went to Kenya until the bishop retired, and a more reasonable man took his place.

Upstairs, in one of the Georgian rooms with swags in plaster and wine-coloured drapes, they devoured pizzas, chips and soft drinks while 'Libera Me', the 'Miserere', 'Gabriel's Oboe' and other pieces of music played in the background.

When they stood at the door, the street was filled with promise.

'Happy Easter, Tom.'

'Happy Easter.'

The priest watched while they went off, then he closed the heavy door and left the light on in the hallway, rather than face the dark silence of the house.

Philip and Sam slunk away on their own. A half-moon was hanging over the budding magnolia at the corner of St Stephen's Green where they turned into Grafton Street. They hardly spoke lest they break the spell.

In front of the Central Bank, they stopped and held each other, and sealed their covenant to the plans already laid in the Georgian room: when they graduated, they would go for a year

to Tanzania to help Philip's uncle, Father Anselm, who was building a health clinic and a new school there.

Now, as he sits in the isolation of his BMW, gazing out at the
empty bay, Philip remembers the letter he wrote Anselm about
how much he enjoyed the summers he spent in Tanzania, and
that he would go out for a year to help him build the clinic. That
was when Una stepped in.

'Better get your Master's first, Philip. Yes, good to help Father
Anselm, but what seems bad to us … well, those people are used
to that way of life.'

'They feel hunger like anyone else; and they die so young.
Surely one should try and – '

'Yes, but … you'd then be forfeiting your Smurfit scholarship.
Have you thought of that?'

'I've promised him.'

'Who?' She was irritated.

'Father Anselm.'

'Oh, Father Anselm will understand.'

'Easy to say.'

Being the eldest child, Philip enjoyed a firm bond with his
mother. She relied on him more than the others, even sharing
small worries, so he was reluctant to spoil that privilege. Nevertheless, he held out, and for a week or so they were skirting
around each other.

Eventually he came round. 'You may be right,' he conceded
when they were alone again in the kitchen. 'Next year. I'll go
next year.'

'Yes. Good decision, Philip.' She was relieved to see the look
of acceptance on her favourite child's face.

In the same kitchen many years before, he had rushed in while
she was peeling potatoes: 'Mam, we had a priest in our class today
to tell about the hungry boys and girls in Africa.'

'Oh, had you?'

'When I grow up, Mam, there won't be any hungry boys and
girls. I'll get them food.'

'Good man yourself, but go up to your room now and do your homework, and I'll go over it with you.'

Sam was doing her Masters also; both, along with Egan, had got scholarships to the Smurfit Business School. And during that year, the Holy Thursday night of Option for the Poor and soup for the down-and-outs got crushed beneath a pyramid of glittering prizes for the young and talented, when the slump came to an end; or if not at home, then in London or Boston. The excitement of marketing ideas, of the bond market, share prices, and bonuses at Christmas was too tempting to resist.

That was the lean nineteen eighties: they couldn't afford to spend any more time on Option for the Poor, not for the present anyway – what mattered was getting a job. When Barclays replied to his application, Philip, along with Egan, hopped on the stepping stones. Sam was changing also – working long hours. Already she was making her mark with High Res. In Doheny & Nesbitt's, college friends told her she was made for it; she purred and sipped her gin and tonic.

Before Philip and Egan left for London, the Newman Group got together for a farewell party in Kirwan's pub. They were clean-shaven and in suits: no sign of torn jeans anywhere, and no mention of the Admiral. When someone said in a throwaway manner that Thatcher was needed to put some control on the UK economy, that the trade unions were holding the country to ransom, there was general agreement.

Philip and Sam phoned each other every Friday; their promises were still on course, but over time the phone calls became less frequent. He joined Egan on the town. Weekends were for the chase: summer evenings when their pints of beer were golden outside The White Hart, where the new wave of Irish drank with their English colleagues. The slanting sun was glancing off the side mirrors of London taxis when they were swinging round the corner or stopping for a fare.

Many of the Irish had postgraduate degrees, and one or two European languages. They shared little with their countrymen who dug trenches and laid cables for Murphy around Willesden and Camden Town. They came across a Longford chap, Dolan, who worked for HSBC, who told them about Haughey's talk of a financial centre for the Dublin docks.

'Go on, pull the other one,' said Egan.

'Honestly, cross my heart,' said Dolan. 'Things are looking up. I'm going back to get a piece of the action. My own brokerage in Dublin. There's a guy over from Ireland; he's recruiting for … let me see.' He took a business card from his wallet and peered at it: 'Sharkey,' he declared. 'Looking for guys for a new bank just down the road from the RDS: small outfit, but if my hunch is right – not for long.' He put his pint to his lips and then rested it on the window ledge. 'Sly-looking bollix, but, hey, you're not going to marry him, so if the price is right …' He shrugged.

The following evening, Sharkey appeared. 'Will you stay farting around here for the rest of your lives, giving out credit cards, chequebooks and arranging mortgages?'

'No.'

'I've done my homework on you, and if you're prepared to work, guys, I'm talking big bucks. Not wasting your life with little old ladies and their savings.' He announced his primary rule of life: 'Guys: *you are what you have,*' and went on to set out his stall. 'Medium-sized companies are my target, but I'll not rest. I've no interest in sprat. I'm going after fucking Moby-Dick. Now if you come on board – and you'd be very stupid not to – you'll meet the bank chairman, St John Dunleavy. Anglo-Irish type of gent – went to that school …' He lowered his head. 'Downside Abbey. Anyway, OK behind it all.'

He wasted no time. 'Now here's the deal. No fucking unions. Amalgamated will remain open during lunchtime. Lookit, fuck up and I shoot you.' He had authority from the board to hire and fire. 'There's a gap which I aim to fill. Ireland is getting back on its feet. No longer the sick man of Europe.' He grinned. 'Companies need loans in a hurry: the big guns keep them waiting. We Harvard men don't believe in sitting on our brains.'

He had other commandments: *No* to those who want a loan to go with their families to see Mickey Mouse in California; *no* to those who want to convert the fucking attic.'

His raw strength and charm excited them. They would give it a whirl.

'What about the interview?' Philip asked as Sharkey was going away. 'Where will it be held?'

'The interview!' Sharkey turned and for the first time they heard his famous guffaw. '*This* is the fucking interview.' He had to raise his voice to be heard above the din. 'I've already boned up on you, guys. I know my men when I've had a pint with them … By the way, do you play poker?'

'Kevin is your man,' said Philip. 'Count me out.'

'Oh, we'll have to teach you then. Won't we, Kevin? How can anyone be a banker if he doesn't play poker? Risk is the name of the game, guys. Calculated risk. The nature of the beast, Philip. The buzz. See you in Dublin if you've any sense. Stay here and become a fucking cabbage; the knitted cardigan in forty years' time, when you're pissing yourself. Join me and you won't be sorry. Remember, guys, Sharkey's motto: *You are what you have.*'

Philip turns the key in the ignition, and the high-powered motor springs to life. He makes a quick plan for the evening. With Sam away in London until the following day, he has no intention of mooching around the house on his own, getting angrier by the minute with Dylan if he is upstairs with his deafening music.

La Salle is silent when he steps inside his hall door. Through the French windows at the back, he can see Zara and her friends having a great laugh: one of them is doing a mock version of a model on the catwalk. Thank God, at least, she's not in a state. He makes a salad, pops a burger in the microwave, and sits in front of the flat screen, surfing the channels while he eats. Ramsay is swearing at kitchen staff whenever they make a mistake; a couple has found bliss in moving from Dunleer to the south of France; they've even started a vineyard. 'Getting away from the rat race; best decision we ever made. Mimosa in our garden in February,' says the woman. Another couple is standing outside their converted dream house in west Cork: 'this is it' they are saying to the design expert. 'All my boxes ticked now. And the water feature *really, really* works.'

He knows the script from memory, so he stands, takes his tray to the draining board and decides, after making a final call to Robin Hill about the American Evening, he will go for a long cycle: one that will exhaust every muscle in his body, and take him away from the suffocating world of contracts for difference, share prices and the guff about water features that *really, really* work.

11

ON INDEPENDENCE DAY, ever since American companies had settled in the country – the gateway to Europe
– Nat Am has hosted a barbecue in one of the golf clubs where
a senior Nat Am man is a member.

The Nat Am man on these occasions arranges with his golf
club to set up the barbecue and tables outside if the weather is
fine; then he and his colleagues cook the meat and help the bar
staff serve the drinks. The American Evening was Sharkey's idea:
'Hospitality to our US friends, and also our big hitters: the
premier league, you know what I mean,' he told a few managers
one night in The Unicorn.

The arrangement suited the various golf committees: they
got extra revenue from the bar and were keen to meet bankers
who might help them with their next loan application. Already
they had benefited from Sharkey's invitation 'not to be a stranger.
Come and see us.' Indeed, in many cases, club members had
joined the gold rush, when he had been urging them to invest
in the bank: 'If you've a few thousand to spare, put it in Nat Am.
Trust me, it'll be twice the value this time next year,' slipping
them his business card. Everyone, it seemed, was investing in Nat
Am – the bank that had put it up the noses of the Big Guns. A
surgeon, who played golf at Woodbrook with Kevin Egan, a
friend since their time together in 'Rock, had invested a quarter
of a million Euro.

The American Evening is overcast: low clouds hang over The

Sleeping Giant; nevertheless, it is warm enough to sit out among the palm trees that stand tall on the front lawn of Robin Hill Golf Club. Those who haven't played in the tournament and have arrived early sit on the wickerwork chairs, or stand around with glasses in their hands. They have a full view of the others cruising into the car park in Mercs and Volvos. The Stars and Stripes and the Tricolour lie limp on the flagpole.

The golfers – mostly men – are bankers and their clients, and a sprinkling of friends from Intel, Hewlett Packard and the pharmaceuticals Pfizer and Imamed. Hair-gelled and full of chat after their shower, the younger men saunter back from the locker rooms with Clifford and a few of the club members Philip had invited along. Some have had time for a massage from Gwen or Tanya in the leisure centre.

The lawn fills up. A long table covered with a white cloth and laden with bottles of spirits, soft drinks, and bowls of fruit serves as a focal point. Earlier, one of the bar staff had positioned clusters of chairs at various points on the patio and the grass.

The white mansion with lemon trim around the windows provides a radiant backdrop for the men in bright linen suits, and the women in summer dresses moving about, some with wide-rimmed cocktail glasses, others seated at the table chatting. For someone looking in from the main road, the Stars and Stripes on the lawn, the plastic boaters, young men tossing around an American football could easily convey a sense of a rich Rhode Island suburb, rather than Robin Hill.

Loud laughter about someone's missed chance out on the course and the chink of ice cubes dropping into drinking glasses creates a buzz of excitement among the palm trees. Cigar smoke mingles with the smell of cooking meat from the barbecues. Now and again, the edges of the white tablecloth rise and fall.

Sharkey makes himself useful by bringing bottles of beer to the small fridge they have set up beside the table; he and others from Nat Am collect empties and set out more clean glasses. In this, they are showing that they are genuine blokes who are not above getting down and dirty. And the American Evening also gives Sharkey the chance to show off his skill in mixing cocktails.

'As everyone knows,' he tells a couple of Nat Am clients, 'a cocktail's not a cocktail without maraschinos.'

'Sorry?'

'Maraschino cherries – make all the difference.'

'I'm with you.'

Brennan is distracted by the flight of a helicopter passing over. 'Look,' he says, poking with his thumb towards the sky: 'We're ahead of the UK.'

'How's that?' asks the club president, who is working the lawn.

'More choppers.'

'*Yes*. One up on the Brits.'

'Glad we went Boston rather than Berlin.'

'And so say all of us,' says Sharkey, who is agitating the silver cocktail shaker like a professional. 'And if ever the well runs dry, we can always become the fifty-first state of the Union.'

'And what about our sovereignty?' One of the group teases him. 'What our forefathers died for!'

'Sovereignty my arse. When you walk into a showroom, you can't buy a fucking new 5 Series Beemer with sovereignty.'

'Got me there, Aengus.'

Sharkey has now recovered from his rage at failing to be among the top scorers in the golf tournament, as he's been in other years. He had been walloped by a former Galway hurler. After a few holes, when he realizes he can't beat the Galway man, he produces the bag of tricks he had been using over the years, and showed – as always on the golf course – that his desire to win is an exact copy of his determination to succeed by whatever means in the banking world.

He started by praising his opponent's strokes – 'you're shit hot today, Liam'. Usually this caused an opponent to become so self-conscious that he invariably fluffed his shots from then on. Then he took to tearing at the Velcro of his glove, or walked ahead to the next tee before Liam had finished his putt. Neither worked. So he jangled coins in his pocket when the hurler was lining up a shot.

On the eighteenth green, the Galway man sank the ball, and turned a sunny smile on Sharkey. He was one under par; Sharkey was two over, yet he grinned and did a high-five. 'On song today, Liam,' he said.

'You know, Aengus,' said the hurler, hoisting his golf bag on to the trolley, and laughing, 'you're some noisy bastard on the course.'

A swirling breeze whips up the delicious smell of meat on the grill, where Philip and another banker are turning hot dogs and spare ribs.

The whiskeys and Sharkey's highballs are gradually taking effect on the men sitting by the barbecue. They are in total agreement: O'Leary should be running this country. He'd soon enough get rid of the quangos. Yes. Give O'Leary his head.

Conrad Brennan takes great pleasure in telling his favourite Mick story: how he cracked the morning traffic problem by slapping a taxi plate on his Merc, and now he can glide along in the bus lane. He looks around for approval.

'Mick would make those civil servants move their arses for a change,' says Wheeler.

'Ah yes, indeed he would – *Romantic Ireland's dead and gone. It's with O'Leary in the grave.* Throw me over a saussie, Philip, like a good man.' True to form, the priest, McKeever, has stolen up on them. He is a wide-eyed child wandering into a game whose rules he doesn't know. Since his arrival earlier, he has been mooching around, dipping in and out of conversations, accepting a glass of wine or a handful of nuts, and laughing, as if to himself.

'More choppers than the Brits,' he chuckles.

They ignore him, but he continues. 'My apologies, I couldn't take up your invitation for the golf.'

'Just as well, Tom,' says Philip. 'These guys were hot.'

The priest succeeds in making common ground and for a while earns their grudging regard through his knowledge of golf: they talk about Harrington, but Tiger Woods is still the top cat.

McKeever begins to wander off again. 'Ah yes. Such is life: more choppers than the Brits. I don't know. Hope it lasts.'

Philip calls him: 'Now, it's ready.'

'Thanks, Philip.'

While laying mustard on the hotdog, he intones to himself: ' "What then?" sang Plato's ghost. "What then?" Hah! Funny old world, *what then?*'

Behind the priest's back, one of the group raises his hand to his temple and does a *screw loose* dumb show. McKeever comes back to them: 'Must be fascinating for you, gentlemen,' he is smiling. 'I mean the world of power, wealth and influence – the way you can shape people's future. I often wake in the night, and ask myself: imagine if we didn't have good people in our banking system.' They are slowly warming to his charm. 'I look up at the IFSC when I'm driving into town and say to myself: *What a place!*'

He has a twinkle in his eye when he tells them what he has read recently. 'In *The Economist* of all places. It was about traders. Men of substance – just like yourselves.' A trace of mustard clings to the side of his mouth. 'Some professor of – I think it was anthropology. Anyway, he noticed that when the traders have a good day, they punch the air, and do – what's it called?' He raises his open palm.

'High fives,' Sharkey grunts.

'High fives,' McKeever repeats. 'Anyway, this professor compared the behaviour of traders to … you won't believe this, I mean it's so ridiculous – rutting stags.' He chuckles. Seems the professor went around swabbing the mouths of traders after a big win to measure testosterone. 'And guess what? Now you'll find this outlandish. It was at the same level as stags in heat.'

The penny drops for Sharkey: his sneer returns, but McKeever continues about how stags fight each other for the female. If they win, they challenge other combatants and the testosterone keeps rising and they take more risks.

Conrad Brennan, ever watchful for Sharkey's reactions, notices a cynical curl to his superior's lip. He mutters to Sharkey and sniggers, like a schoolboy, but McKeever is undeterred.

'The stags continue winning until one day they are defeated. *Kaput.*' He snaps his fingers. 'They've gone too far.' He looks at them. 'I mean can anyone believe this? Who pays any attention to these guys with their heads stuck in books.'

'Rubbish,' says Brennan.

'Anyway, let me finish my story.' Another hormone makes an appearance, and assumes control. A hormone called cortisol. Fear and suspicion grabs the herd of stags, and they huddle by a lakeside. McKeever chuckles. 'I suppose you could say, their water cooler; ah well, there you have it,' and he sidles off again, calling to Philip over his shoulder. 'Back for one of them great-looking steaks.'

'Wouldn't you think the way they've been behaving lately – like animals – they'd disappear off the radar,' says Wheeler, casting baleful looks at the priest's back.

Philip is standing back to avoid a sudden plume of smoke rising from the grill. He affects a lack of interest. 'I wouldn't mind him. Doesn't know where he is half the time. Was rapped on the knuckles by his bishop – took it badly. Great guy when we were in college. Can be funny at times.' He turns the steaks. 'Nearly there now.'

'Jesus! Religion,' says Wheeler. 'What a load of cobblers. Why don't they keep it to themselves, and not be bothering us? That crap belongs to the dark ages, or for guys about to pop their clogs. All my generation wants is to get your MBA, have the Beemer, and the cool babe in the sack.'

'As far as I'm concerned, Kyran,' Sharkey grins, and uses a throwaway he'd heard once and thought very clever, '*they can do whatever they like in their own houses so long as they don't do it out in the street and frighten the horses.*'

After they have eaten, they saunter around; some go to the bar and others relax in the clusters of chairs placed around the lawn. And gradually the light fades without their noticing. Close by the garden heaters, groups prolong the dying pleasures of the evening. One or two are exchanging business cards. The gas flame catches the shine on the golfers' sunburnt faces; their nodding heads look comical on the front wall of the clubhouse.

Sharkey, who had made sure to work his way through all the guests from the American companies, is strolling up and down the lawn with a group of men; once in a while they stop and listen to him. He is using his hands a lot; when his listeners draw on their cigars, the red tips brighten and then fade into the gathering darkness.

'Went from a force two to at least seven or eight in a flash,' he is saying, but interrupts his story to introduce his Intel friends to Doc Clifford and others from Robin Hill. Now with a wider audience he continues: 'The waves were – I kid you not – humongous. Bats out of hell we were – lurching and holding on for dear life while we lowered the main sail, tied buckets to the end of ropes and threw them out to act as anchors. Luckily I've a great crew – two of my sons and their mates – Trinity Blues.'

Darkness has fallen when Sam and her tennis friends take the cloths off the tables; while they work, they cast long shadows in the amber light that streams across the lawn from the clubhouse.

'By the way,' someone says, 'we need a fourth for a doubles on Monday night; we're playing away to Greystones.'

Sam makes a face: 'Sorry. Duty calls. I'll be out of the country for most of the week.'

'Where this time?' one of the others asks.

'We're doing a shoot in a little village close to St Tropez.'

They do a collective whine of mock sympathy.

'My heart bleeds for you, Sam.'

'Looking out at the Mediterranean every day. Ah, isn't that just so unfair.'

12

'I WAS GETTING big points for two things that go down well with High Res – loyalty and availability.' Sam is telling one of the models about her time with High Res. They have wrapped up the shoot in the village near St Tropez and the team is basking on the hotel veranda. In the warm sunshine, others of the crew are standing around having a drink before the mini-bus arrives to take them to Nice, and then home the following morning. The relief shows in the rise and fall of laughter and in the laid-back conversations. Champagne and cocktail glasses sparkle. Below them lush rows of pink, crimson and white bougainvillea surround vineyards ripening while they sleep in the sun. Some lavish god has sprinkled the Mediterranean with a thousand glittering diamonds. Big yachts are resting in the bay.

You could put your shirt on Sam; never lets you down. The Sam brand does what it says on the packet. At the beginning her job was to make sure the models were there on time, book the flights, hire the stylist, get local camera staff if needed, and make the reservations in the hotel. 'I'm a call girl – a dogsbody,' she used to joke to Philip when she spoke on the phone to London.

Different now from when she first joined High Res, when she was straight from the Smurfit with an honours diploma – fourth in a class of twenty-seven – with no intention of remaining a dogsbody. She had her sights set on the creative director's job, but, as a commerce graduate, she was at a disadvantage, since her rivals had come from schools of art and design, or had a background in literature and drama. Still, she had her foot in the door, and she would do anything – be at their beck and call, if needs be.

A blip in the Rome shoot, Sam. Need you to go on the next flight.
Sure.

London, Oslo, the Cliffs of Moher. Wherever. She would jump through the hoops. Having helped to fix the problem, she then waited while the cameraman got the light to his satisfaction, or when the art director and a temperamental photographer were being bitchy about the way a shoot should be done. Jaded from fixing and peace-keeping, she would trudge to her hotel room after dinner.

Sam was drawing a fair weather picture for the model: she was hiding the ruthless streak that meant that she would stop at nothing to get her way.

As when she paid close attention to what Pamela, the creative director, was doing for 80k. She could do it better, so when Pamela went on maternity leave, Sam was asked if she would fill in – on a temporary basis – and for less money. The board admired her attitude: they took a mental note. She had determination and was willing to help them out. *Loyal to the company – a good sign.*

Sam grabbed the baton and ran with it, and by the time Pamela returned, she had made her mark: she was smart and cost-effective. And most of all – not a pain in the arse, like Pamela could be at times with her snooty English ways. Eventually, Sam edged out Pamela, who left High Res to start up a public relations business.

On the way to Nice in the bus, they chat with the others, but after dinner contrive to be on their own to walk along the Promenade des Anglais, and then go for drinks to a quiet bar away from the hotel.

The crew was doing a final wrap-up of what was her concept in the first place, so she was able to stand back, like someone admiring the house she herself had designed; and had time also to look closely at the faces of the models, who seemed bored until they were called to smile, or stare, or pout. The way the director took control of a model infuriated her: a touch under the chin; a hand around the small of her back to bring her breasts into prominence, as if she were just another item in the miscellany of equipment.

The director cut several times. The photographer wanted more knee showing: the female model was to lean back against the oak tree. The male model, in a dress suit, needed to position his leg between hers. 'And show off the watch, Ross – that's the whole fucking point of the shoot,' the director called out as he pranced around, sizing them up from different angles. As if watching a circus in which she herself was the ringmaster, Sam wanted to slap the director across the face.

In the almost empty bar, she shares her contempt with the model. Some distance away, a woman about her own age, with a strained look, is staring intently at a computer, typing some more and then taking a sip from her glass.

Sam had always liked talking with the model; they had done a shoot in the Lake District, and the Aran sweaters one in Killarney. Now the martini is working its velvety way into their bloodstreams. The mask of restraint Sam wears each morning in the office is slipping, and the reserve she maintains with all professionals is dissolving in martinis: another successful shoot in the can, for which she and High Res will be paid handsomely.

In the background, a muted Frank Sinatra is 'spreading the news' about New York.

'You get weary at times.' She shrugs. 'Maybe it's me.'

'No,' says the model, 'you're dead sound. We're there for the sake of a fucking product to be foisted on people. Airheads who leaf through the Sunday supplement and imagine they'll be transported to a desert island because of some brand of drink we're supposed to be enjoying. And we're expected to be all over a self-preening guy who happens to look like George Clooney.' A smile breaks about her lips. 'All the drink will do is to rot their liver, and George Clooney, more often than not, is either gay, or a moron who thinks you're dying to get in the sack with him.'

'Wow,' says Sam. 'Some speech!'

'I know you're heavily invested in the business, Sam, but it's a fucking lie. Enticing some sap to think that she will be changed by wearing what we're peddling.'

'Why then?'

'Why what?'

'Model.'

'Yeah, well, this is my last shoot. Going back to teachers' training college: should've stayed there in the first place. A clothes peg. You strut your stuff on the cat walk. Today it's some brand of watch, tomorrow it's a bra and knickers. Not for me any longer – no way. In any case, models have a limited shelf life and then you're for the landfill.'

After two more martinis, Sam is intimating that all is not well with Philip and herself, and how her children are proving to be a handful lately, especially Zara. Her chief source of comfort now is her therapist. 'I'd be lost without the weekly visit. Same as Mam's generation went to confession on a Saturday evening, except that my therapist won't consign me to hellfire if I fuck up.'

'It helps?'

'Yes. Things don't ... well ... don't go according to plan,' she hears herself saying. 'You know about all the separations, but you tell yourself it won't happen to you. No, your marriage will be different. You're so well matched, made for each other.' She lowers her head, and plays with the olive stick in her drink: 'I don't think I'm into the maternal thing that much either. Never was. And I kind of know what's behind the marriage issue.'

'Meaning?'

'The price I'm paying for giving everything to the job. I can't stop myself now. Like a junkie.' A weak smile plays about her mouth; she runs her finger up and down the stem of the glass: '*I owe my soul to the company store.* We both sold out. Going to La Salle was supposed to change things. A fresh start.' She raises her glass: 'Anyway, I vowed when I joined High Res I would one day – *one day* become a creative director, and then have my feet beneath the table.'

But she brightens, and both are laughing a lot when they return to the hotel in the balmy night. Across the bay, planes are landing and taking off; the airport lights cast orange streamers on the water, and the scent of rosemary fills the air.

'*Come on, girls, we haven't got all day*', says Sam suddenly, putting on the high-pitched tone of Desmond the cameraman. She struts ahead, one hand on her hip. Both of them are now in fits. Sam continues to swagger until she stumbles, causing the model to reach out and save her from falling. They hug for a moment in a way that is warm and instinctive.

'Thanks for the chat,' Sam whispers into her ear.

The following morning, they sit with the others at one of the breakfast tables. The model is catching a flight for Paris, where she has another shoot; Sam is returning to Dublin with the crew. In the lobby, the air is filled with the faint smell of coffee drifting from the dining room, and with announcements of taxis arriving. Guests are booking in; others are leaving. A stack of bags on a trolley stands to one side of the elevator; the hotel staff, behind the desk, are filling in forms and answering telephone calls.

Sam rests her hand on the model's forearm: 'Thanks for listening. We'll do it again.'

'Sure, I'll be in college in September.'

'Right. Bewley's. That's a promise.'

13

WHILE TIGER is having martinis with the model, Philip is carefully scrutinizing the draft of another €70 million loan to James Feeney, who wants to extend his portfolio in a shopping mall in Coventry. The following morning he will hand it back to Kimberley and the legal team for a final scan, and then he will meet the developer to sign just before close of business. Treasury and the Risk Committee have already done a vetting.

Feeney is in the company of Mary Pat, a financial controller, his lawyer, and an architect when they arrive at Nat Am. He is having a government minister to his house that evening, so he can't take up Philip's invitation to dinner in The Shelbourne. Consequently, when the documents are in order, they all go up to the executive floor for sandwiches and coffee.

'Me and the minister have been through many an oul rough boreen.' He winks at Philip as they are travelling up in the lift. 'Good and bad. Anyway, with the oul ticker, I've to keep well back from the table. Green tea and spring water is all my doctor will allow me now. Jaysus! Green tea, like them Chinese. Did you ever hear the like a' that?'

'Now,' he says to Philip, as they sit at the table, 'one good turns deserves another. I've a couple of horses runnin in Galway next week, and if you're in town I'd like to invite you down to the races.'

'Very kind of you,' Philip says. 'I'll have to get my secretary to check the diary before you leave. What day are we talking about, James?'

'Thursday.'

Feeney holds up a glass of Ballygowan and examines it: 'If the oul lad, God rest him, knew that we're now buyin water in bottles and puttin ice and lemon in it, he'd be spinnin in his grave.'

Mary Pat looks at Philip, and rolls her eyes. 'Here we go again, Dad – back to the old days.' Her smart London accent, polished at a convent school in Liverpool with England's Catholic elite, contrasts with her father's Leitrim drawl, still intact after sixty years of building a multi-million pound empire.

'Right then, Philip. Gentlemen,' Feeney raises his glass. 'In the fairs long ago around Mohill and Ballinamore, the oul lad used spit in his hand and the cattle dealer would slap his open palm. But this is Dublin 4, and we're now Europeans.' He looks around with a twinkle in his eye.

They all raise their glasses.

'Your health.'

'Good luck.'

'Long live Nat Am,' says Feeney.

'And may the Feeney empire continue to flourish,' Philip returns the compliment.

When they are saying their goodbyes downstairs in the foyer, Philip assures them that the documents will be processed first thing in the morning.

That evening the city is booting up for the weekend when Philip takes a taxi into town where he is to meet Egan and a few others to round off the week with a drink at Neary's. On his way into the pub, a herd of men with loud English accents stop him. 'Hey, mate,' one of them asks, 'which way to …' he turns to the others. 'Wot's the place called?'

'Templars … something. Temple Inn.'

'Temple Bar?'

'That's it, mate.'

He gives them directions.

Egan is holding forth about a last hand of poker that re-deemed his losses the previous night when Philip arrives with news of the Feeney deal being clinched and the invitation to the Galway Races.

'How could you, Lalor?' Egan speaks in a tone of mock regret.

The others join in a chorus of good-natured teasing.

'The lowest.'

'Never would I see myself doing a thing like that.'

'Sell your soul, Lalor?'

'All done out of loyalty to Nat Am,' says Philip, leaning against the counter. 'You guys are sorely lacking in loyalty.'

'I mean *the tent*,' says Egan. 'Jesus. That's surely a breach of banking ethics.'

One of the group is a dentist in Dundrum. Like everyone else who has been seduced by the spiel of making the best use of his money, he has invested some of his life's savings in Nat Am shares. Weary from looking into open mouths and calming children, he looks forward to retiring early. He wants to know why Feeney would be borrowing so much: 'A rich chap like him. Doesn't make sense.'

'You're behind the game,' Egan intervenes while Philip is ordering a round. 'Won't cost him a penny. You must know by now: the rich pay for nothing. He'll make a killing in two or three years' time if he sells, and if the wind is at his back. Property has been increasing by twenty per cent every year. Then there's the rent.' He does a quick calculation: 'Five per cent. You're talking six million annually. That's unless this whole thing goes belly up.'

The dentist is interested.

'Put it another way,' says Egan. 'Feeney will secure ninety per cent of the loan from Nat Am. He'll find investors to make up the deficit. They'll receive their cut, the bank and the brokers will get their slice. And guess what? The Honourable James Feeney will make about twenty million without investing a Euro.' He laughs 'Are you with me, Doc?'

'Very much so, and if he needs an investor, don't be shy in picking up the phone.'

'Consider it done,' Egan says, raising the glass to his lips.

A couple of days later, Feeney's personal secretary phones Philip to say that a car will pick him up to take him to Weston Airfield.

'Mr Feeney would like you to know that he will be travelling down to Galway with you in the helicopter.'

When Philip arrives in the chauffeur-driven car the following Thursday, Feeney is already out on the airstrip, speaking into his mobile phone, and strolling between Cessnas and Pipers. A rush of wind from the propellers of a helicopter in the distance has blown his red tie over his shoulder. Waiting for him to finish are Mary Pat and a tall and ungainly man with hunched shoulders and a head of silver hair. Mary Pat introduces him. 'Murt – Dad's friend.' She grins: 'They built the London skyline, don't you know.'

All are in a cheerful mood as they climb into the helicopter. 'We soldiered around Kilburn in the good old days,' says Feeney, laying a work-hardened hand on Murt's shoulder. 'Dug Her Majesty's trenches. Right, auld stock?'

Wispy hairs sprout from Murt's ears, and a wide gap shows between his teeth when he smiles. 'Great woman. Fed us when we were half-starved.'

'I've given our pilot instructions to do the scenic route; I want to show Philip here the beautiful county of Leitrim.'

The pilot, a young man with gelled hair and a diffident look, welcomes them on board, and then gives his complete attention to traffic control: 'Good afternoon, Weston Tower. Request permission to lift.' He speaks into the headpiece and waits for clearance. 'Going towards Straffan ...' The helicopter rises, and all the while the pilot is receiving instructions about weather conditions for the journey. 'Sunny in Ballybrit,' he relays to his passengers. 'Good,' says Feeney, 'that'll suit The Gunner Brady. His mother was a topper on the firm sod.' They fly over prosperous farmhouses, painted sheds and gleaming silos, over stud-fenced fields of Kildare with thoroughbreds grazing in rich pastures, their sleek coats catching the light whenever they bolt or race around the paddocks.

The scene spread out below them changes: they cross over the lake country of Westmeath and then the small craggy fields of the West. In silence, Feeney is taking it all in, until he makes out the spire of the parish church of his youth. 'There it is.' He springs to life. 'The home place. You see that, Philip.' He stretches and points towards the patchwork quilt beneath them: small fields and a scattering of lakes and groves. 'If I had the price of forty or fifty acres of that land to add to the father's bit of bog, I'd never have left Ballinamore, and John Bull would never have seen me.'

He is in high spirits, and doesn't hear Murt joking: 'Weren't you the lucky man to get away from the bit of bog, James?'

'That little parish,' he points again, 'produced a man who became an archbishop out in America, several priests and nuns, includin one of my own sisters; three of us who hit London, and I don't mind sayin it – we did fairly well. And look,' he says with a sweep of his hand over the well-tilled fields, 'you wouldn't have seen that fifty or sixty years ago – only hunger and misery, when shoals of us were takin *The Princess Maud.*' They pass over more villages and small towns with ribbon developments.

'D'you know,' Feeney chuckles, 'that half the houses built in this country over the past few years are for rent or for re-sale.' He turns to Murt. 'Lucky thing, if a family had a roof over their heads that wasn't leakin when we were young lads ... Ah well, suits us fine. We'll give them all the houses they want, Murt.' He's the tour guide from now on: showing them all the fields that were flooded in winter. 'And we didn't see them from a helicopter, hardly had the price of the train. Nothin but cryin and olagonin at the railway stations in them days.'

'Great credit due to you,' Philip says.

'Hard graft, Philip. Hard graft.'

When they land in Ballybrit, they are taken straight to the marquee in a limousine, where a man in a well-tailored suit – a county councillor – is waiting to greet them. 'He'll get the nomination the next time; in with the right gang,' says Feeney out of the side of his mouth. 'A bit too slick for my likin; give me the old war horses like Haughey any day.'

Inside, it's party time: bursts of laughter rise from the tables; drinking glasses and women's jewellery glitter beneath the naked light bulbs. Men, with wine-red faces, are wolfing down Boeuf de Corrib; women in showy hats and black dresses, which set off their Riviera tans, are grandstanding. The din of conversation is drowning out the Barber Shop Four, who are waving their straw hats and singing for all their worth.

As the county councillor leads them to their table, a man leans over and shakes Feeney's hand: 'Good luck today, James, and good to see you looking so well.'

'Porridge, Mick,' says Feeney with a glint in his eye. 'And a clear conscience.' They laugh. 'And a banana in the mornin to keep the ould potassium right. My doc tells me I should make the ton at this rate. See you after the last race, Mick auld stock. We'll chew the cud, and maybe you'll give us a bar or two of your song.'

'Yerra, why wait until the evenin,' Mick guffaws and breaks into 'The West's Awake', much to the delight of the table, who join him in the chorus. The Barber Shop singers give way, and, when Mick is finished, they too join in the applause. Shouts of 'Up Roscommon' fill the tent.

'And Leitrim.'

'Up Ballintubber, boy.' His red face glistening, Mick stands and raises his glass. 'The West's Awake.'

Feeney leans close to hear what a man, tagged with a trainer's label hanging from his buttonhole, is saying to him; Murt and Mary Pat greet others. Feeney straightens and beckons to Philip: 'Come here and meet a man who has been my good friend for longer than I care to remember. Francie Stack.' Like a middleman trying to seal a bargain at a cattle fair, Feeney draws the two men together; they are so close that Philip can smell the other man's whiskey breath. 'A man who keeps his word, even if the hoor is from Cork itself.' While they speak, racing tips are being exchanged across the table, 'JP's horse is out of it; pulled up in training.'

'Jaysus. I was going to put my shirt on him.'

'Is Bertie here?'

'Tomorrow. He's comin tomorrow. Has a meetin that he can't miss.'

'Meetin? Chrisht, sure there's no meetin more important than this one.' Any remark now is enough to set the table into hoots of laughter.

'Go an eat your dinner, boy.' Feeney taps Stack on the arm. 'Only a few of us left now, Francie. We need to keep the strength up.' The Barber Shop singers resume their spirited performance.

Feeney leans over to Philip: 'You might do business with Stack. Gilt edge.'

'I'll remember that.' Philip scans the menu: crayfish terrine, medallions de Boeuf de Corrib, baked Cajun sea bass with Sauvignon Bergerac, Merlot vin de pays de l'Aude from the Cathar region. Dessert is apricot Bavarois Napolieene.

Out of the corner of his eye, he spots a man stretching behind another man's back to give racing advice to a pretty-looking woman with a low-cut dress and a pillbox hat. 'A ton on Jim Bolger's horse, Rachael, for the Guinness – won't go astray. A monkey on the Sheikh's for the *Connacht Tribune*. Dead cert.' The others at the table are so taken up in some play on words about jockeys and women, they don't notice the man reaching for her hand, and winking. All around are faces Philip has seen or met before in Dublin: the RDS, Croke Park on All Ireland day, or in the Horseshoe Bar at Christmas. Some are Nat Am clients: those they have poached from other banks since they have acquired a reputation for giving out loans without any fuss, or lengthy waiting periods, or sometimes even devising an ad-hoc credit committee while the client is waiting in the executive lounge.

'Been comin here to Galway for over forty years now. My kind of people.' Feeney laughs and, with a cagey look, scans the tent. 'Haven't seen *him* in ages.' He indicates with a discreet movement of his thumb a man in whose hands the knife and fork are pieces from a child's dinner set. Hanging from the back of his chair is a pair of field glasses. He grins: 'Far away from binoculars he was reared – and me too for that matter. John Bull with only a cardboard suitcase fit to fall asunder.' He leans towards Philip. 'Most of us here never saw the inside of a second-ary school.' He chuckles. 'But we made up for it.' He nods towards nearby tables. 'He was a plasterer; and your man with the young dolly was a carpenter. They're both on the rich list of the *Independent*. Costs 4k for a table here, but no matter. This is the fast track to influence. You understand these things, Philip.'

'Sure.'

'And d'you know what? I couldn't – or many others here – couldn't give a fiddler's who's in the Dáil, so long as we've an open door to power.' A roguish look shows on his flushed face.

The buzz word is The Radisson. Don't miss it – the craic will be mighty. Goes on till the small hours. 'Brian will be there – gas man after a few pints. He'll have you in stitches. Tidy footballer in his young days.'

They share a private box with a few of Feeney's friends to watch his horse, The Gunner Brady, with wins under his belt at Punchestown and Roscommon, coming in second in the Guinness Handicap. Mohill Lass is well down the field in the Guinness Storehouse.

Later in the day, between races, while Mary Pat is again on her mobile, Feeney leans over to Philip. 'I might be speakin out of turn here, but if you could offer a better deal to Stack than the arrangement he has, he'd like to hear from you. We had a short business conference in the tent.' Again he winks.

'He can call me any time; maybe we'll meet before the day is out.'

They do. In a crowded lounge of The Radisson where Stack explains about the new processing plant he is opening in New Mexico. He 'would be interested in talkin business'.

Philip reaches into his back pocket and slips a card from his wallet. 'Any time, Francie, any time. In fact, why not tomorrow or after? I'll get my secretary to set up a meeting in the bank – maybe a bite to eat. As the chap said, Francie, "money never sleeps".'

The following morning Philip does a search of Stack's business profile. At fourteen, he had started as a drover for prosperous farmers in north Cork, listened to deals being made at the fairs, and when he was old enough, started buying a few calves which he put to graze in a bachelor uncle's farm. Now his parent company, Viking, is one of the bigger cattle exporters in the country, with food-processing plants in Ireland and Britain.

As soon as Stack returns from Galway, he too gets his accountant and financial adviser to do a trawl of Nat Am possibilities. At the final meeting on the following Monday, when Philip signs off the loan, Sharkey sits in, as well as one of the accountants, Kimberley from the legal team, and Karen to record the minutes.

That evening, Philip sends round an email informing the others in corporate finance that he has just negotiated a thirty-five million loan with Viking plc. 'The contract is in the bag. Good day for Stack – no more hanging around for a word from our rivals. Good day for Nat Am. Celebration lunch tomorrow at La Mer – nothing fancy. Anyone who's free, most welcome.'

Sharkey usually attends such lunches: he regards them as a reflection of his leadership, and makes sure everyone knows. This time he is absent. And the following morning he summons Philip to his office.

The pout says it all. When Philip steps inside the door, he keeps on working at his computer. 'Stay clear of the Incredible Sulk when the pout shows' is the received wisdom around Nat Am. Without taking his eyes off the screen, he motions for Philip to take one of the vacant chairs in front of his desk. Then he continues his two-finger typing, leaving Philip to stare at the balding crown and putting him in mind of the day he was returning from lunch and spotted Sharkey in his Merc using the rear-view mirror, and licking his fingers to plaster the few remaining strands across his scalp.

Now, without a word, Sharkey holds up the email Philip had sent around the previous day. 'What's this?' he asks, and purses his lips again. 'Would you mind reading it out to me?'

'Read it out to you? I'm not a schoolboy, Aengus.'

Sharkey lets it drop on the desk.

'So what's the issue?' Philip asks.

'The issue,' he repeats with mock dismay. 'The issue! Why did you send this out without my sanction?'

'Feel good, Aengus. "Good for company morale" you always say. We should "Hoot and Holler", you say, like they do on Wall Street when they make a killing.'

Sharkey sneers. '*Feel good* for Nat Am, or for Philip Lalor's ego?'

'That's over the top.' Philip knows that the more Sharkey loses control, the more he himself has the whip hand.

'No, it's not.' Sharkey's beefy hands grip the edge of the desk.

'In the interests of fairness, Aengus, we should deal with this in a businesslike way.'

Sharkey glares at him, and his index finger does a windscreen wiper in front of his face: 'You don't ever lecture me!' His voice becomes high-pitched: 'Nor ever attempt to tell me about the ways of business. Remember,' the finger stops, 'I gave you and many others here a leg up.' He raises his voice: 'I *made* you, but I can also *break* you.'

Philip glances through the venetian blind to catch heads dipping: children caught out by the teacher.

'This should have been submitted to me for clearance. The credit committee should have been informed.' Sharkey holds out the email between finger and thumb.

'With all due respect, you are forgetting an essential piece of the equation. When I said we should check it out with the credit committee, you said – and I distinctly remember your words: "Fuck the credit committee. This bloke needs money in a hurry." You had precious little to do with the project apart from attending the initial meeting.' Philip is now going for broke. 'Also, you're forgetting what you yourself have done on many occasions: opened others' files and claimed the honours yourself. You hooted and hollered about other people's work – that's hardly ethical behaviour.'

'Are you trying to undermine my position in an institution that I made the showpiece of banking in Europe?' Sharkey now loses all sense, and begins to shout. 'Don't you dare, don't you ever, ever attempt to lecture me on banking ethics! When it comes to international banking, you're a nobody.' He springs from his desk and paces around the office like a trapped animal.

Philip gives as good as he gets. 'You did it with the Harrison file – that was *my* portfolio. When my back was turned last summer, you accessed my files and sent around an email – very similar to what you've got in your hand, and – '

'If you fuck up from now on, I'll have your ass before the Red Braces.' Sharkey makes a ball of the email and aims it at the paper basket, but fails to make the target. Then, sinking into his chair, he returns to his computer: 'I've work to do.'

The following morning he greets Philip as if the blow-up had never happened; and in that, he is living in accordance with his motto, announced one evening in the Davenport Hotel, when he and Philip and a few others were waiting for a developer up from the country: 'No matter what the row, this is about money, guys. We can't afford feelings or grudges. This is about … dear and glorious Mammon.' A sly look appears on his face. 'As Frankie Dettori once said: *better than sex*. No time for feelings: business as usual when the blood is mopped up.'

14

DESPITE DANGER signals on the horizon, such as the fall of Northern Rock in the UK and Bear Stearns in America, the clear directive in Nat Am and in other banks is to keep up the policy of lending, and to turn a blind eye to the economists. 'It's in our fucking make-up to moan' is Sharkey's explanation. He is in ebullient mood one Monday morning after clinching another multi-million loan at the Glen on the previous Friday, and the afterglow of his success shows in his topped-up suntan.

This time the loan is to Halos, a pharmaceutical company from Illinois, which wants to open another factory in Ireland. Three years before, it had been granted fifty million Euro from Nat Am to expand its portfolio. On that occasion Halos had succeeded, by means of an ingenious advertising campaign, to scare the public about the safe levels of cholesterol in order to promote the company's latest product called Statinmol Plus – to be sold over the counter.

'Somewhere way back – the Famine or some such place,' Sharkey puts on the whining voice of ancient Ireland, and quotes an old Irish lament,' "*We'll all be rooned*", says Hanrahan, "*before the year is out.*" Moaning is a national fucking pastime.'

He holds to that even when one of Nat Am's big clients, a developer, has a whole row of empty houses out near Clonsilla. For that project, Wheeler and Brennan had granted a multi-million loan after they had finished eighteen holes with the developer's son and his quantity surveyor at Mount Juliet one Saturday afternoon.

Towards the end of that week, one of the major shareholders drops a bombshell by withdrawing his ten percent interest in Nat Am. He had heard the whisper doing the rounds in The Shelbourne that Nat Am is skating on thin ice – loaning like there's no tomorrow, when the markets elsewhere are contracting. 'The chickens are coming home to roost,' he was told. 'Once a maverick always a maverick.'

St John Dunleavy is all for riding out the storm, but Sharkey has a plan which he unveils to a few of the managers, including Philip, in the executive lounge. He would give some of the big fish a loan to invest in Nat Am through stockbrokers; in that way, it would show the market that Nat Am is in a healthy condition. Their investment would be regarded as a customer deposit.

'Is that kosher, Aengus?' Egan asks. 'It seems a little odd. After all, it's our asset reserves that are being put at the service of these clients. And look at what Providence Investment Services came up with the other day – *thirty-five per cent downside risk to commercial property values* – one has to factor that in.'

Sharkey ignores Egan and appeals to St John Dunleavy: 'We've too much to lose; another drop in the share price and investors will be looking closely at the bank. It's either that, Breffni, or we're toast, and we've all put too much into Nat Am to let that happen.'

'Still, isn't it robbing Peter to pay Paul?' Egan persists.

The half-dozen managers ignore Egan and turn to St John Dunleavy, who asks Sharkey: 'How are you going to get that off the ground?'

'I've got the big guns lined up; they're ready to come in,' Sharkey assures him.

St John Dunleavy looks worried. 'Well, I don't know. Let's put it to the board.'

'Breffni,' Sharkey says, 'I think we should park that for the present. The less they know at board level, the better – until this whole thing cools. The market will recover. Only a blip. A couple of the clients I've lined up are on holidays. Conrad Brennan is in

Madrid talking to one, and Kyran Wheeler has flown to Barbados to talk to two others. But – trust me – I have it in the bag.'

Sharkey tries to put Dunleavy's mind at rest. 'They're all guys who made a fortune through tax breaks in the urban renewal scheme. You know – hotels, private hospitals, third-level colleges – that sort of thing. But we gave them the lolly, so they owe us one.'

'Quite so, Aengus, quite so.' Dunleavy seems a little relieved.

Like people skating to their heart's content, and who suddenly hear the dreadful crack somewhere out in the lake, and know now it's too late, investors and loan-holders in the banks listen in horror to the crushing news about the Wall Street collapse, and how it's only a matter of time before Europe also goes down. People who wouldn't bid each other the time of day on the DART are chatting like members of a support group who have an alcoholic in the family.

Farmers on their high-powered John Deere tractors are stopping on country roads to console one another and share their grief. Instead of lamenting about the poor prices for their milk and livestock, they are exchanging the latest piece of information from news bulletins; they know that Standard & Poor's has downgraded Nat Am.

Plasterers and taxi drivers with properties in Spain and Portugal are telling their bartenders that the politicians should be put up against a wall and shot for allowing such a state of affairs to happen.

Panic-stricken people are phoning in to chat shows for advice: should they transfer to the post office? Is anything safe now? Old women afraid of losing everything ask: 'Should I withdraw and hide my life savings in the mattress?' Self-appointed banking experts who sit together in bars with pints and chasers on the counter declare that it's only a matter of time before the multinationals pull out of Ireland.

Questions sprout that frighten the living daylights out of couples, and tear at the jaunty masks they wear for lunchtime Ballsbridge. Couples who had been given full loans to buy the 'must-have' mews, and dine with Saturday night friends in one of the café bars along Ranelagh Road, are cracking.

Reports of road accidents are brought to the tense plaza over cups of coffee: *nothing serious, just a lapse in concentration.* Someone else had a bad dose of flu, or fell and fractured her wrist. The nightmare is spreading: words like 'redundancy' and 'unemployment', which most people thought had been dead and buried, are sprouting with a vengeance. And can you believe it? Shanahan's on the Green is down thirty percent. Oh my God.

On his way home from work one evening, Philip glances at the sheaf of newspapers carried back and forth between the lanes of traffic by the Hungarian woman at Sutton Cross; he picks up the banner headline before the lights turn green: 'Banks on Life-Support Machine'.

Kevin Egan – holding on to his job by his fingernails – wakes one morning with a strange feeling in his head. At first, he puts it down to a hangover, but the dizzy sensation hasn't gone by evening and now he is beginning to have double vision and a blinding headache. He drops in to his GP, who arranges for him to be admitted immediately to the hospital for tests.

Egan's blood pressure is sky high. The tests also show he has diabetes, so he is kept in hospital against his will, and then advised to rest at home for a week or so. 'Your stress level seems high,' the consultant tells him, 'and that may have contributed to your condition.'

The following day, Philip sits with him in the lounge of the hospital where soft lights and easy listening music cause visitors to talk in low voices; patients in dressing gowns drag their feet along the deep pile carpet.

'I'm scared shitless that bastard will edge me out. Can't afford to retire, Philip,' Egan tells him. 'Nor can I afford to spend a week resting. The houses in Galway and France – neither paid for – and then the loan for the shares that Sharkey was ladling out.'

'But your health …'

Egan is all the while tapping his fingers on the lamp stand beside him. He straightens. 'This is only a wake-up call. I'll be careful from now on.'

As twelve-year-olds, they had started secondary school to-gether. In their late teens, they had busked a couple of summers underneath the Eiffel Tower and, in all that time, Egan had always maintained a laid-back attitude, and rarely spoken about his worries to Philip, except the time when he feared Gillian was going to run off with the builder of their holiday home in Oughterard.

So, even now, he sidesteps his sickness with the latest joke. 'I'll be out of here in no time; all I need is to get the weight down, and then …' he grins and raises an index finger, 'I'll be taking money off you at the Glen. '

15

LATER THAT WEEK, Sharkey calls after Philip as he is crossing the plaza, heading for his office. 'Time for a coffee, Philip, Just to shoot the breeze? Let's go upstairs, quieter there.'

'Yeah, why not? This can wait.' He indicates the bulky file under his arm.

Sharkey is at his charming best. At meetings both men take up a professional manner, but Philip has been steering clear of him, apart from the occasional drink with others; then they are both polite, for Mammon's sake.

They sit at one of the corner seats in the executive lounge. Sharkey sets the pitch. He was only thinking to himself the other day how quickly time passes. 'What was the name of that pub in London where I came across Kevin and yourself?'

'The White Hart.'

'I often think the early days were the best days. You know, when we were raising the bar and the Big Guns were calling us buccaneers, and laughing at us in The Moira over their gins and tonic.'

He changes tack: the progress his own children are making – Conor, doing his articles with PricewaterhouseCoopers, and Vicki, about to be apprenticed to Mahon & Quinn – mostly family law. His youngest, he says with a shake of his head: 'He's, well, considering his options. Young people today – for the life of me – I just can't … oh, I won't *go* there.' The office rumour is that the lad has failed his law exams for the second time and has gone to live with Sharkey's estranged wife and her partner. And that he is prowling around Ranelagh village peddling hash.

Sharkey leans back and sweeps the lounge with his eyes. 'A step up from Andrew Street, wouldn't you say?'

'A giant leap, Aengus.'

Three Asian men in business suits and carrying briefcases come and sit at a side table. With them is one of the bankers from Treasury; a glint from a gold cufflink shows when he raises a manicured hand in greeting. He is smiling broadly at the Asians, but beneath the table his shining shoes have a restless life of their own.

Sharkey stirs his coffee and says in a low voice: 'Conrad contacts, would you believe? He put them on to Treasury.'

'My goodness.'

Then with put-on sympathy, Sharkey says: 'Poor Kevin. So sorry for him. Like yourself, he was one of our brightest and best. What a shame! Will need to take it easy from now on.'

'Oh, I'm very glad to say there's been a big improvement. No reason why he shouldn't be back. Sure, half the country is suffering from blood pressure. The doctors are very pleased.'

'Still,' says Sharkey, and his face grows solemn, 'when these things, like blood pressure … and then the added complication – diabetes on top of that. Writing on the wall.'

'You know, time was when such ailments were … as you say, danger signals. But now …' he raises his arms, 'you see people with a good quality of life, holding down a job, right up until retirement age.'

'Correct, but our world, well, so competitive – more so of late. We've got to be on top of our game. Shareholders … I needn't tell you, Philip.' He leans forward. 'We'll have to think of something. Yeah. Thing is: where do we fit him in?'

Philip refuses to be drawn into what he knows is Sharkey's bogus concern.

'His consultant says he'll be as right as rain in no time.'

While throwing a shifty glance at the Asians, Sharkey listens. 'Oh, but of course,' he leans again towards Philip, 'we'll welcome him back. And I'll get one of the Young Turks to give him a hand with some of the contracts – just to ease the burden. Oh, God, of course we look after our own.'

A boy in a white jacket is serving coffee from a silver pot to the Asians and the Treasury man, who is in full flight, using his hands a lot, and passing around pages. The others are bent over their computers. Sharkey puts up one hand to the side of his face: 'If our man here can't get them to bite, no one can.'

Spreading his hands wide in a gesture of candour, he returns to their conversation. 'You know what the Braces are like.'

Both men finish their coffee and stand. 'Good to have this private chat,' Sharkey says. 'With the pace of life as it is, we hardly get time to say hello.'

Before Philip returns to his office he glances after Sharkey's self-satisfied swagger: he is overstating his concern about the Red Braces. Even if at times they look down their noses at him, they also know that he is the lighting rod that has transformed the bank, and made it what it is. They give him authority and freedom denied to anyone else.

He is intent on maintaining the position Nat Am holds in the banking world, no matter who becomes a casualty. The personal fortune he has acquired, big investments in the Docklands development, and a couple of shopping malls in Britain – all these would have been sufficient for another man to take his foot off the pedal – play golf, visit art auctions, and take leisurely lunches in Patrick Guilbaud's.

At a black tie dinner in Carton House the previous November, a government minister presented him with the Banker of the Year award, and in his speech called him 'one of the men who kick-started this economy: a mover and shaker, badly needed in this country'.

Later, when the dance was in full swing, Sharkey leaned over the Waterford Glass trophy mounted on gold, and boasted to a couple of them, including Brennan: 'For all the posturing the Red Braces do in The Horseshoe Bar, Nat Am would be a fucking two-bit money lending outfit if it hadn't been for yours truly.' He jabbed his thumb towards his starched shirt-front. 'It was only when they became scared that I might be poached that they came up with the top job.'

When the adrenalin is rushing, his well-concealed hurt shows.

He knew that even though he was a 'Harvard man', the top brass in the other banks never fully accepted him, and that they preferred the company of their own sort: especially those from long-established banking families.

'I should've got my feet under the table long ago. Fuck them,' he laughs and looks fondly at the award. 'Dunleavy never got one of these babies, and never will. Guys like him with tennis and Robinsons Barley Water in the back garden – they never had the hunger.' He straightened up in the chair. 'The Davos award last year was big, but this baby – this is special.' And yes, he was aware too of the nickname other banks had given him when he joined Amalgamated and door-stepped debtors: The Marino Bootboy.

'But I brought home the bacon.' And he had wiped their eye, taken some of their biggest customers, and had set up in business those who would have been left scratching their arses, and maybe never getting the start they needed.

Like others of his generation and poor background who were clever, and had the strut of newfound success in the construction industry and in politics, Sharkey believed his star would continue to rise. He spoke their language, and was willing to take risks in a country no longer relying on farming for its mainstay. They were street-wise, and could work with each other precisely because of a shared desire for the prize that was dangling before them.

During the summer months they went on the occasional golfing trip to Lahinch and across to Wales, and also to corporate boxes at Old Trafford. And when the football game was over, Alex Ferguson came to say hello, and invited them for a drink. And wherever Sharkey went, his disciples followed. When Conrad appeared with them at Bellamy's for the first time, Egan quipped from his high stool, 'Who's Sharkey's new fucking food-taster?'

Egan was too open and careless; behind his back, the lackeys were all the while giving a blow-by-blow account to their master. And when Egan was passed over for a promotion for which he was eminently suited, he began to use his sharp wit even more to raise a laugh at Sharkey's expense. The two men maintained a professional manner at work, but the poker games ceased.

While Egan is resting at the nursing home out in Dalkey, Sharkey calls a meeting. 'Just a short get-together, guys, nothing formal. Take a pew.' The disciples are there, as well as one or two from Corporate Finance and Treasury. 'One of our clients is causing me some sleepless nights,' he tells them. On his desk is a file. 'McCarthy here.' He rests one hand on the file. 'He's been our client for donkey's years. Now he's failing to make the cut. Only four occupied out of a whole development in Tullamore.'

Like a walk-on actor who has been waiting for his cue, Brennan comes in with: 'Who was processing the loan, Aengus?'

'Well,' Sharkey, stares at the file and, with put-on reluctance to betray a colleague, says: 'Kevin actually.' He heaves a sigh: 'Didn't crunch the numbers, I'm sorry to say.'

He allows one of his deadly silences to fill the room. 'Maybe he was a bit below par, and we're all concerned about poor Kevin, but we've to run a bank. Nat Am will be history if we don't get the finger out. He won't be back until Monday and I just got this info this morning. Unfortunately, these things can't wait or we'll be in the manure business. So we have to press on. I'll take this up with Kevin on his return.'

Sitting to one side, Philip is raging, but he has to be cautious. Eventually, he speaks. 'Aengus, to be fair about it, a few of us, including your good self, had a look at that application. Don't you remember – afterwards we took McCarthy and his lawyer to Thornton's. So it's hardly fair …'

Reptile-like, Sharkey's tongue shows at the side of his mouth and slides along his lower lip: an involuntary action, and by now a dead giveaway to all who know him that he is about to fly into one of his tantrums.

'Yes, here in your office.' Philip adds. 'We *all* fell short in not crunching the numbers.'

The temperature drops.

Sharkey affects a moderate tone. 'Come on, Philip – Kevin was the one who signed off. Lookit, you all know the rules by now.' He looks around for support. 'Whoever signs off owns the loan.'

'Right on, Aengus,' says Brennan.

'So with the greatest respect,' he whips a letter out of the bundle, and casts it in front of Philip, then leans back in his chair. 'Yes, I know Kevin is a life-long friend, and it's admirable to see you stand up for him, but from that, you'll see who signed off.'

'Kevin will be back on Monday. Can we not put it on hold until then?' Philip says, handing back the letter.

'No, we can't put it on hold.' Sharkey's anger is rising. 'If I don't take steps to deal with this, we're in Queer Street and *my* ass is on the line. It isn't by putting things on hold that has made Nat Am what it is.'

'I'm with you there,' says Wheeler.

One of the women on Egan's team for processing loans reaches for her inhaler and, in the silence, can be heard drawing in the tense air.

'The buck stops here. Let no one think otherwise.' Sharkey passes around the file. 'See for yourselves, guys.'

The asthmatic lets a sheaf of papers fall to the ground; she is full of apologies. 'No prob,' Sharkey says, 'we're all stressed.' Then he sits in a broody silence, as the file is given a cursory examination.

'No reference at all to market research from estate agents for the project,' says Wheeler.

'So now you see the pickle we're in, guys,' Sharkey slaps the file for emphasis and places his two hands on the desk to signal the end to the meeting. 'That's it. Any ideas, send them in.'

As they are leaving, Philip lingers, and, in a low voice, asks Sharkey if he might have a word.

'Well then, what is it? I'm busy.' He starts to play with the string that is securing the folder.

'No reference to the meeting we had.'

'Meeting? What meeting?'

'The meeting you held right here in your office with Mc-Carthy. Kyran and Conrad were here also.'

'Don't know what you're talking about.'

The cold dark eyes are looking away towards Dun Laoghaire. Then he turns and speaks slowly and deliberately. 'I've been nearly thirty years in banking and I've never been called a liar until now.'

'I'm not calling – '

'You are impugning my character.'

'No. I am reminding you of a meeting here with McCarthy to point out that Kevin did not go out on a limb.'

'Kevin has been dragging his heels in this bank for a while now, and I've no intention of carrying the can for him any more.' He holds Philip in a penetrating gaze. 'A piece of advice, Philip. I'd tread very carefully if I were you.'

Philip doesn't reply but opens his briefcase, removes a page and places it in front of Sharkey. 'There,' he says; 'that might jog your memory. It's a photocopy. I've been boning up on this file – just to help out an old friend, you might say.'

Sharkey stares at a copy of a letter that had been in the file, but was not included in the one the staff has just seen. It is a letter from McCarthy's personal assistant thanking Sharkey and Kevin Egan for approving Mr McCarthy's loan application, and inviting them both to his box at the Curragh on Derby Day.

'You know what this means,' Sharkey hisses.

'No. What does it mean?'

'You know I can scupper your prospects with Nat Am.' The hissing voice becomes more intense. 'No one, but no one, crosses me and gets away with it.'

Philip has one more card left to play.

'Right,' he says calmly. 'You're playing with the gloves off. Here's something else to jog your memory. Remember Jacqui?'

'Jacqui?' A hunted look appears in Sharkey's small eyes.

'Jacqui who used to work in IT. Left us a couple of years ago. I think you remember her alright. Not easy to forget Jacqui: dark and *very* pretty. Oh yes. Anyway, she remembers you, and she has an interesting story about … let's call it your extra-curricular interest in Googling.'

Sharkey's shoulders begin to droop; his hands get busy, tying and untying the string that keeps the file together.

Philip puts him on the rack. 'Didn't I bump into Jacqui a few weeks ago in Upper Mount Street. She works with the Bank of Ireland now. Said she got a hard time here after her third baby was born. Had to decamp.'

'Your point? I don't have all day.'

'She invited me to Scruffy Murphy's for coffee. She used to help out here when Karen was under pressure. Anyway, she tells this strange story. Said you were called out of the office one evening. It was a Friday, near to close of business. And didn't she take a peek at your computer? Didn't like what she saw – not one bit, Aengus. You were off to Berlin on business the following Monday, and it seems you weren't exactly looking up the nearest chapel for morning Mass.'

Sharkey glares him. His mouth hangs loose and, like a scowling child tidying up his toys, he begins, slowly, to align the file on his desk. 'I never thought you'd stoop so low. Never,' he mutters.

'Neither did I. You see, Aengus, Jacqui is my insurance.'

After a moment's staring at the file, Sharkey's face brightens; he has the look of a chess player who has hit on a move to stymie his opponent. 'Jacqui has fuck-all proof.'

'Right there, Aengus, except that if she began to blab – and I persuaded her not to – but if she did, well now …. But, Aengus, I know how to handle Jacqui. Of course, there's the reputation of the bank … And the Braces.'

'An all-time low. A fucking all-time low.'

'Agreed, but we live in a jungle.'

Very slowly, and without raising his head, Sharkey says to the *Gatsby* photo on his desk: 'This meeting's over.'

Sharkey comes to an agreement with regard to McCarthy's liability to the bank which worked to the satisfaction of both, and Jacqui never again comes up in conversation.

16

E GAN TAKES A TURN in the nursing home and has to be
removed to the Blackrock Clinic, where stents are inserted
into his coronary arteries. Then he is back again at Our Lady's
Manor. When he is well enough to see visitors, Philip drives out
one sultry evening after close of business. Cones are forming on
the chestnut trees inside the walls of Blackrock College: the slow
turning point of the year is creeping towards autumn.

Every landmark and turn in the road is suffused with
memories shared with Egan. Like the summer they had snogged
the dark-haired Louise and Clodagh, her friend, from Sion Hill.
With Louise, he had felt, for the first time, the luxury of young
love's extravagance in the lane that ran along one side of the
college, while a few yards away Egan was canoodling with
Clodagh.

They took them home from hops, met up after tennis games
in Sandycove, and came back with them from the Sunday
evening folk Mass at Merrion Road Church. On those Sunday
evenings they went for ice cream to Blackrock Village, but nearly
always ended up on the lane.

The images are still fresh in his head when he arrives at the
nursing home where cars are parking, or pulling up by the line
of beeches at the side of the low building. Inside, the sun lounge
has retained the heat of the day and fresh flowers on the ledge
along the glass panels fill the air with a summer perfume. At the
reception area, table lamps cast a soft glow on the lime green

carpet. An old woman sits on a couch, flanked by two younger women: she is crying. One of the women is holding her hand; the other is talking softly and stroking the old woman's wispy hair.

The receptionist, in a tight-fitting suit, is on the phone behind the desk.

'How may I help you, sir?' she wants to know from Philip, when she puts down the phone, but at that moment, he spots Egan's bulk down the corridor. A nurse is helping him to shuffle along the carpet.

A man about his own age appears around a corner, trudging behind a frame. At his side is a nurse with a wheedling voice: 'Very good, Matthew, very good. Now we'll go back again. Good man, Matthew.' A plastic bag with his urine is clipped to the frame, the connecting tube lost to sight beneath his dressing gown.

'Would you look at what the cat brought in?' Egan says when he hears Philip tell the receptionist how she might help him. Speaking as if she too had been issued with the same Mammy voice in her training school, Egan's nurse suggests they go to another lounge, or to the coffee shop at the other end of the hallway. 'It's quiet there now. That alright, Kevin?'

'Perfect, nurse.'

'The old charm hasn't deserted you,' Philip says, and nods in the direction of the shapely figure tripping down the corridor. He glances at Egan: a few days have added ten years to his life – one eye is bloodshot, and purple patches mark the loose hanging flesh of his face.

After trying to reassure Philip that his doctor is very pleased with his progress, Egan forecloses on any further talk about his condition. So from then on they keep at arm's length the smell of sickness, and the slow-moving figures with the stare of death making their way to the lounge. There, on the television, Goosen is lining up his shot for a birdie, but he is largely ignored by the patients and their visitors. Mingling with the murmur of conversations and the genteel clink of china, the commentator is speaking in the tone of voice they use for the state funeral of a president.

Apart from a few words about his feeling of tiredness, 'which will go in no time', Egan resumes his jokey manner. They give an airing to their London days: the time the accountant chap – JJ from Scariff – met the Jamaican at the King's Arms, and made a date for the following night. Wearing the new shirt and tie he had bought that day, he had spent hours getting ready – and checking his reflection in the mirror. He was over the moon going off to meet her: 'best-looking bird in town'. The smell of hair gel lingered in the hallway when he slammed the door behind him. They both laugh again when they recall that *the best-looking bird* turned out to be a Jamaican man of nineteen.

Other patients in dressing gowns are shuffling in. They glance at the television and, with much groaning, lower themselves into the armchairs. The interest is back to Goosen, until it is time for Philip to go.

Although the two men have a deep fondness for each other, Egan holds such a grip on the conversation with jokes and anecdotes about London that Philip, much to his regret, hasn't the heart to bring up any further reference to his condition as they stroll through the sun lounge and out to the front where they can hear cars speeding by on the main road.

There, Egan's act falls to pieces: 'Don't know if I'll make it, Philip,' his chin begins to quiver, 'and I'm scared shitless.'

Philip gives him space.

'I'm frightened. I never thought ... yes, Gillian will survive,' he says with a snort. 'And the boys are nearly there, but it's Roisín ...' His eyes fill up, but he makes a brave effort to stifle a rising surge of sadness.

'None of us ever thinks of ... well, sure it's only for old people.' Philip is searching for a foothold; he lays a hand on Egan's arm. The patients wave to the departing cars and then turn to the front door where the smiles fade.

'I have to stick around for another while – for their sakes, anyway.'

'They'll be fine, Kev. They'll be fine. Look after yourself.'

'They'll be grand.' He dries his eyes with the back of his hand as a child would. 'And I'll be back to the office before you can say "Dickhead Sharkey", and taking money off you at Robin Hill.' The slanting sun shows up the colour of death in his eyes.

Before he enters an opening in the hedge leading to the car park, Philip turns back to wave to his friend, but he has turned away; his whole body has sagged – an actor drained after a long performance.

17

DURING THE SUMMER, whenever Philip and Sam are away, such as at their house in Antibes, they ensure they are never on their own. They bring along Zara and her friends, or else Philip manages to talk his brother, or his father, into making up a party. Una went once, but the atmosphere between her and Sam was so tense, they were all in need of another holiday when they landed back at Dublin airport. For Dylan, the novelty of going to France has worn off; and since the family moved to Auburn, he much prefers to hang around Cooper's Hill, or down at the harbour with his friends.

He is all too familiar with his parents' rows. One night, a couple of years before they had moved to La Salle, he heard them while he was trying to get to sleep. 'If you think I'm prepared to forget you and your banker-whore,' she was screaming at him, 'you'd better think again!'

'You drove me to it. All that counts for you is to be head-honcho.'

'Ah, go and fuck yourself. Guess what? I don't know what she saw in you because you are boring. Really, really boring.'

The front door slams shut and Dylan hears Sam's car driving off. And though he succeeds most of the time in putting it out of his mind, playing his rock music with Jamie, Mark and Rob, he dreads the day when they will call him and Zara to the kitchen table to announce that they are going to go their separate ways. Yet, even with his best mates, he likes to give the impression that Philip and Sam are off having a super time. When the weather is fair for sailing, he and his friends spend most of the day in the dinghy they all chipped in for.

While attending to his bees or weeding the flowerbeds, Doctor Clifford becomes aware of their shouts, or the rush of their feet when they play tag rugby. And whenever their ball soars over the hedge, he tosses it back to them. 'Sorry, Doctor Clifford. Sorry.' Then the scamper of feet and the shouts of excitement start all over again.

Jamie is gangly with a sheepish grin. Mark, the most handsome of the three, is never without a girl hanging out of him in front of the Mace store, or sitting in one of the sun-trap recesses at the harbour. And Rob, with his spiky hair and studs, nearly always wears black. If Clifford comes across them by chance when they are lazing in the heather with their girlfriends, they chat, so their awareness of each other is casual and easy.

On his own, and loitering around the entrance to the pier one day, Mark is anxious to talk, in a way that takes Clifford by surprise. 'I want to travel; do graphic design when I get back, but my dad won't hear of it.' He keeps gazing out to sea. 'Dad says I have to go to Trinity and then join him. He says, "You'll be the fourth generation to work in the family law firm. It would be unthinkable for our proud name to disappear from the front door plate".'

'But law isn't what you have in mind.'

'Is this all I mean to him – someone whose name is on the fucking plate?' Mark had just matriculated with the highest points in the class, but he isn't in a mood of celebration. His eyes look as if he has been crying, prompting Clifford to remember a neighbour's word in his ear: 'They're smoking that … that marijuana thing. I can smell it. It's those newcomers who brought that around.'

True enough: when Philip and Sam are away, Clifford catches the sharp whiff that brings him back to his own student days – summers when he had got an internship at the Beth Abraham Hospital in the Bronx, and a few of them would hit Greenwich Village, or attend concerts in Central Park, all the while keeping a weather eye out for the police.

The laid-back look Mark had paraded for various girlfriends is gone. 'All they can think about is fucking prestige.' With his foot, he takes aim at a pebble. It soars over the edge of the pier and plops into the water.

All Clifford says is, 'I know parents want the best for their children, Mark, and yours are no different, but it's *your* future.'

That weekend Auburn is stunned with the news that Mark is dead. He had been found unconscious in his father's new Jaguar after crashing against a tree, on a straight stretch of the road near Tara. When the fire brigade arrived, steam was rising from the car's creased bonnet. An ambulance, with the engine running and blue lights flashing, waited on the road; the Guards put up diversion signs.

As soon as the fire brigade had cut him free, covered in blood, and shards of glass, the ambulance rushed him to Navan Hospital, where a surgeon and her team tried to save his life but failed.

An hour later his family stands sobbing around his cold body in the silence of a room off the surgical ward. All the urgency of young life has now drained from him. Gripped by shock and grief, they are deaf to the occasional clang of a trolley out in the corridor, or one nurse calling to another about an accident victim in casualty, followed by a commotion down the corridor. A young nurse hovers in the background and makes reassuring sounds when Mark's father mutters to himself: 'Why you didn't wear the seat belt, son, I'll never know.'

At the Requiem Mass, Mark's friends bring up his guitar, a rugby ball and a copy of his sketches of The Sleeping Giant and others of Dublin Bay that he had been doing over the summer. The priest says that Mark was 'a young man with promise, gifted and generous, whose death leaves a deep sadness in his family and in our community'.

A picture of the funeral appears in *The Irish Times*; beneath it is a heading for a short report: 'Son of Well-Known Lawyer is Laid to Rest'.

Hair-gelled and serious and wearing dark glasses, Dylan, Jamie and Rob walk behind the coffin, black ties loose at the necks of their white shirts. The girls support each other. Sunlight glances off the hearse as it passes between two lines of students from Goldsmith Park forming a guard of honour in the church grounds.

In the sailing club, after the funeral, the guests are full of sympathy for Mark's family. His friends, they say, as they stand around with glasses of wine, were so dignified – the way they took part in the ceremony – reading the intercessory prayers and forming the offertory procession.

Poor Mark. It just doesn't make sense.

What?

You know. Well –

Oh yes, of course. The roads. Yes, the roads are lethal nowadays. And those powerful cars.

For a week or so, the back garden of La Salle, and indeed the neighbourhood, is hollow and deserted, until one evening when Clifford answers a knock on his door. They are outside: Dylan, Jamie and Rob, and two of their girlfriends wearing teeth braces, dark eyeshadow and sad looks. After an awkward moment, when they don't know what to do next, one of the girls ventures: 'Could we ask you something, Doctor Clifford?'

'Of course. Where are my manners? Come in.'

Over coffee, they speak more easily in the sunny kitchen about exams and university, until Jamie plucks up the courage to ask the doctor the question that has prompted their visit. Has he seen many people die?

'Yes, especially when I was an intern in the Mater, and later as a registrar.'

'What's it like? Dying, I mean.'

'One can never be certain,' Clifford tries to read their thoughts, 'but in the case of a tragic … a sudden death, there is little or no pain.'

'Little or no pain,' one of the young women repeats in an abstracted way.

'Yes.'

'You slip off.' They exchange looks. One of the girls begins to sniffle.

'So, Mark?' Jamie raises his head from his coffee mug.

'No, as far as I know… Mark became unconscious on impact, so no, there wouldn't be any…'

'That at least is …'

All the while Dylan is silent, searching Cliffords's face, as if he might find some clue to this hammer blow that has ruptured their plans of having a great time in Lanzarote, then hitting Trinity in a couple of weeks. He raises his head. 'And could it be that Mark … ? That the car went out of control, as the Guards said.'

'Yes. Yes indeed.'

They leave as quietly as they had arrived. Before closing the door, Clifford watches them as they shuffle down the driveway.

A couple of weeks after Mark's funeral, a mournful howl wakes Clifford with a start. At first, he thinks it's a dog or a fox. Foxes often steal down the hill looking for food, and sometimes, a callous neighbour, who keeps hens, lays traps for them. After a while, he realizes he's not listening to a dying fox but to a human cry coming from the direction of La Salle.

He parts the curtains and when his eyes grow used to the dark, he is able to make out the figure of Dylan lurching around the terraced garden, a bottle in his grasp. A couple of times he almost topples over while repeating the same tormented wail: 'No fucking reason.'

He takes another swig from the bottle. Lights go on in the house and show up the pond, the sheen on the barbecue, the Valentia slate of the garden shed, and on his washed-out face looking up at the sky. A hoarse cry rises from deep in his chest: 'Mark, why? Fucking why? I loved you, man. Now …' He falls, but manages to hold on to the bottle while trying to struggle to his feet.

The patio doors burst open, and Sam, followed by Zara, both in their dressing gowns, appear and run to where he is lying.

'Dylan, lovey,' Sam pleads and hunkers down beside him, putting her hand around his head, 'come into the house.'

But he shrugs her away and tries to get to his feet, only to collapse again.

Clifford throws on his clothes, rushes down the stairs and is met at the door by Zara, crying and pleading with him: 'Please, Doctor Clifford, please. Dylan is *so* out of it. Come and help us.'

Ahead of her, he hurries down the drive and around by the back of La Salle and to where Sam is talking to her son, who is now flat out on the grass. 'I hope you don't mind my – '

'Oh, Ned, oh, please ...' On her knees and holding his head, Sam turns and stretches out her hand.

'Let me,' Clifford crouches on the grass beside Dylan.

'Philip is down the country. Please, whatever you can do.'

Clifford turns him on his side. 'Dylan,' he calls. 'Dylan, we'll take good care of you, so don't be worried about anything.' His pulse is too weak for Clifford's liking. 'A torch, quick, a torch.' He reaches out towards Zara who runs into the house, and returns with a torch. One look at the dilated pupil is enough.

'Dylan, Dylan? Do you know where you are?'

Dylan mutters as if trying to make contact with reality, but all he wants is an answer from the grave: 'Why, Mark, why? I ... we loved you.'

The whiskey bottle lying at a slant on the grass catches Clifford's eye. It is more than half-empty. 'Casualty, Samantha,' He whispers. 'We have to. Better to be on the safe side.'

'You ... our mate. Why?'

In less than five minutes an ambulance screams up Beresford Road. Without fuss and with a few practised words of reassurance, the ambulance men place Dylan on a stretcher, and cover him with a blanket. Standing behind Sam as if for protection, Zara, now in a tracksuit, is sobbing quietly. Strands of her long hair are matted to her face.

Sam travels with Dylan in the ambulance; Zara drives with Doc Clifford. Before long the ambulance loses them.

'Will he be alright, Doctor Clifford?' she asks a couple of times in a snuffling tone.

'He'll be fine, Zara. This is just a precaution. He'll be fine.'

She grows silent, blows her nose and sinks back into the seat.

'I knew something bad, like, was going to happen,' she says out of the silence.

'How do you mean?'

'Miss Myers, who teaches us physics, and she was, like, telling us before the summer holidays about birds falling out of the sky in some parts of the world, and that's, like, a bad sign. And …'

'Yes, Zara.'

'I've been.' She glances at him. 'You won't tell Mum or Dad.'

'Not if you don't want me to.'

'I've been dreaming that a whole shower of small birds fell on our back garden. And I tried to help them but they were *so* dead. Are birds able to sleep at night?'

'Yes. In the trees.'

'I'm glad.' She grows silent for a while and then pipes up with: 'Dylan's been on the lash all day, and he's also on … I'm scared, Doctor Clifford.'

'Of what?'

She dries her eyes. 'We've everything, and we've, like, nothing.'

Lest he place too much on her young shoulders, Clifford considers his reply. He had grown fond of them, but the ingrained habit of the clinician he cannot put aside. 'Perhaps this is a chance – a wake-up call – to do something about that, Zara.' They are stopped at a red light in Fairview: 'But you might let Dylan get better first.'

At the junction of North Circular Road and Eccles Street, they notice a head-to-head between a man and a woman in their thirties. The man swings his arm and strikes the woman on the face, sending her reeling. Another man, who is in their company, comes to the woman's defence and receives a punch to the head for his gallantry. He teeters on the edge of the footpath and barely escapes being hit by an oncoming car; blood streams from his nose. The woman is screaming for them to stop. A police car, with blue lights flashing, screeches to a halt. Two young policemen in shirtsleeves jump out and break up the row.

Inside, the emergency unit is bedlam. From behind closed curtains come groans and shouts for assistance: 'Me fuckin brain is stickin out, nurse,' and from another end of the ward: 'Is anyone goin to come and look after me? I'm fuckin dyin.'

With jigging stethoscopes around their necks, doctors and

nurses are rushing in and out of the curtained bays, a blur of white uniforms. Some are examining those lying on trolleys; others are trying to calm frightened patients. 'Keep steady... Good man. Hold your arm out straight ... Good.' Stale drink and hospital smells mingle with the whiff of urine.

Dylan has been wheeled into a bay. Inside closed curtains, a doctor and a nurse are attending to him. After some time, the nurse brings Sam, Zara and Clifford to an alcove, and reassures them that Dylan will be fine: that when he vomited, he got rid of some of the drink, and won't have to be pumped out.

The shouting continues outside: 'Am I goin to die in this fuckin place?'

A hospital orderly – mullet head planted on beefy shoulders – saunters to the bay, eases back one of the curtains, and says in a low voice. 'Shut the fuck up. A doctor or a nurse will be with you as soon as they can.' He closes the curtain and winks at a nurse hurrying by with a scissors and bandages on a tray.

Relieved by what the nurse has said, both Sam and Zara rest against each other: all they have to do now is wait until Dylan is ready. Clifford stands: 'Back in a minute.' Sam reaches out for his hand. 'I don't know what we'd have done without you, Ned. Thanks.'

'Dylan will be fine, Samantha.'

He walks down the aisle between the curtains towards the door where another ambulance has backed up. The doors are thrown open and a man in a trolley is lifted out; around his waist is a blood-soaked bandage.

A young doctor, his white coat thrown open is shouting. 'Theatre, quick, come on, out of the way.' The orderly is also shouting and opening doors. 'Stand back. Patient for theatre.'

A group of young women are sitting close on a bench in the waiting area, their arms around each other. One is crying, causing her eyeshadow to smear her face; another is at the admissions hatch arguing with a nurse. 'We're students; we can't afford to go to a chemist ... It's just not on.' The nurse is trying to tell them that they are busy right now, but will get to them later.

The mullet comes back and is now giving the girls the once-over. He smiles and whispers to Clifford: 'The stampede for the morning-after is beginning early tonight. You always pay for your whoopee.'

There's a shout from inside one of the curtains: 'I'm losing him: get the defib.' Immediately there's a flurry of feet, and a rumble of the defibrillator machine along the centre aisle.

'Stand back,' a nurse orders.

Chubby and out of breath, a young priest comes dashing in; he is clutching a purple stole and a silver phial, one end of his clerical collar hangs loose. When he makes a move towards the patient, a nurse snaps at him: 'Stand back, I said.' With a sheepish look on his plump face, the priest slinks behind the resuscitation team.

When the intern lays the pads on the patient's chest, another nurse turns a switch on the machine; the patient's chest jerks and falls again.

On the journey home, they are mostly silent. Every so often, Sam, who is sitting close to Dylan in the back, asks him how he is feeling.

'Grand, Mum. Grand now.'

'That's good, lovey.'

Clifford parks beside Sam's SUV and waits while they trudge towards the front door, where they stand: a forlorn sight. 'Thanks, Ned,' Sam says in a hushed tone. She raises her hand and then lets it fall to her side. 'Talk to you tomorrow.'

In a low voice also, Clifford says: 'Have a good rest, Dylan.'

'Thanks, Doctor Clifford.'

A 'good rest' is echoing in Clifford's mind when he wakes in the dark, and the scenes of the previous few weeks form an odd *mélange* in his head. He gets up, puts on his dressing gown and saunters to his study where he looks across at the gloomy outline of La Salle. There he remains in the dark, trying to sort out the knotted skein until he is disturbed by one of his dogs yelping in a dream.

18

OVER THE LATE SUMMER Sharkey is merciless in making redundancies. Apart from back office staff, senior members are given the option of a golden handshake. If they refuse, they suffer the *Sharkey treatment* until they crack. Those jobs that can be are outsourced; empty desks are removed. In their place, palms and latticed partitions decorate the open office plan on one or two of the floors in the six-storey building. And when the purge is slowing down, and the bulk of the back office has gone elsewhere, the fear of other cutbacks, like the aftermath of a contagion, continues to generate anxiety.

In the private dining room, St John Dunleavy is in denial. 'Don't come to me with problems. Come with solutions' is his motto, and so he listens closely when Sharkey reveals his plan for a Corporate Bonding Conference: 'I've seen them go down a bomb in the US. Just the ticket to get us all out of this slump. Good for staff. Good for Nat Am.'

Sharkey also knows that the best man to lead the conference is Scott Montgomery. 'Charisma is his middle name, Breffni. A few years ago, I shared a platform with him at Brown while I was up in Providence foraging for Nat Am investments.'

'Leave it with me,' says St John Dunleavy. 'I'll work on my board' is followed by his trademark wink. 'By the way,' he says when Sharkey has his hand on the door knob, 'when you are selecting other speakers – warm-up men, as they say in America – give a wide berth to those jumped-up economists one has to endure on the television these days. Their lot is doing harm to our economy and to our banking system, making it out to be a basket case when it's nothing of the sort.'

'Consider it done, Breffni.'

To organize the conference, Sharkey gathers round him a few junior bankers who are to be available at all times. He leaves them in no doubt about the serious nature of the event: 'I've done some groundwork; now you're on your own. You've got your BlackBerries; I want a 24/7 response. Gun to tape, and no lagging behind. Get it?'

They stand in front of his desk. 'If you blow this,' he tells them, 'you are showing me you can't organize a piss-up.' And he cocks his forefinger towards the venetian blinds, where members of staff are moving about the office floor with papers while others scrutinize their computer screens. 'See,' he says, 'I can get several out there to step up to the plate.'

The conference would be held out at Windermere Hall, a hotel with two hundred acres of golf course off the motorway for the South. Before the boom, the owner had been a bricklayer out in Sallins. One morning he walked into Sharkey's office and asked for thirty million Euro to invest in a housing project in Kells. Within three years he was in the premier league of developers, Windermere Hall becoming one of his trophies.

'It's what I have in common with Maggie Thatcher,' Sharkey boasted in the executive floor dining room after a Sunday paper had named his client 'a Celtic Tiger success'. The subtitle read: 'Another first for Nat Am'. 'Maggie could size up a guy in thirty seconds. I'm the same. I liked the guy; he has balls.'

By email, Sharkey keeps the staff in touch with the preparations. He sends a final one close to the event:

> Listen up, people. You are to be at the foyer by 8 AM on Saturday morning for Scott Montgomery's arrival. Scott doesn't come cheap. 8 bells. Go well.

When they step out of Mercs, Volvos and corporate taxis, at the front door of Windermere Hall, a few of the directors and senior managers who weren't able to make the previous night's dinner are in a cheerful mood, laughing and shaking hands with each other. Porters stand at a discreet distance, ready to help. 'I hope the traffic was light this morning, gentlemen,' one of them says in a sycophantic manner to two executives. The concern is ignored.

'Is there anything I can do for you, sir?'

'Yes.' A director points to his bags on the tarmac. 'Fetch them.'

'Be glad to, sir.'

Windermere Hall rolls out the red carpet for the guest of honour. Inside the glass panels, the bank personnel affect a buoyant mood while they wait for his arrival. Then, with a loud whirr that sends a rush of wind through the hedge, the helicopter descends on the pad across from the driveway. The engine is shut off and the propellers come to rest.

Something about Montgomery's name and the reputation that Sharkey has built up leads them to expect a large-limbed figure, so they are greatly surprised when, instead of John Wayne, Dustin Hoffman with Bono glasses emerges out of the giant fly.

In the conference hall, Dunleavy gives the opening address, followed by Sharkey, who says: 'It is only right that one Harvard man should add a word of welcome to another.' He gives a glowing account of Montgomery's achievements, and how fortunate they are to have him deliver the keynote address. Sitting at the front facing the stage, Montgomery gets to his feet and turns to the assembly; his arms shoot up in a Richard Nixon salute.

For openers, he speaks about *can-do* and *taking no prisoners*. 'You see, folks, a founding principle in my country is that all men and women are equal. All have an equal chance of success. And that's why the free market is the way to do business. On my way over in the plane, I boned up some more on your economy, and came across a speech by one of your government ministers. I like what that man has to say.' He refers to his paper. 'Here it is. "I make no apology to anyone in declaring my strong defence of the free market. What we need in this country is *light touch* regulation. It releases entrepreneurial skills in anyone willing to get off his backside and work." Now, folks – there's a man after my own heart.'

By now, mobiles in handbags, or held discreetly on laps, are lighting up. Encounters that began at the bar the previous night are still simmering.

What wud u like 4 dessert? xxx. Hugh

What's on the menu? xxx Melody

Do u c the high heels on the little runt? Well hello.

When Montgomery has finished, he does a Nixon pose again. Sharkey leads the applause and reminds them that they are to be back in the conference room in fifteen minutes. Mock protests like pupils deprived of time-off rise from the floor. 'Guys, golf or trips to Castletown House or Carton in the afternoon.'

Sharkey, who had been the first to leave the bar the previous evening, had, along with Karen, set up the PowerPoint, and checked that the material was in the right order. They did a trial run of the pages: sales figures, current market share and diagrams, showing how Nat Am ranked with other financial institutions.

St John Dunleavy, and one or two of the other directors, speak about the major contribution Nat Am is making towards the Celtic Tiger, how it maintains the highest ethical standards in line with good banking policy, and at the same time delivers prompt service to its clients, especially 'those willing to take risks for the sake of this country's future, for its towns and cities.'

Again, Sharkey becomes the warm-up man for Montgomery. He nods to Karen to open a page showing an image of the redbrick house on Andrew Street where Nat Am had started out as Amalgamated. 'A million and a half pounds in the kitty,' he says. 'Buttons.'

He beams at his audience. 'Now, under the guiding hand of our chairman, we're the envy of the banking world. Fifteen billion in gross assets. Morgan Stanley, Bank of Ireland, Bank of Montreal – the big guns among our register of shareholders. We bought out First Union in Philly, Lyon Paribas in France, Royal Mutual in Berlin. They laughed at us over their gin and sour in the Four Seasons, called us buccaneers.' He leans into the microphone, and raises his voice. 'They're not laughing now.' A burst of applause drowns him out, so he has to repeat himself: 'We did it through being faithful to the highest standards in banking ethics: *efficiency, integrity* and *confidentiality.*'

Karen turns over another page that shows just the three words. She tracks progress with the mouse, and stops where Nat Am lies in the table of market shares.

'See who the leader is, guys. Now, are we going to lag behind that lot?' Then louder: 'Are we going to lag behind? Are we happy to be lying fourth or third or even second?'

A surge of voices fills the hall: 'No, we're not.'

Mobiles are lighting up again:

In d ro bhind u, Hilary. Gd body structure. Any guided tours?

Dpends who d tourist is.

The market share is left frozen on the computer as all eyes watch the thickset figure of Montgomery climb again to the stage.

'My daddy was a West Point man, who fought with Mac-Arthur in Korea,' he begins. 'Fact is – I carry the proud Montgomery name: the name that is honoured for bravery in wars going back to the Alamo. Yes sir, an illustrious ancestor fought beside Sam Houston against the marauding Mexicans and became a byword for courage, and Texan can-do.'

Hot last nite, babes. Justin.

&u. More wre tht came from.

'My daddy,' Montgomery continues. 'He used to say: "Whenever the troops are happy, something has gone wrong." I understand you're not a hundred percent happy right now. Well, maybe that's because this great financial institution is making decisions that will be to your good and the good of the company in the long run.'

Pacing, he extemporizes for a while and in that way lives up to Sharkey's glowing praise: 'No one, but no one does *ad lib* like Montgomery.'

'Positive thinking,' Montgomery declares, 'it's the only game in town, folks. A get-up-and-go attitude, along with loyalty to your company. I want to quote a great Irish-American, and a welcomed visitor to the shores of his ancestors: President Ronald Reagan:

Trust the people. The societies that have achieved the most spectacular broad-based progress are neither the most highly controlled nor the biggest in size. No, what unites them all is their willingness to believe in the magic of the market.

Karen brings up the key words on the screen: *The magic of the market.*

'Yes, the former President, God bless him, was a firm believer in the free market; and the boundless opportunities for every man and woman who wishes to succeed. Be proud of Nat Am, and be loyal – it's what has made the United States of America the most powerful nation on earth. And by the way, if needs be,' a broad smile shows on his tanned face, 'kick ass. Best motivator in the book. The banking world is no tea party. Never was. You've got to fight for it on Main Street; come on you guys!'

Sharkey picks up a radio microphone: 'Everyone. Let's show Scott we Irish can appreciate the best motivator you'll ever hear.' With jerky movements of his two hands, he indicates that they give Montgomery a standing ovation.

When they settle down again, Montgomery opens a file and delivers his paper: more about loyalty and the free market, and quotations from Ronald Reagan and Margaret Thatcher.

Mobiles continue to light up.

Some play golf that afternoon, others catch up on lost sleep or go to the pool. The women avail of the Ocean Spirit spa, facials or the sauna; some opt for exfoliation and massage.

That evening, waiters in black jackets and bow ties dim the chandeliers in the dining room and then at each of the round tables they light candles in glass bowls as the chattering guests arrive. Women's necklaces and bracelets sparkle in the candle-light. The Georgian windows with their tied back drapes give a wide view of dusk falling on the golf course.

The waiters move smartly around the tables with bottles of wine; they take orders and reply in the accents of Eastern Europe. Later when the wine begins to take effect, they have to endure self-styled comedians, who make cheap jokes at their expense. 'Did you come for the weather, mate?' At one corner, a pianist plays a range of music from Beethoven to Cole Porter to The Beatles. The pianist, an ex-Christian Brother, has been hired by the hotel to play at weddings and conferences. On a good week, with tips included, he brings home more than a teacher's pay.

The after-dinner speeches are brief. St John Dunleavy calls for a toast to Mr Scott Montgomery and the 'great United States of America, our closest and best friend'. The ex-Brother plays a few bars of 'America the Beautiful': all stand and raise their glasses.

Some of the directors, and those, like Conrad Brennan, who never miss an opportunity to advance their careers, saunter out on to the smoking salon with Montgomery; St John Dunleavy has given the speaker a box of Havanas. His cheque would be sent on the following week.

Philip and the others intend to have one or two drinks, get an early night and meet for a swim and a work-out in the early morning; but, like any group with a shared history, they have stories to tell, and one rolls onto the next, especially about the time when they returned to Haughey's daring new world of financial services. They were climbing the greasy pole then: keeping ahead of the mortgage, the loan on the new Volvo, and getting the boys down for Belvedere where they would meet 'the right sort'.

Before he leaves for Dublin airport on the Sunday morning, Montgomery delivers his final inspirational speech. He ends with a parable. His wife's grandfather arrived at Ellis Island from Lithuania on a bleak February morning in 1904. All he had was a shirt, long johns and a pair of socks in a brown paper parcel.

'But Margaret's granddad didn't sit on his hands. No sir. He raised a family, became a steeplejack in the Bronx, then a builder, made several fortunes, so that his family went to Columbia and Fordham. And his granddaughter – my lovely wife – made it to Yale, and is now a highly respected lawyer. Can-do, guys. Buckets of can-do. All men and women are equal in the United States of America.'

With his fellow Harvard man leading the applause, and others rising from their seats, Montgomery raises his voice: 'Go get it, guys, go get it. And make sure you always get bang for your buck.'

When he is leaving, everyone goes out to the foyer again to wave goodbye. Halfway across the avenue he turns and waves: 'Remember Speaker Moynihan folks: "No one ever lost an election by underestimating the intelligence of the public." ' The full-on propellers cause a flurry in the high hedge as the helicopter rises into the sky.

A short session on the Sunday morning is devoted to a mission statement. This is St John Dunleavy's idea: one of his old Benedictine teachers had suggested it to him at their last Downside reunion. 'And it will consolidate the spirit of bonding that was evident these past two days,' he declares.

Sharkey has no time for mission statements. 'Is it converting black babies we're at now?' he says to his retinue while they are having breakfast. 'Give me investments, net-worth, and equity, and fuck your mission statement. What do monks know about anything? If I hadn't grabbed Amalgamated by the balls, well … guys,' he says as he stirs his coffee, *'you are what you have in this world.* Yes, and by Jesus, you hold on to it.'

'Seems to be part of this Catholic thing he's so proud of.'

Sharkey ignores the comment. 'Here's my mission statement, guys. First commandment of banking: You shall be judged by the profit you bring in. That's what the shareholders demand and rightfully expect. The second commandment: Hold your client. Sin against one of those two commandments and I shoot you.'

19

PHILIP AND SAM used to invite Father Tom for a meal when he returned from the missions. Afterwards, they would sit with him and a remnant of the Newman House group and, over a glass of wine, look through photos of themselves, at the Phoenix Park and in Galway during the Pope's visit. One had been taken on Christmas Eve morning outside the Bank of Ireland when they were coming off their forty-eight-hour fast – their breath showing in the frosty air. And every time they scanned these photos, they had a good laugh at the one of Sam challenging a Garda inspector in her fight for Nicaragua.

They would return to Mass when Dylan was making his First Communion. Indeed, they composed sunny images of themselves climbing the lichen steps of Raheny Church on a Sunday morning: Dylan beside his father, and Zara hanging on to her mother's hand.

But Sunday was their only time to have a lie-in while they clambered up the ladder at a rate beyond their wildest dreams. After a while, the invitations to Father Tom and the Newman remnant fell away.

The relentless progress was consuming them, body and soul. Their determination to climb higher was as fervent as their one-time commitment to the soup run. They were winning trophies too: the house at Antibes, a growing trust fund for Dylan and Zara, the SUV and the Beemer in the driveway. Encouraged by Sharkey, Philip, like most Nat Am staff, had taken out half a million Euro to invest in the bank.

The Lalors were changing: Sam would stop at nothing for a chance to sit at the directors' table. Philip had been bending the rules, like being up to his neck with Sharkey, and a few others in conspiring to hide the millions Sharkey was taking out on loans from Nat Am. He was also in on the bank policy of advising clients to avoid DIRT, by helping them to open non-resident accounts.

When Philip saw how money was draining out of the country, he hit upon the idea of opening a branch in the tax-free Isle of Man to attract investors, and talked it over with Sharkey and Kevin one night in Shanahan's on the Green. He had to do some clever footwork, and get around Sharkey, who usually shot down any idea that wasn't his own.

'Don't you remember, Aengus, what you said there a couple of months ago about some way of getting our clients to avoid a penal tax bill?'

'Yes ... Yes, I did.'

'And you said something about the chance of opening in the Isle of Man.'

'Now that you mention it, I was about to get around to it this week.'

At that time both Philip and Kevin were among the disciples. Philip was getting good at justifying what he was doing: other banks were in on the act and, anyway, hard-working people were being fleeced with punitive taxes. So, apart from Philip's education project for Tanzania, the slow drift away from the Holy Thursday ideals got lost in the welter of plans they devised as they drove home in the dark after picking up the children.

They considered themselves lucky when they got Crina from Romania, who acted as nanny and housekeeper. Crina lived in a Baldoyle apartment with her husband, Lars. When Sam went back to work after having Dylan, Crina looked after the baby; the same when Zara came along. She also did the housework, washed and ironed, and the children loved her. She arrived each morning before Philip and Sam had gone to work, and when they returned, she drove away in her twelve-year-old Nissan Micra.

And when Philip and Sam went out for a meal or to the

theatre with the Egans, or other colleagues, the children were glad to have Crina for a few more hours. Lars, who worked in construction at the airport, came now and again to cut the grass, trim shrubs and bushes, and tend to the flowerbeds.

For a week or so, when Crina flew back to Bucharest to see her father, who had suffered a stroke, Philip's mother, Una, volunteered to come and stay at the house. At such short notice, Sam couldn't get anyone she trusted, so she gave in.

The two women had never warmed to each other: Una always maintained that Philip gave Sam too much authority over their affairs. 'There's no doubt who wears the trousers in that household,' she confided early on to her sister the nun as they paced Sandymount Strand. 'And that father …' She made a face. 'Something strange about that boyo. God forgive me for talking like this. You should hear him go on about his 'property portfolio' in Alicante. Upstart.'

A practical woman, not given to too much reflection, Una believed that Philip could have done better. The two families met for the first time when Philip and Sam graduated; they all went to Dobbin's Bistro for a meal. Although Ollie and Myra wore expensive clothes, Una feared the worst: Philip would marry beneath him. Used car business or not, they were working-class through and through: the father, with his suntan, was still the spray painter from Crumlin.

The following Saturday, in the convent parlour, she gave a blow-by-blow account to her sister. 'You should see the get-up of him, with his rings and his bracelets. Like one of them swarthy fellows you'd come across trying to sell you carpets of a Saturday in Roscrea.'

Soon after, Philip brought Sam home for the first time; one look for Una was enough to know that it was too late now to stop him, yet she let Sam know where she stood in her affections. For most of the evening she talked to Philip and ignored her. At the dinner table, Una served her son a steak; Sam was given a salad. As the years went by, the gap between the two women grew wider, but by sheer effort and fearing the consequences, they stifled their mutual hatred. That effort – in a perverse way

– fuelled their loathing. Una harped on to her sister about Sam's obsession with dieting and how the blender is always at the ready on the kitchen island. 'This vegetarian nonsense, and not a pick on her. I wouldn't be at all surprised if she didn't have one of those – you know – eating disorders. And Dylan and Zara,' she snorted. 'What sort of names are they?'

Conversely, everything about Una set her daughter-in-law's teeth on edge. Like the way she wrong-footed them at the table, making a lot of crossing herself and saying Grace Before Meals, when Sam was about to tuck into her food.

At the beginning, Sam coped by referring to her jokingly as the Queen Bee, and Philip took no offence then, but later, when they became snappy with each other, and the rows became bitter, she raged at him: 'You're fucking well in thrall to her … the Queen Bee.'

'At least she acts her age, not like your silly mother, mutton dressed as lamb.'

When Crina had to fly to Bucharest, Sam was in a corner; not easy to get someone on a temporary basis to whom the children would adapt, and while Dylan was quiet and biddable, Zara was already proving a handful. Besides, Sam was now due for promotion, and taking time off wouldn't go down well. Even with just two children, she had to endure the snide remarks of some of the men about women wanting it both ways. Like Nat Am, High Res demanded unconditional loyalty.

So on the evening before Sam left for London on a shoot that would take three days, Una and Seamus moved in to the house in Raheny. The arrangement seemed good for everyone: Seamus would potter about the garden, weeding flowerbeds and cutting the grass. He would also bring his poetry collections: Wordsworth, Tennyson and Yeats – a life-long interest, which Una saw as a waste of time.

The weekend would become Una's chance to put into action what she had been hatching for some time: to do something about the children's lack of any religious formation. Philip and Sam's decision to send the children to *that place* – the feeder school for Goldsmith Park, had appalled her.

'Sure, there's no religion taught there, by all accounts,' she appealed to her sister. 'And Dylan should be making his First Communion in a year's time.'

The nun made clicking sounds with her tongue.

'Not a sign of a religious picture in the house, but she can go into town and buy dear paintings from that gallery on the Green. It's far from art she was reared.'

As soon as Philip had gone to Druid's Glen with a couple of developers, Una told the children that she had some books they might like to look at. She rooted in her bag, while they stood in front of her with a look of expectation, as if they sensed that something out of the ordinary was about to happen.

'Now,' she said, 'let us all sit and look at these.'

Very quietly they eased themselves on to the couch at each side of her.

'Dylan and Zara, here's pictures you will know. That's who?'

They looked up with blank expressions. 'I don't know, Nana. Who *is* he?'

'That's Jesus, of course,' she told them with an edge to her tone.

'Oh Nana,' Dylan grinned, sinking back into the couch. 'You – ' He covered his face with a comic book; Zara copied him. 'You *shouldn't* be saying that word. That's a curse.' They sniggered behind their comics.

'What, child?' She let the book about Jesus sink into her lap.

'My friend, Josh,' Dylan told her, 'said that word when he fell, and his child-minder said not to be saying *that* word.'

Zara thought it was very funny and started running around repeating: 'Jesus, Jesus, Jesus.'

Una closed the book, and in the measured way she would explain the rules to fractious pupils in her school, she said: 'Come here, Zara.' Her lips tightened. The children stood in front of her.

'Children, Jesus is a *good* word, a holy word, and it should be spoken only when you are praying. It is the name of the Son of God. He came to save us from our sins.'

Zara liked the sound of 'praying'. She moved against her grandmother's knee, and kept repeating the word.

When Sam returned from London, Dylan was bursting with news of Nana's books, of men having dinner on one side of a table, with Jesus in the middle. 'And Jesus is a good word, a holy word.'

'Oh, really' was all that Sam said, but Una received a frosty reception when she dropped in the following week. Philip had gone out on his bike, so they had the house to themselves. Both women stood in the kitchen contriving to make small talk, aware of what hung between them. Eventually Sam spoke her mind.

'There's an issue … and I'll not sit here and pretend it hasn't happened, especially since it concerns my children's education.'

Una's mouth tightened. 'Yes, Samantha.'

Both had experience in dealing with conflict: Sam at work; Una, when irate parents came to her office to complain that their children were being treated unjustly.

'Then I must insist that you will never again interfere.'

'Interfere?'

'Yes. It is *our* right as parents to introduce them to religion, if we so wish.'

'So you think it is right to deprive them of the true faith that has served this country so well for centuries?'

Sam raised her voice: 'Dylan and Zara are *our* children. We have the primary responsibility for their upbringing. I don't share your ideas. Ireland has moved on. I've nothing in principle against religion but, as far as I'm concerned, it's a private matter. For your information, Dylan will make his First Communion, and so will Zara. A priest comes to Goldsmith Junior; it's not the heathen place that some make it out to be.'

Looking composed, Una was about to give battle, when she spotted Zara, who had come into the kitchen and was looking up at them. 'Nana,' she muttered, with her thumb in her mouth, 'will you read us another story about the man with the beard?'

'Lovey,' Sam said, in a low voice, 'go and play with Dylan. I'm talking to Nana.'

The two women were silent for a moment after Zara had left, both avoiding each other's look. Una was the first to speak:

'I owe you an apology, Samantha. You are perfectly right. Dylan and Zara are your children.'

Sam sank onto the couch where they sat as a family to watch a small television until the children's bedtime. 'It's just the way I see things nowadays.'

Clutching her handbag, Una remained standing near the cupboards, but when she spoke, the edge had left her voice. 'I may be stepping out of line here, but weren't you and Philip very much involved with that priest in college? Masses and the soup round, and so on.'

Despite her resolve, Sam found herself becoming tearful; she began to play with a tassel of the throw. 'It was ... oh, I don't know, I suppose a student thing. Stand up for the poor. But it didn't really cost us anything. And we had the luxury of knowing we'd never be in their situation – or, most certainly, never have to live near them.'

The serious look on Una's face was dissolving. '*A cool* thing to do as people say nowadays.'

'Exactly. Thirty-six hour fasts. Change the world. Philip more than me. Some of the time I was only going along for his sake.'

Sam had another reason, which she wouldn't reveal to Una. While she was ladling out soup to vagrants, she felt superior: her own worries seemed to disappear. She smoothed down the throw: 'The world changed us, I'm afraid.'

It was a side of Sam Una had never seen before, but she made ready to go. 'I just called in for a minute while Seamus is browsing around the library,' she said. 'I feel I need to apologize. As you say, your children are your responsibility.'

'Thank you.'

It was a reconciliation of sorts, but the two women would never be friends, never stroll up Grafton Street on a Saturday morning, looking at shoes and then drop into Bewley's for a cup of coffee and a croissant. And Una would never again bring books about the bearded man who came to save us from our sins.

20

WORD GETS TO EGAN in the nursing home that Sharkey has farmed out some of his files to a young graduate from the Smurfit School – a chap who plays tag rugby with Brennan in Donnybrook. The files in question did not require urgent attention.

So, despite his doctor's strict advice that he take a month off, Egan returns to work, brushing aside well-meaning words of caution from friends at Nat Am about not rushing things, and how 'Deansgrange Cemetery is full of those who couldn't slow down'. As always, he makes light of such advice, and resumes his high stool at Paddy Cullen's, even if he is now limited to tomato juice or mineral water. 'Never felt better,' he lies when they ask how he is. Laughing off his illness, he says: 'Remember John Maynard Keynes, fellas: "In the long run we're all dead." The padded box is waiting for us all, so what's the fuss?'

With Philip, though, he drops the devil-may-care routine. 'I have to, Philip. Sharkey will edge me out: he's already given some of my portfolios to a mate of that creep Brennan.'

He hides as well as he can his chest pains and his insomnia. But Philip can see through the act: 'Go easy, Kev,' he tells him one evening while they are having a coffee in the plaza.

'No worries.' Egan shifts in the chair, and fixes his glance somewhere in the distance. 'Not going to make Gillian a widow quite so soon.' He adds sheepishly, 'Although that mightn't be something she would find too much to cope with. No, I feel I'm regaining my strength.'

Philip listens while he continues to talk about how he is walking out the Blackrock Road every evening. 'You won't believe this. I do a few rounds of the old Alma Mater, and sometimes drop into the chapel. A couple of weeks in the clinic sets you thinking about … well … the God thing.'

'Not like you. You thought we were all bonkers – the Charismatic Masses, braving the freezing nights.'

'Look,' says Egan, anxious to change the subject, 'we haven't done Picasso's in ages – I mean the four of us.' He takes his BlackBerry from his inside pocket. 'We'll get more time to shoot the breeze.'

'I'm on for that.'

'Saturday night then.'

In the early years, the four of them had gone out frequently together; then it tapered out. Although they were cordial, sometimes even effusive, neither of their two wives liked each other. From the beginning, Sam envied Gillian's sensuous beauty and the way, even when she had thrown on whatever clothes were near at hand, and was without a trace of make-up, she was the one whom men openly stared at when they were walking down a street together.

On the Saturday night the four of them have a drink at the bar of Picasso's while waiting for their table. As always, the two women are demonstrative in their greeting and air kissing.

Great to catch up, Sammy.

You're looking fab.

So are you. New hairstyle looks … just right for you.

After the meal, when they are relaxing at the bar counter and the two women are flitting from holidays to House of Ireland and Brown Thomas, Philip learns the full extent of the pressure Sharkey is exerting on Egan: either take a golden handshake or else be put on a two-day week. He describes to Philip what happened earlier that day when Sharkey called him in. ' "You'll have more time on your hands, Kevin", he says. "Get out there on the golf course. Wouldn't mind that myself." Then the gobshite stands up and starts doing air swings. "Yes, that would be the life. You've no idea the shit I've to put up with in here.

We'll call it a retirement that you opted for. Time out to smell the roses. No loss of face that way." ' Egan's round shoulders are hunched, his stout neck sunk into his chest, and beneath the restaurant lighting, perspiration glistens on his forehead.

Leaving the restaurant, the women get back to how great it is to catch up.

Must do this more often.

Absolutely. I'll look forward to that.

'Why don't we do a weekend at Kelly's?' Gillian suggests. 'Brilliant down there.'

'You're on, I'd like nothing better,' says Sam, knowing it will never happen. 'Rosslare here we go, Gill.'

Egan puts back on the sunny mask as the four of them head for taxis waiting outside on Vernon Avenue. 'Golf very soon, Philip. I'm shit hot now after the break, probably should give you a handicap.'

'Very soon at the Glen, Kev,' says Philip.

Very soon at the Glen never comes for Egan. The following Sunday morning, as he is setting off for his walk around the grounds of Blackrock College, he slumps over at the foot of the stairs.

The Pakistani doctor at the Clinic is very sympathetic to Gillian, their two sons and Roisín, their daughter. He brings them into a private room. 'So sorry, Mrs Egan.' He steals a glance at the clipboard. 'Gillian. We did all we could.' He holds her hand while he speaks.

The following day, after a night of fitful sleep, Philip makes the dreaded visit to the funeral parlour where his dead friend is reposing. 'Oh, yes, of course. I'll take you to view the deceased,' says the funeral director, a pale man with priestly gestures. He leads him down a carpeted hallway, where churchy music is playing softly. The dark-suited funeral director opens the double doors of a room that smells faintly of varnished wood. At the centre of the floor stands a coffin on its own; the brass fittings glint in the light from the amber table lamps.

'So you were life-long friends. My goodness, how sad. And a relatively young man.' The funeral director's discreet tone is conditioned by day-in-day-out contact with death. He goes around the room, fussing over the flower vases, picking up fallen petals with ladylike hands.

Philip walks slowly to the coffin. 'School. College. Best-man and then work.'

Egan's grey face looks swollen and is blotched with purple patches.

'Yes. Ever since ...'

'My condolences.'

'Yes ... thank you.'

Streaks of light show on the opposite wall when the funeral director half-opens the venetian blinds. Philip finds himself tracing the sign of the cross on Egan's cold forehead; he tries to shape some prayer, but his mind wanders. An angry curl has replaced the constant smile Egan had shown to the world: must have seen death stealing up on him, and he resisted with whatever strength he had left.

'Here's a chair, Mr Lalor, I'll leave you for a minute.' says the funeral director.

'Thank you.'

Play-acting for Egan is over, but Philip still sees the team mate who would always be the sturdy schoolboy covered in mud as they leave the Donnybrook pitch, telling everyone how he nailed the 'little Gonzaga bollix and the ref never saw it'.

After some time, he touches Egan's waxen hand, and stands.

The funeral Mass begins with a procession of priests up the nave, accompanied by the full swell of the pipe organ from overhead. Philip is seated beside Sam about halfway down the church. The priests are shuffling in the way of those affected by arthritis; one or two carry walking sticks. They are the decrepit remnant of the men who only yesterday coached cup-winning rugby teams, and tripped along the corridors of Blackrock College.

The main celebrant talks about Kevin Egan's faith. 'And Jesus, by his rising from the dead, makes it possible for us to see death as entering a glorious eschatological state.'

Philip switches off – the same rigmarole. Would he be so full of the eschatological claptrap if he were in a cardiac unit, wired up to monitors and waiting for an update on his condition?

'A man with an abiding commitment to his family,' the priest continues.

Philip had hoped to hear even a word or two that might show that the priest too would be as scared as everyone else in the church if a consultant had asked him to take a seat in his office, and had muttered about 'showing up in the scan' and 'further tests'.

Sharkey is seated a few rows ahead with Phoebe, his partner, and a few others from Nat Am. He hasn't changed much over the years – the same comb-over from a low parting just above his ear.

Right through the ceremony, those few who are daily Mass-goers know when to stand, when to sit, and when to kneel. The majority, for whom the Church's rubrics are now a foreign language, glance over their shoulders and follow their example, so that, like a slow motion Mexican wave, the signal to stand eventually reaches the front where Gillian and the family are still sitting until they sense movement all around them.

Sam discreetly checks the lit-up screen of her BlackBerry and sends a reply. Philip remains kneeling, not in prayer but playing in his head the upset of the previous days from the time of Gillian's hysterical phone call. 'Near the stairs … and fell … Come over. Oh God, Philip.'

From the organ gallery comes a beautiful rendering of Fauré's 'Pie Jesu' by the soprano who had sung the Mass; the odd cough or shuffle or the whooshing sound when the door opens is all that disturbs the silence until she fades out. Then after a nod from the celebrant, Roisín steps up to the lectern to deliver the eulogy.

She thanks all who have been a support to the family in their grief, especially her father's life-long friend, Philip Lalor. 'Kevin was a dreamer, whose dreams didn't always bring him the reward he had envisaged.' Looking out at the congregation, she speaks with a steady voice. 'In fact, he should never have been a banker. My dad's spirit was too expansive for balance sheets and for fumbling in the greasy till. The Celtic Tiger devoured my dad.' She quotes Auden:

He was my North, my South, my East and West,
My working week and my Sunday rest,
My noon, my midnight, my talk, my song;
I thought that love would last for ever: I was wrong.

'Goodnight, Dad. For me you will be forever among the stars.'

The main celebrant stands and recites the Final Prayers of Commendation.

May the angels lead you into paradise,
May the martyrs come to welcome you.

A woman in front of Philip leans towards the man beside her. 'She was the apple of his eye, you know.'

And take you to the holy city
The new and eternal Jerusalem.

'Poor Roisín will have to live in the real world, and forget her poetry.'

'No money in poetry,' the man says out of the side of his mouth; his shoulders shake.

His voice shall bid me rise again
Unending joy unceasing praise …

After the burial in Deansgrange, Gillian hosts a lunch at a Dun Laoghaire restaurant overlooking the harbour. Out in the marina, yachts are bobbing and swaying; the scratch of rigging and a tinkle of bells fill the late summer sunshine. A faint smell of the sea rises from the water.

Some have to return to work, but a few stragglers stay behind talking in the sun. On the way out, Sharkey and his cronies stop to admire a crew navigating towards the harbour, at the same moment that Roisín and her friends from UCD appear at the front door. When she sees Sharkey, her body stiffens. He goes over to renew his sympathy. 'Again my sincerest … Roisín, you can be very proud of your dad.'

She glares at him, refuses his outstretched hand and, before her friends can intervene, says: 'And I hope you're proud of yourself. I hope you are very proud of yourself, because you brought about my dad's death.'

The other women usher her past him, but she stops and says: 'How you could turn up here today shows you've got some brass neck. There's more to life than money, but you'll never understand that.'

21

ON THE NIGHTS following Egan's funeral, Philip sleeps badly, and even when he tries going to bed late, he is still waking at three or four. From then on, he tosses and turns in a welter of anger and sadness, searching for a more comfortable position so that he might drift off with some resolution to his questions. Roisín was right: her father was a casualty of Sharkey's merciless ways.

During the day Philip is spent, especially in the afternoon, when he is struggling to keep his eyes open. He knows that his work or his health will suffer if this continues. And even if he is bringing home the bacon for Nat Am, the Young Turks are snapping at his heels. He could easily become the next wounded zebra in the jungle.

A few days after the funeral, he is stepping out of the lift in the Plaza, when he comes upon Sharkey, who, with a chopping motion of his hand, seems to be issuing instructions to Karen. When he sees Philip, Sharkey excuses himself and rushes over. 'We will all miss him. Big loss. Pity, Roisín … but then the poor girl was upset. Have you time for a coffee? Let's go upstairs to the lounge after work.'

'Not today, Aengus. I'm going straight home after seeing a client; he's in my office right now.'

'Sure. Yes. Very understandable in the circumstances.'

Driving out the coast road, he wants to walk for miles with rain lashing down on him, and a fresh wind blowing in from the sea, as if only an outpouring of nature could wash away the previous few days.

As soon as he changes into casual clothes, he sets off for the Head but, rather than a downpour, the sun shines between the filmy clouds that drift across the sky. He takes the long walk around by the perimeter of the golf club, and down into Keel Strand. Sand clings to his trainers, and the ends of his chinos are drenched from crossing rippled streams. On his way back through the village, he rests on a low wall and stares out at The Sleeping Giant; the walk has failed to shift the tiredness in his heart. He shades his eyes from the sun and glances up at the dark Gothic arch of St Kilian's Church.

Then – as if compelled by some unknown force – he crosses the road and walks up the steps, but before going in, lingers in the porch, casting his eye over the notices. *Meals-on-wheels: care to help?* The Vincent de Paul Society is looking for new members. Something old and puny stirs within him, but he puts his hand to the worn brass handle, and pulls open the door.

Inside, the church is cold and smells like all old churches: furniture polish and the lingering scent of funerals; it gives the impression that nothing much goes on there now. To the left side of the door, an old woman is dropping coins into a box in front of St Anthony's statue.

He sits at the back and gazes at the altar, and the deep red of the sanctuary lamp suspended from a silver chain. The churchy smells and shafts of light are dragging him back in time, and the stillness is all the more pronounced by the occasional sounds from the street: car engines or children on skates rattling down the hill.

He eases into a pew and looks around at the haloed figures in the stained-glass windows. The Virgin Mary, all in blue with clouds at her feet, is floating up to heaven.

The door opens behind him, followed by much whispering and shunting; then the roll of wheels on the age-dented tiles. With a child tagging along beside her, a woman pushes a buggy up the nave. The woman sits at the outside of a pew: both have a hand resting on the buggy. The child baby-talks into the hood of the buggy, then takes in her surroundings, straining her neck to the ceiling. She stares at him, loses interest and wheels around towards the sanctuary. After a while she points to the stained-glass image of the Virgin rising to heaven on the cushions, with the apostles looking up at her. 'What is that? Who is the woman, Mum? And the men with the dresses?'

Mum raises her head.

'What are they doing?' The child is now standing in the middle of the nave and, as she gazes at the altar, she raises her arms to form a cross like the figure of Jesus in a panel of the lancet window. She laughs at her own imitation, and turns her attention to the Stations of the Cross along the wall. The smile on her face becomes a frown. 'What are they doing to the man?'

Her mother looks at the station where Roman soldiers have whips raised. 'Jesus,' says her mother. 'That's Jesus and they are soldiers.'

'Why are they doing that?' The child is getting impatient for an answer, but the baby begins to cry, and so the mother stands. 'I don't know, Britney sweetheart. Now we have to go. We'll Google it all when we get back to the house.'

Pouting, the child looks at her copybook: 'Mum,' she pleads, 'Miss O'Meara wants us to find out how many apostles Jesus had. How many did he have?'

'Ten … I think.'

Philip sits for a while after they have gone, and then, in the silence, a dreadful sense of being trapped in a cave with no way out, or of being cut off from everyone takes him by surprise. He tries to wriggle away from the questions that spring to the surface of his mind from some menacing jester. Who are you? What are you doing? His impulse is to make a break for the front door, and take refuge in the street, but he is caught – almost paralyzed – in the grip of anxiety. His chest seems to be contracting, as if he is going to suffocate, but he manages to distract himself by fixing his mind on the child. Her mother. The bad men beating Jesus. We'll Google. Britney.

The weird feeling persists and now he can hear the rapid pounding of his heart. This will pass, he keeps reassuring himself.

Calm. A heart attack. Christ. Can it be? Doesn't he work out in the gym twice a week? And forty or more k on the bike around the peninsula. Would have happened there, surely. Too young and fit. Calm. He breathes slowly.

After a while, his heartbeat returns to its normal rhythm, but he is weak and perspiring. His forehead is cold. When he stands, he is light-headed, like looking down from the top of a mountain.

Up the hill to his home, the terror has subsided, but he is worn out; he trudges as if he had run many times around the Head. A bit calmer, he is now able to look at the weird sensation – a heart attack wouldn't have gone away that quickly? Or would it? He catches a glimpse of the redbrick chimneystacks of Doc Clifford's house. A chat. Throw it in casually.

Clifford is about to phone the receptionist at the Greystones clinic for the results of a breast-screening test for a patient when Philip phones him. Something in his tone of voice, and the time of day it is, puts the doctor on the alert. Well used to the cover-up ways of patients, he says: 'I'm at a loose end anyway. Yeah, please join me.'

'Good.'

As an ice-breaker, Clifford leads the conversation about his bees, and how he had read in the paper that bees are dying in some parts of the world, all the while placing a filter in the coffee pot, ladling out a couple of spoons, and setting the coffee to brew on the kitchen counter.

He picks up his mobile: 'These boyos, according to an expert, are causing the trouble.'

'What's that, Ned?'

'Mobile phones are causing bees to die in certain parts of the world. So I believe. Something to do with radiation. What was it Einstein said – when the bees go, then it's endgame for us all.'

'Oh, yes.'

'Anyway, here I am rattling on about bees. My sympathy on your friend's death.'

'Thanks.'

'Too young.'

'Kevin was his own worst enemy. Couldn't play the game, and he got zapped.' While Philip talks about their long friendship, Clifford pours two mugs of coffee, slices a ginger cake and puts it on the table. And in the manner of a throwaway, he says: 'You look a bit peaky.'

Philip lowers his head and stirs his coffee.

'Sorry, Philip. Can't help noticing … Professional thing.'

It is the opening Philip is waiting for; he describes the scary feeling that came over him in the church. 'Come to think of it, I had something like it a couple of weeks ago. Woke one night, and had to go to the bathroom for a drink. Feeling of suffocation, or going to die and couldn't do anything about it. Probably a bad dream.' He makes an effort to smile. 'I think it was after a visit to Kevin out in the nursing home. Don't suppose it's anything serious. Would probably be stone dead by now.'

While Philip is speaking, Doc Clifford glances at him for any telltale sign: a lesson never forgotten from a pompous professor. 'Ladies and gentlemen, "*There's no art to find the mind's construction in the face*", according to Shakespeare. I agree up to a point, but with experience, you will pick up signals – the eyes, for example.'

'Any feeling of sickness? Pain in your left arm? Anything like that?'

'No.'

'From what you tell me,' Clifford studies his face again, 'most likely we are talking here about panic. I'll have a quick look. Roll up your sleeve and open your shirt. Back in a minute.'

Clifford returns with his stethoscope and blood pressure sphyg and, after a careful examination, he says in an abstracted way: 'Well, you seem fine in these departments.' And while winding the connection of the blood pressure sphyg around the dial, he adds: 'This is by no means a thorough check-up, just to put your mind at rest. But I strongly recommend that you pop in to your own GP. Just to be sure.' The two men sit at the table again and sip their coffee. 'And I doubt there's any heart problem.'

From where he sits, Philip has a side view of La Salle: it looks deserted – Sam managing a shoot outside the Ritz in London. Their children are God knows where.

'Panic can happen when one is stressed,' he hears Clifford telling him. 'It mimics a heart attack, so that people sometimes think, my goodness, this is it.'

Philip returns to Egan. ' "It's like a brace tightening around your head," he told me in Our Lady's Manor. "Sharkey and his henchmen twist and you feel they will crush your skull." ' And he goes on to describe the fracas outside the restaurant after the funeral: how Roisín had had a go at Sharkey. 'She was spot on,' he reflects, still staring across at La Salle.

'I know, but ultimately ... well, I mean ... was your friend helping himself by returning so soon.'

Philip turns away from La Salle and looks at Clifford. 'He was scared, Ned. Everyone is scared. I've seen it happen. You're disposable in there, especially when you reach a certain age. We play a part – sure, we dress up and drive the Merc or the Cherokee to work, but the question in everyone's mind is: who's next for the chop?'

'Interesting you should say that,' Clifford says. 'Since all this talk about a downturn has happened, I've never written more prescriptions for depression and anxiety in my entire career. Nearly a third increase in anti-depressives nationally.'

'I've a strong suspicion,' says Philip after a pause, 'that there's worse coming down the line. No matter how much posturing Sharkey and his like are doing about Ireland being safe.'

Satisfied that he hasn't suffered a heart attack, Philip relaxes and talks on about the uncertainty now sweeping through Nat Am. When he has finished, Doc Clifford reassures him again: 'No, it wouldn't be unusual for someone living with all that tension, and then losing his best friend, to have a panic attack. 'Death, well ... *never send to know for whom the bell tolls*. We're all threatened by that old hooded bastard with the sickle. I don't want to second guess what's going on inside you, Philip, but the panic attack – at least that's what I think it is – is saying as much. It's like a message from in here.' Clifford taps his head. 'Some rumble telling us all's not well. And you could go on medication, but ...' Clifford glances at him to see how he is reacting, 'some things need more than pills.'

'Meaning?'

'Look, Philip, I'm not a philosopher – goodness knows, I've made some howlers in my time, but I've learnt a thing or two; one of them is – if you burn the candle at both ends, well …'

'How do you mean?'

'Breathing space.'

'Not easy. There's so much …'

'I know. The pace of life and all that.'

Philip straightens in the chair. 'I feel better, much better. I've taken up enough of your time.'

'I'm glad that the Medicine Man can still serve some function. We can chat again: I'm time rich nowadays.'

22

SAM IS DISAPPOINTED when she steps on to the bathroom scales of her Kensington hotel. After all her efforts, including denying herself chocolate, she has put on nearly a pound in a week. So exercise has been on her mind all day, and as soon as she finishes work at the shoot, she returns to her hotel and plans her route.

After a light dinner, she will power-walk, down as far as Victoria Station, then along by the Thames, turn at Battersea Bridge and back to sweat it off in the sauna, then as many lengths of the pool as she can manage.

Kensington has settled down after the growl of evening traffic. Although she is used to the district by now, and feels safe among the rows of Regency houses, with their cream-columned porches – the legacy of empire and old money – she is always wary. A woman on her own, one never knows. The community of cyclists, however, and power-walking women like herself who take over the streets after close of business set her mind at rest.

The mild evening has brought out more walkers and joggers than usual, and couples too on bicycles, some with a child in the carrier. They are availing of the last few days before the schoolchildren go back after the summer holidays. When a pub door opens, the din of conversations and the whiff of beer flow out to the cobbled street. Working up to a brisk pace, she passes a man and a woman in well-cut suits, whose row is so intense, they are heedless of their surroundings. The woman is giving him a piece of her mind. 'Yes, that's you – the centre of the bloody … ah, what's the use?'

In their wake, they leave behind the echo of their cut-glass accents.

After twenty lengths of the pool – the last few a self-punishment for the midday chocolate – another setback – she takes her laptop to the dining-room to check over her presentation for the following day's meeting.

She has a system worked out for these business trips abroad, when she is on her own without a copywriter or an art director: time to work out her meetings and time to exercise. For the most part she manages to silence the mischievous whispering from the wings and to shut out Peggy Lee's world-weary song.

She is determined, however, to keep the prize in her sight, her place at the table, and never to become her mother, looking in shop windows for another pair of dancing shoes.

After returning from the dining room, Sam lights the sandalwood and lavender candles she had bought as she was jogging back to the hotel, pours a glass of wine and places it on her bedside locker, then takes her well-thumbed copy of *Unleash the Power Within* from her briefcase. At the gym in Raheny, everyone was praising the book to high heaven. She has a whole shelf of books like it at home; each, more or less, promising to transform the reader's life in ten weeks. About to settle the pillows in a comfortable position, she notices a concert ticket falling from the book – their first symphony concert when Philip returned from London.

'Toner's,' he had announced to her over the phone, when he told her of Sharkey's offer to him and Egan. 'Saturday night. Big homecoming.'

Some of the gang from UCD – those who had got jobs – turned up. They had the latest news: Emer and Don have parted company; he's gone to Zambia to work on a hydroelectric power plant. Ann-Marie is in line for a consultancy at Tallaght Hospital. The International Financial Services Centre is up and running: 'Here's to Haughey.' They raised their glasses.

To Haughey.

And Desmond.

Here's to Desmond.

Dawn was breaking over Ireland: there was talk of computer companies setting up, house prices were showing a slight improvement and the country kept winning the Eurovision Song Contest. Sam and Philip had a lot of catching up to do with others now back from Sydney and New York. They laughed at their student campaign to change the world, their protest rallies and their decision to join the Labour Party.

By the way, has anyone seen Father Tom?

Gone to Africa, I believe. Couldn't hack a bossy bishop.

Oh well. Same old, same old. What are you having there?

A pint.

Yeah. Tom's a great guy.

Wasted in the priesthood.

Agreed.

Like actors following a script, the circle broke for the next scene, and, as in the past, Philip and Sam found themselves together: she perched on a high stool, her wine glass on the counter, he standing beside her with a pint of Guinness. The others keep their distance. But Egan, jubilant after his engagement to Gillian, said what they were all thinking: 'Thank goodness, some things never change, like pints of Guinness, or Philip and Sam.' He raised his glass; the whoop of the gang becomes a Greek chorus: 'Yeah, made for each other you are.'

'Not the marrying kind,' Sam calls out, 'too much on my plate right now.'

Less than a year later, on the same high stool, Sam announced their engagement. 'We can have it all, girls. Why not? Career and two kids. Right?'

'Career, the house on the hill – let's drink to that,' said one of the girls.

'And in control of our own destiny.'

They were married in the church of Our Lady, Mother of Divine Grace, Raheny. After the ceremony, when Philip and Sam stood at the front door of the church, surrounded by their laughing friends, motorists, waiting on the Howth Road for the lights to change, hooted. Philip's uncle, Father Anselm, took holidays from his missionary work in Tanzania to officiate at the wedding. Ollie told everyone that he was sparing no expense for the wedding of his one and only precious daughter, so the reception was held at The Shelbourne Hotel. In his after-dinner speech, Father Anselm joked that 'marriages are supposed to be made in heaven, but this one was made in the Commerce Soc. at UCD.' Everyone laughed except Una.

We can have it all, girls. Sam tears the concert ticket in two and tosses it in the bin. She gets off the bed and slouches to the desk where she opens her laptop to check her messages: among the twenty or so is a *Good luck tomorrow* from Philip. She replies to the most urgent, but while working on her laptop, images in her head break her concentration.

The one of Philip, herself and the children at Kelly's Hotel in Rosslare rises to the surface. Crina had taken their photo in front of the pool. Neither Dylan nor Zara wanted to go unless Crina went too. This was the first telltale sign of how much her career had cost Sam.

Crina had been looking after Dylan since he was five months old when Sam returned to work with a flat stomach after keeping to the drill her coach at the gym had drawn up. And when Crina herself had had a baby, and so had to stay in her rented apartment in Killester, Philip or Sam would drop Dylan off each weekday morning.

'New baby, Cee-ah new baby, new baby Cee-ah,' he chirped from the back of the car each evening when they were driving home in the dark. And what wasn't lost on Sam was the way he clung to Crina when she was tucking him up in his coat and scarf, but she still stuck to her guns: *just a natural fondness, and shouldn't I be glad to have found her?*

When Zara came along, she would spend the day in the apartment while Crina washed and ironed, and her daughter played with Zara in the sunny kitchen. And whenever Sam had had a day to herself, she had the weird sense of being an interloper in her children's lives.

Then one evening coming up to Christmas, Sam was driving home to Raheny, with Dylan beside her and Zara in the back of the car, and *Drivetime* on the car radio was yakking on about Ireland's latest success in an economic survey – something about GDP and how it was the highest in Europe apart from Luxembourg.

'Mummy,' Zara calls from deep in the back seat, 'Mummy, Mummy,' her tone had become urgent.

'Yes, lovey.'

'Mummy, can Crina come to our house on Christmas Day?'

'What?'

Dylan joins in. 'Oh please, Mummy, ask her, Mummy.'

'Yes, and we'll get a second turkey, won't we, Mummy?' Zara is clapping her hands in the way of children who are excited by a sudden notion.

At Raheny village, the lights are against them. Both children have an opportunity now to make a joint attack, so, to pacify them, Sam says: 'Yes, Mummy will ask, but you know, Crina may be going to Bucharest to be with her own mummy.'

Zara becomes peevish and frowns at Sam's eye in the mirror: 'No, she won't be going to Book-a-es. No she won't.'

'Lovey,' Sam says, 'Daddy and I will make sure Santa Claus gets you whatever you want on Christmas morning. The best present you ever had.'

Zara is working at the door handle, and muttering: 'I don't want Santa Claus. I want Crina.' She starts knocking her feet against the back of Sam's seat.

'Right, Miss,' Sam says, losing her patience, 'one more word out of you, and I'll get another nanny for you.'

'I hate you! I hate you! I want Crina for my mummy!' Zara shrieks.

Sam raises the volume on the radio. Wide-eyed, Dylan now sinks deeper into his seat as the rain spits against the windscreen.

Sam finishes off replying to the other messages, closes down her laptop and wanders around the room. An ambulance siren gets louder as it tears up the road, past her London hotel.

She fills a glass with wine, goes to her bag for a bar of chocolate, eighty percent cocoa – it helps to lower cholesterol; one or two pieces won't do her any harm. Later, when the wine has worked its way into her veins, she will call one of the girls to give a glowing account of her trip, and the luxury of the sauna and chablis.

23

SINCE SHE HAD ACHIEVED her dream of having her feet under the directors' table at High Res, Sam is getting home later than ever. Philip, too, sends her last-minute texts about meetings and blips that require his attention: 'Under pressure again'. So, right through the summer, deadlines and the desire to climb higher surpass the sun-drenched promises they had made in Nice.

On the Thursday evening after her business trip to Kensington, she is driving home well after eight, when it dawns on her that she and Philip haven't had a conversation or sat together at the table in almost a week – breakfast on the run, if either is at home. As often as not, one of them has an early meeting: Philip, like the other senior lending managers, is trying to salvage some equity from a defaulting client. Sam is off in London.

She swings into the cobbleblock front of La Salle, parks facing the party hedge, and sits to admire the house, while rubbing her finger along the SUV fob. Her eye is drawn to the elegant front door, the double-hung sash windows perfectly proportioned and, beneath the roof, the decorative mouldings on the cornices.

While savouring the view, she becomes aware with a start that she has forgotten to make the booking for the following night. Dinner for the two of them at The King Sitric, another attempt at *Philip and Sam quality time*.

She continues to stare at the house that ticks all her and Philip's boxes. *Masters of our own destiny*. The attempts they have made to rekindle the love they once shared have come to nothing, like the disastrous sessions they had taken with marriage counsellors when they were on the edge of separating; then, as a last throw of the dice, phoning Father Tom, who had just returned from Africa.

In his frugal kitchen, they chatted about college days and the soup run. 'A lot of that died out after your time; study took over, and, I don't know …' He paused while taking down a tin of biscuits from an overhead cupboard. 'Exams, I suppose, and getting a job. Anyway – as you know – I went Kenya side.'

Philip was the one who explained why they had come. 'Sorry to trouble you with this, we thought that … Well, you know us for yonks.'

They went over the same ground as they did with the counsellor: great at the beginning, then the arrival of Dylan and Zara seemed to drive a wedge between them. Sam grew jealous of the attention Philip was paying to the children. 'What's for me here any more?' she sobbed one evening after he had put them to bed. Still in her business suit, she was sitting up on the couch, her briefcase beside her, like a visitor who wasn't going to stay long. They lost interest in each other: indifference became fault-finding and bickering, but when they managed a reconciliation of sorts, they put it all down to pressure of work. They were worn out every night, and then went their separate ways in the early morning.

When they had finished, Tom didn't spare them. 'I don't have magic, nor am I a trained counsellor, but I'll not mince words, and you won't like me after this, but you asked for my opinion.

'You've chosen to follow different drummers, ones neither of you is going to lessen your hold on. And until that happens … well, who knows?'

There was no trace of the eccentric cleric, who, a few years later, would mooch around La Salle at the house-warming, quoting Yeats to himself.

'What are you talking about?' Sam asks.

'Gods, agendas – call it what you like. It has taken a grip: work, promotion, status – that's a very crowded pitch. How could you meet each other with that mob taking up all your time and effort?'

Going home, they stare at the road ahead, and are in agreement about one thing: what the fuck does he know about married life?

He's changed.

Not like he used to be.

No, he's definitely not like he used to be.

Lost his sparkle.

The malaria.

That's it. The malaria.

And did you see the poor state of the house?

Sam checks her BlackBerry, and downloads her social appointments. To her great relief, she sees that the Auburn fashion show is down for Friday, and is already forming an excuse: *After the effort the girls put into it, just couldn't let them down. Isn't that a bummer?*

Her BlackBerry on the passenger seat springs into life, causing her to stir. She reads Philip's message. *Loose ends 2 b tidied, grab something on my way home. C U later x.* She closes her BlackBerry. They are both at the same game.

As she picks up her briefcase and makes to open the car door, she remembers that Dylan will be with his rock band friends: her golden chance to talk to Zara, whom she has been worrying about lately.

They have a lasagne and salad, and a fitful conversation, kept alive by Sam, but even then Zara is lapsing into silence, so that they are suffocating each other. To Sam's relief, Zara finishes her meal.

The evening is warm, and once, when she glances at her daughter's flushed face and the pullover with the Goldsmith Park crest, she says: 'Do you need to wear your jumper on an evening like this?'

The flash of alarm that shows on Zara's face causes Sam to fear the worst. The talk – she'd heard it at wine-tasting nights: kids stoned at house parties while parents were at their villa in France. Ecstasy and worse. Needles.

Zara rattles on about Aoife: her parents promised her a new Toyota if she gets enough points for medicine when she sits her Leaving Certificate examination. Tara is working as an *au pair* in France next summer. And Keelin is the latest to have a trust fund, but it's all tied up until she's twenty-one and in Trinity.

It isn't until Zara stretches for the coffee pot that Sam sees the reason for her daughter's odd behaviour of the previous months, and her nervous chatter. The terracotta sleeve of her pullover has slid up to reveal tram lines scoring her daughter's forearm.

Panic-stricken, she hears her child rattle on about her hockey teacher, and how she herself was *so* looking forward to going on the school outing to Paris.

That talk for parents in Goldsmith Park comes winging back to her. The psychiatrist at the podium, his glasses perched on his nose, taking questions from the audience. Clipped accents failing to hide the terror: 'Why, doctor? Why is teenage binging becoming so prevalent?'

'As a society we've no time for each other any more; consequently, there's a lot of depression about. The World Health Organization puts the statistic at one in five. I estimate that one in every ten people may be on anti-depressants.'

A polite grumble spreads through the hall. A woman raises her hand: 'An estimate but not cold hard facts. Wouldn't you say so, doctor?

His voice grows more resolute: 'Life is disposable; people are disposable in today's world. You're only what you have or what you do. This leaves young people very unsure about themselves. Thousands of young people are self-mutilating – slashing their arms with razorblades, piercing their thighs with needles to deflect from a greater pain. Psychiatry has lost the fight against mental illness.'

'Thousands, doctor?'

'Yes, thousands.'

Earlier, he had shown a piece of film. Ambulance sirens screeching, police in high visibility jackets trying to steady drunken young men outside a night club, garish lights flashing.

Girls in skimpy dresses and high heels were swaying and staggering on a wet street in the early hours of the morning, their heads thrown back in drunken laughter. Barely able to stand, a young man with his shirt hanging out reaches for one of them, and just when she is falling into his clutches, she swings her handbag and hits him right in the face. The others are now in stitches as he crumples to the ground, blood pouring from his nose.

Sam knows she has to be careful here, and not make a bad situation worse. So it isn't until they are filling the dishwasher that she makes another remark: 'How you can wear a sweater on an evening like this beats me.'

Zara turns away, and looks out through the window in the direction of the bay. Seagulls are scavenging for food. 'Oh, I just forgot. D'you think it's, like, *warm?*' With a wary look, she tugs at her sleeve. Sam then does what she will sorely regret afterwards: she swings around from the dishwasher, grabs her daughter's arm and pulls up her sleeve.

'That's the reason!' she flares.

With a look of terror in her eye, Zara manages to pull away and makes for the doorway, but Sam cuts her off.

'You tell me right now. Right now!' she is shrieking, 'or I'll have you down to Doctor Mullen in the morning. Fine gratitude after all your dad and I have been doing for you and for Dylan.'

When she recovers from the shock, Zara also flies into a rage at the way her mother has torn open her dreaded secret: '*You* do stuff for yourself, not for Dylan and me.' She becomes like a trapped bird, dashing around the kitchen looking for an escape.

Her back to the door, Sam glares at her: 'You thankless bitch! After all we've given you.'

'Yeah, things you gave us. Things to make *you* feel good. You're either in London or, like, some other place! Following your career, because that's what counts.' She is darting around the kitchen again.

Sam springs from the doorway, raises her hand, but stops; she lurches to the nearest chair and sinks into it. A row they'd had when Zara was about twelve flashes across her mind: 'Yeah, go on, hit me, and I'll be *so* on to Childline, you'll be sorry.'

The doorway is now free, but Zara stands still for a moment, and then slips into a chair beside her mother. They are both frightened and drained of energy, and, like two combatants between whom a curious bonding has taken place, they rest in a silence, broken only by Zara's sobbing and Sam's heavy breathing. After a while, Sam shuffles to the counter and puts a box of tissues in front of her daughter. 'There,' she says quietly.

Zara takes a fresh tissue from the box and blows her nose; and, in an abstracted way, her fingers work at a second tissue until it falls to pieces on the cream tiles. She is all clogged up when she speaks: 'I won't do it ever again, Mum. Sorry.' They look at each other, and Zara falls at her mother's lap, and embraces her. 'For the thing I said about – like – you and Dad.'

Only occasionally is Sam open and natural in her expressions of affection to her children, and this inability has hardened over the years, as if life, or the cut and thrust of business, has annulled her womanly instinct. Both children had been born with the help of an epidural, and, much to Philip's surprise, Sam decided against breast-feeding, so that they would take to the bottle and Philip could get up in the middle of the night to feed them. He also did much of the nappy-changing, and tried to get them to sleep by casting funny shadows of laughing foxes on the wall with his hands, and telling stories, just like his own father did with him and his brother when their mother was downstairs correcting her pupils' homework.

Sam now clings to Zara out of fear of what is happening to her and the family: out of fear that it's all unravelling before her eyes. 'It's ok, lovey, it's ok,' she keeps reassuring her. They are both crying. 'Promise me, lovey, that you won't do that again.'

'I promise.' And her grip tightens around her mother's neck.

'Our secret, Zara lovey, our secret.'

They sit back. Zara draws her feet beneath her and begins to rock, forgetting that the scars she had hidden are now visible through the soft hairs of her forearm. Sam's anger falls away also; she remains seated next to her daughter and again, tentatively, puts an arm around her shoulder.

'What's it about, lovey?' Her tone grows soft. 'You can tell me. I won't go to Doctor Mullen, but please tell me.'

'A few of us.' Zara removes her thumb from her mouth; she is still sobbing, 'we just, like, heard about it on the internet and went down to the grove behind Robin Hill, and – '

'You went … oh, Zara, darling, why?'

'I'm sorry. We were only, like, experimenting. Just the once.'

Zara is lying. They had been going to the grove for a few months, and also taking Solpadine for the buzz; the group has been able to get a supply by stealing from their parents' medical chests, or doing the rounds of chemists as far as Clontarf, Fairview and beyond. Whenever their parents were away for weekend breaks, they texted around in haste: *free hse Fri nite. Bring ur own.*

Sam and Zara lapse into silence again; Zara stops rocking. 'Right, lovey. We've been missing each other. You know, your dad and I have to work hard for all this.' Her arm sweeps over the cream tiles, the basalt stone top of the island, and stops at the French windows leading out onto the garden.

'I know, Mum,' says Zara, leaning her head towards her mother again.

'Well, we're going to put all this behind us. Right? And we're going to have more time for each other.'

Zara forces a smile: 'We are.'

'You and I are going to have ourselves one great day out on Saturday. It'll be our women's day.'

Frightened now at the enormity of what she has been doing, Zara is willing to go along with her mother's suggestion; she puts an arm around her shoulder and snuggles into her.

'Our secret, lovey,' says Sam. 'Our secret.'

No sooner had Zara gone upstairs than Sam receives a message on her BlackBerry from Ciara Bell, her boss. She phones her back, and learns that Volvo had seen the work Sam has done for Arrow in New York and wants to talk about a shoot in Stockholm. 'We need you to go to speak to them; André won't be back from London until Wednesday. Big fish, Sam. They're not in the habit of being kept waiting, so it looks like you're the only one with the experience. Consider this a favour that will not go unnoticed.'

'When?'

'Has to be tomorrow afternoon. I've got your flights booked.'

Sam and Bell had started together at High Res, and had got on well until Sam began to climb the ladder. From then on Bell no longer invited her to Searson's or The Lansdowne for the Friday evening drink, where they occasionally met up with clients and business contacts. She knew Bell had pushed André's bid for the Creative Director's job, but when Sam pulled off another highly acclaimed advertisement that was displayed in *Marie Claire*, it was impossible to hold back her claim.

Sam sinks into a chair and, her elbows on the table, joins her hands in front of her face, like someone in the act of praying, and remains like that for some time, puzzling over the best way to make an apology to her daughter for heading off to Sweden the next day.

24

A S SOON AS the children go back to school after the summer holidays, the weather turns sunny and the US government lets the axe fall on Lehman Brothers. Overnight the worst fears of the previous months become a grim reality. Television pictures show stockbrokers leaning against the fronts of buildings in Wall Street. In the reflected light from Sky News at Paddy Cullen's, upturned faces look jaundiced. *Lehman*. Sudden death. I mean, *Jesus*, they've been in business since the American Civil War. What's going on?

Like children frightened of the bogeyman, staff hang around the water coolers, or stand outside in the sun-drenched forecourt sucking on cigarettes, unmindful of the bronze eagle at the centre of the fountain and Dunleavy's *Renovabitur ut aquilae iuventus tua*. Every lunchtime, in the Ballsbridge pubs and restaurants, they devour the news updates coming from the ticker tape on the television screen. And, like a blood test that comes back from the lab with the dreaded result, each bulletin is rolling out shock and dismay: 'Banks worldwide have been sold a sandwich with a rat's tail'. Still, government ministers are asserting that 'Our banks are well capitalized. No worries here.'

Television images show sullen traders in blue overalls leaning against monitors on the trading floors, or staring at screens with sleep-starved eyes. Others are shuffling around punch-drunk – in and out of offices or smoking cigarettes on the Wall Street sidewalk. The bronze bull poised to attack is an absurd reminder of the hubris of other days.

Although he affects confidence 'in the market', Sharkey is worried – he has more to lose than most at Nat Am. Developers are bringing him bad news about whole rows of empty houses. Through his brokers he gets rid of Phoebe's and his children's shares in the bank, but his own – which run into millions – he couldn't pull without bringing down the whole house of cards. Moreover, the millions he has covertly taken out to invest in a Canadian mining company, without the approval of the credit committee, would come to light if an investigation were to follow.

His friend, Muldoon, the chief of National Custodian, had colluded with him each year in transferring his loan, while the Nat Am auditors were doing their annual examination of the accounts. In that way shareholders and prospective investors were in the dark about the true state of the loan book.

Every August, as his loans from Nat Am rocketed, Sharkey hosted a lunch for his disciples at Icarus Hall, at which Muldoon had pride of place. There they discussed the 'guest-housing deal': Sharkey's name for the arrangement. Having tossed back their liqueurs, they returned to their cars at the Royal Irish Automobile Club. Everything was hunky-dory until the next audit. In buoyant mood, they confirmed golfing arrangements for Mount Juliet.

The avalanche that began at Lehman causes other giants to fall. Merrill Lynch, J.P. Morgan and other banks are in trouble and have to be bailed out. There is a demon out of the underworld, a ravenous monster, stalking Wall Street, London and Frankfurt. It is now only a matter of time before Irish banks collapse.

Fear is spreading, not just among bankers and shareholders but among all who had fallen to the seduction of becoming 'players' in the market: all who had traded up the hill, bought top of the range cars, right along the chain to Sam's taxi driver, who had bought another house off the plans in Spain.

Government ministers, however, assure the nation that Ireland's banks are secure. We have checks and balances in this country to ensure that things don't get out of hand, they assert.

The fault-line is elsewhere: the sub-prime plague that has hit America stems from the Clinton policy of ensuring that everyone has a home. Other experts declare that the rot had set in with Reagan and Thatcher giving the market too much autonomy.

Images of banks collapsing into the ground and raising a cloud of dust are invading the dreams of those who had been given loans eight times their salary to increase their purchase on the ladder.

Long after offices have closed down for the evening and the sound of vacuum cleaners fills the corridors, Sharkey sits peering at his computer screen as if it might reveal an antidote to the rampaging virus; the desk lamp with its green shade shows up deep furrows on his forehead. Brennan and Wheeler stay back to catch up on work, but more so to keep vigil. Apart from Philip, they are among the few who know the full extent of Sharkey's surreptitious borrowing, but they gave him a hostage to fortune by accepting his offer of getting in on the loans to invest in the Canadian mining company without the sanction of the credit committee.

One night, after a lot of searching, Sharkey hits the off switch on the computer, and stares at the blank screen. Beyond the venetian blinds, the open-plan office is a graveyard of silent computers. The evening growl on the Merrion Road has long gone; pools of amber lie at the foot of street lamps and, way beyond, a twinkle of lights marks the contours of the Dublin Mountains.

'Right, guys,' he says to his cronies, after much stroking of his temple, 'this is going to be our greatest hour. Invasive surgery once again.' A sinister grin appears on his tired face. 'Got to draw blood.' He does a blade-turning act with his hand. 'Don't know about you but I've no intention of giving up what I've slaved for all my life.'

'What will they do?' Wheeler asks meekly. He too has to be careful, knowing that Sharkey would sack his grandmother to save himself.

'Who?'

'Those who are shown the front door.'

Sharkey is cross that he should be asked the question. 'They'll find something out there in this fucking pigs' trough of a world. The senior guys who do less for more will be the first out. I'm not having drones, nor will I carry the can for them any longer. But, guys,' his mind is racing, 'we're so fucking deep in shit, that *that* cost-cutting exercise is only a drop in the ocean. The shareholders have to be kept happy.' He removes his half-lenses and rubs his eyes. 'We need a cash injection. Look,' he spreads wide his palms, 'we're up shit creek for capital. We're talking mergers here, and fast. I'm setting up a meeting with Muldoon of Custodian. I'll tell him it's a liquidity issue; there's a chance he might swallow the bait.'

'Aengus,' Wheeler says, 'he's been a friend to Nat Am. The *guest-housing*, I mean.'

Sharkey glares at him. 'This isn't your fucking Fitzwilliam Tennis Club and drinks in the bar after mixed doubles. This is survival. Do you think you can get your head around that much?'

'Sure, Aengus.'

'Now, where was I? Yes. Conrad, you're for Dubai with a small delegation to talk to the sheikhs. With your sales technique, you might pull it off. We need their oil money and, thanks to Bin Laden, the Arabs are still not exactly flavour of the month in the States, so they need another outlet to spend their billions. The sheikhs bailed us out before.'

He strokes his chin, and an early growth of stubble causes a rasping sound. 'Kyran,' he says, 'I want you to test the waters with our friends in the US. We've contacts at Mayflower in Rhode Island. I've a list: Lakeside Finance Investment Company in Oakland, and others. Tell them we're talking liquidity, not capital. Play poker.'

A cleaning woman knocks on the door. Sharkey ignores her. 'You're the guys I can rely on; you're loyal to Nat Am, and you've always been loyal to me. I'll put it to the board tomorrow. The sheikhs, the US.'

The cleaner knocks again.

'Yes,' he barks.

The woman thrusts her head around the door.

'Will I do your office, Mr Sharkey?'

'Can't you see we're busy?' he snaps at her, but then cools. 'Ten more minutes. Thank you.'

'Right, Mr Sharkey.' She closes the door.

'How will Dunleavy and the Red Braces … ?' Wheeler asks.

'Fuck them. It's every man to the lifeboats now.'

He leans back in his chair and taps the desk. The few strands of hair that formed the comb-over, always smooth across his crown, now hang in a comical way over one ear. Having invented a self on sailing, rugby and Harvard, he is always cautious about his past lest he contradict himself; but now, on the deck of a listing ship, he allows his disciples a different perspective.

'My mother, guys, was a canny Leitrim woman who managed to rent a cubbyhole where she set up shop just off the Howth Road. Sweets, papers, groceries and the like.' He smiles at the memory. 'She worked in that little shop all year round, including Christmas Day. On Christmas Day she charged three times the price for things that people might have forgotten – fairy lights or crackers. Or if they ran out of batteries for toys. I used help her to wrap them up.' He swings around towards his back-up men who look bemused. 'Provided each of us with a good education.'

'She was right to charge the extra. For Christsake, wasn't she working on Christmas Day?' Brennan chirps up, but Sharkey isn't listening: he is back there in the cubbyhole, wrapping up fairy lights that cost three times the retail price. 'She had no other option. The dad … well.' He snorts. 'Let's say he was too fond of the nags. Said he'd make his fortune out of them. And he was too often on the high stool in Fagan's.'

To the surprise of his henchmen, Sharkey continues. 'It was she who got me into Belvedere. Put down my father's occupation as *an engineer*, would you believe?'

Wheeler's laugh is contrived. 'And he wasn't?'

'He was the boilerman at Lemon's sweet factory in Drumcondra.' His attempt to laugh sounds more like a cry from deep inside.

Sharkey's mother, a seamstress at the Janelle sewing factory before she opened the huckster's shop, had walked from Marino to Belvedere College to meet the Rector and fill in the application form. That evening, she asked her friend Patti, from Janelle, to join her in the snug of Kennedy's pub. They raised their sherry glasses in celebration of pulling a fast one over the Jesuit with the posh accent. Now her son would mix with the quality.

'It's the way things are done in this country.' Sharkey has a smug look on his face. 'Stay by the rules and, by Jaysus, you'll be left far behind. Guys, if our ancestors had stayed by the rules, they'd have got zilch out of our English masters.'

'You're dead right,' Wheeler says.

The henchmen allow their boss to savour the memory. After a while Brennan asks: 'What's going to become of us? This is, just – well – a right fucking mess.' He sounds like a boy scout who has lost his compass in the forest.

'Lookit, guys. The banking world has taken the biggest hit since the crash of '29, but you and I won't suffer in the long run. The mother used to say: "Make sure you're one of the in-crowd, Gussie, and then you can never be touched. Jail is only for poor people." If one of the cleaners out there steals a vacuum-cleaner and is caught, she'll be up before the district judge in the morning. That's the way of the world.'

Coming out of his reverie, Sharkey stands and takes his jacket from the back of a chair. 'Nor will Nat Am go to the wall. D'you know why?' He stops, and a slippery look shows on his face: 'Because the government would have too much to lose; because if they let us go to the wall, then we would bring the whole fucking house of cards down with us. So now, what do we do?' He looks from one to the other. 'I've been thinking about that. From now on we're going to give out domestic mortgages like there's no tomorrow. Why? Because the big fish may get away, but the little man will always be screwed. Right?'

'Right, Aengus,' says Wheeler, and the look on his boyish face suggests that he is in the presence of sheer genius.

Brennan is concerned. 'But, Aengus, central banks globally are already pumping billions into emergency liquidity assistance.'

'No panic. Didn't the governor of the Central Bank say we're robust? Jaysus, sure that's the Pope speaking from his golden chair.'

Their laugh eases the tension. 'The little guy will be our banker then.' Brennan looks relieved.

'Right, guys, action stations. No point in pissing around; tomorrow is a new start.' And he picks up his bunch of keys.

When they are leaving, the cleaning woman is at the door. And Sharkey, remarkably kind to the cleaning staff – always remembering them at Christmas with generous gifts, and even setting up a scholarship to get some of their children into secondary education – now offers his sincere apologies for his discourtesy.

'That's alright, Mr Sharkey. I understand. It's them bankers in America. You've a lot on your mind, God love you. You're a great man. I'll say a prayer for you.'

On their way across to Roly's for a light meal, they are ambushed by a television crew that appears from one side of the green-tinted glass tower. A reporter shoves a microphone in front of Sharkey's face.

'The word in the market, Mr Sharkey, is that Nat Am is in trouble: on a life support.'

Always prepared for being door-stepped, Sharkey holds forth. 'On the contrary, Mark,' he smiles, 'the fundamentals are sound. Our loan book is healthy. Seventy-eight percent of our loans are performing. Yes, we may have to write off the rest, but, come on – that's hardly life-support, wouldn't you agree?'

'And the massive bonuses, Mr Sharkey. Did you not bring all this on yourselves?'

'Lookit, our policy in Nat Am is to recruit the brightest and the best, and you're not going to get them without an adequate reward. The old story: give them peanuts and you get monkeys. However,' he cuts in as the newshound is about to fire another question, 'we are tackling that issue at the minute. A threefold operation.' He lists them on his fingers. 'One, a pay cut for executives. Two, a pay freeze for all staff. And three, an end to all bonuses.' He starts to move off, even though the reporter follows him; the cameraman scrambles ahead for a good shot. People who are walking by stop to look.

'The only problem Nat Am has at present is one of liquidity. Lookit, all our clients are sound. Our lending team left no stone unturned when they were researching each loan application. Other than that, I want to say – hand on heart – to your viewers. Rest assured, the fundamentals are sound.' He beams to the camera and side-steps the microphone: 'Thank you for your interest. Now, it's been a long day. Got to nourish the inner man.'

He turns to his hangers-on who are waiting to cross the road: 'That gobshite was in nappies when I was kick-starting this economy.'

The following week the Minister for Finance calls the heads of the major banks, including Sharkey, to a meeting in one of the stately rooms in the Bank of Ireland, which was the Houses of Parliament until the Act of Union of 1801. The meeting is scheduled for nine o'clock in the evening.

When the bankers come through the great columns, a porter wearing a dark blazer with silver buttons down the front shows them into a chamber with a high ceiling and crystal chandeliers: the chamber was once the House of Lords. Faded by time, expansive tapestries hang on the lofty walls: one depicts James II laying siege to Londonderry; opposite, his-son-in-law, William of Orange is triumphant on his horse after the Battle of the Boyne.

The porter indicates the chairs on each side of a long mahogany table. Here they sit and wait. These bankers have millions in investments. They own stud farms, prize-winning racehorses, and shopping malls, and are on the board of major companies in Ireland and Britain. They have been in receipt of Christmas bonuses many times the salary of the US President. They are not used to being kept waiting.

After about an hour, a waiter in a black waistcoat and a white shirt brings in tea, coffee and sandwiches, places them on a sideboard and pours.

The bankers hardly touch the sandwiches, and while sipping

tea or coffee, they fidget like pupils, dreading a severe scolding from the school headmaster. In an effort to break the tension, the AIB man tries gallows humour after counting the chairs along one side of the table. 'Twelve,' he says, 'one for each of the apostles.'

The Bank of Ireland man throws him a jaundiced look: 'I wonder which is the one for Judas.'

Though they know each other well, they are too tense to sustain a conversation and, between long silences, jump from one topic to another, not once mentioning finance, in case, like poker players, they expose their bank's true position.

One man rests his hand on the long mahogany table, and whenever he rubs his chin, leaves a trace of perspiration on the polished surface. Even though all present are responsible for the cycle of reckless lending, their body language, and the sullen looks they throw at him, bespeak their rage with Sharkey for the financial collapse. *He* is Judas.

Coming up to eleven o'clock, a door opens and a senior civil servant comes into the room. Without apology, he announces that the minister is at present on the phone to the President of the European Central Bank and after that he will be answering questions at a late sitting of the Dáil. They are to return the next morning at eight o'clock sharp. While speaking, he shifts his gaze from one tapestry to the other.

One of the bankers grumbles: 'This is preposterous.'

Totally absurd.

Does he think we've nothing else to do?

The tight-lipped civil servant cuts them short. Like a prefect of studies announcing bad exam results to a class, he tells them: 'The minister is working around the clock to rescue our country from financial ruin; you are in no position to make demands. Good-night.' He closes the file.

More vacant places appear in Paddy Cullen's and Crowes public houses; girls who had sat tall and cross-legged on the high stools, and were loud about exfoliation and the weekend in Bruges, vanish like the terns from Sandymount Strand each autumn.

St John Dunleavy calls for a meeting on the following Sunday morning in the conference room, to explain the bank's policy. He is the first speaker; directors and divisional heads, including Sharkey, sit in a row behind him.

Four hundred employees fill the room: students who fear that the principal is going to read them the Riot Act. Dunleavy is glad that the government has taken the right decision to come to the assistance of the banks. 'This is a situation without precedent, one that has been visited upon us,' he declares. 'A situation that came about through reckless and wasteful spending in the international money markets, but we here in Ireland are being made to suffer. However, we have to apply ourselves to the challenge. We are all in this together, so I look to your customary loyalty in bringing about a solution to a crisis that was not of our making.'

He goes on to remind them that the bank has no option but to rationalize. 'It behoves us to restructure, ladies and gentlemen. Nat Am has a reputation for upholding the highest ethical standards in banking. In these stirring times we have to cut our cloth according to the measure. We are reluctant to do this, but the gun is to our heads. Otherwise, in the long term, we would be failing our customers and shareholders who have placed their trust in us.'

When he has finished, St John Dunleavy calls on Sharkey. 'It is my great pleasure,' he declares, 'to hand you over now to our esteemed chief executive, a man with a deserved reputation for leadership and hard work.'

As Sharkey steps up to the rostrum, his cronies work up a spirited applause but it falls flat. He proceeds to sing out of Dunleavy's hymn-sheet: cuts are necessary for survival. We, at executive level, are working 24/7 so that we will recover our proud place as leaders and trendsetters in the world of finance. But we all have to take a hit if we are to remain one of the leading players.

'As I speak, some of our hard-working executives are on missions to Dubai and to the United States to encourage investments: the news so far is promising,' he lies. The reality, known only to Philip and other senior managers, is that Conrad Brennan and his colleagues are coming back from Dubai with their tails between their legs; likewise Wheeler and the delegation to America. Junior executives in these banks are sent out to the foyer to meet them with a terse message from their superiors: *you are on your own.*

When Sam has gone to bed that night, Philip, after consuming two double-whiskeys, sits in the living room with only a reading lamp on beside his armchair. Sam's relaxing music is playing on the Bose. He stands and mooches around the house, staring at the furniture, the Graham Knuttels, pictures of the family in classic monochrome taken in the Grafton Street studio one Saturday morning. He looks at everything as if he is a stranger, seeing it all for the first time.

In the kitchen, he switches on the arc-light over the Richmond range set into the tiled recess of the wall. A must-have in Auburn, the duel fuel range hasn't been used since Zara's sixteenth birthday party at the beginning of August. Before that, it was for the house-warming. A ring of dust shows when he lifts one of the hotplates. The light catches the gleam on the copper pots and pans hanging overhead. 'No kitchens now in the new apartments in Manhattan' was a bit of news one of his colleagues brought home after a business trip to New York.

For an hour or more, Philip stares out at the dim horizon and the sombre outline of Lambay Island away in the distance, before switching off the Bose and dragging his feet upstairs.

The noose is tightening. Economists are calling for Nat Am to be treated as a scapegoat, bearing the misdeeds of all banks so that these may recover. The Hungarian woman with a sheaf of evening papers at Sutton Cross is sandwiched between laminated headlines: 'Nat Am: Bin It'.

Instead, towards the end of November, the government nationalizes Nat Am and appoints financial experts and university professors to the board of each major bank. The open sore that Sharkey and a few others had managed to hide is now revealed in all its horrifying features. He had borrowed €160 million without the sanction of the credit committee or the directors.

The net closes in around him. Over coffee in the plaza, junior staff and those with limited experience of the ways of banking are shocked; they are too young to remember the DIRT episode, and the times when Nat Am and other banks were found guilty of overcharging customers. Didn't he have a banking brain that was without equal? Jesus, didn't the guy get that big European award in Davos? Wasn't he Banker of the Year at the Carton House bash, for God's sake?

Investors cause a run on Nat Am: in a week, the bank loses two and a half billion Euro. But that's not all. Working late, when everyone else has gone to tag rugby and Pilates, an auditor appointed by the government discovers that Sharkey had been ferrying ten billion back and forth across the Irish Sea from four different banks, two in the City, and one in Jersey, to make it look as if they were customers' deposits and, in that way, boost the bank's profile in the market. It is only a matter of time before the Minister for Justice sets up a Garda inquiry.

The hushed word around the plaza is that St John Dunleavy has marked Sharkey's card; that his position at the bank is reduced to appearing before the directors to give details of his wrong-doing. He is a lame duck chief executive. Dunleavy is hosting dinners at his Monkstown mansion, they whisper, where the real board meetings are taking place without Sharkey. Any day now, they predict, Dunleavy and the directors will dump him.

Sharkey, during this time, is living the life of a recluse. He drives into work in the morning, goes straight to his office, has lunch with the satellites on Fridays, and works on until everyone has gone home. At this stage, it is no longer in anyone's interest to be identified with him. Brennan is the first to skip the Friday lunch. He has a set of excuses: the youngest child is teething. Awake all night! You know yourself, Aengus. Wheeler backs out also. 'Up to my tonsils, honestly, with the wedding coming up, and now with tennis practice nearly every fizzin night in Fitzwilliam – ' he raises his hands in despair.

The government guarantee eases the anxiety among Nat Am staff – at least it seems now that jobs are secure, although many have lost thousands in investments, and some are in negative equity. So in deference to an enraged public, and because fewer put down their names, the Christmas party is held at Icarus Hall rather than in the Four Seasons.

A fall of snow – unusual for early December – touches off a festive cheer, and causes the guests to arrive determined to put aside all thought of the credit crunch at least for one night. Many had come straight from Neary's or Davy Byrne's so the younger bankers are in a giddy mood when they approach the front door. Women clean their shoes of slush on the foot scraper, and while they're doing that, men make much of holding on to them so that they don't lose their balance. Their laughter is loud and crisp in the night air.

When the party is in full swing, Sharkey makes an appearance. Smiling, he works the room as usual, and then stands on the second step of a wide staircase. The staff gathers round with drinking glasses; one of the caterers rings a bell for attention, the music dies. He thanks the guests for their loyalty to Nat Am and assures them that 'we are already coming out of our darkest hour; we'll be motoring again as soon as this credit crunch comes to an end. *And come to an end it will, guys.*' For a moment, a glint of the brash Sharkey shows on his face.

But, quick to spot trouble, the smile fades. Karen is squeezing her way through the gathering; she speaks close to his ear, and hands him a page torn from a ring binder. He glances at the page. 'Thanks, Karen,' he says quietly. 'I'll attend to that presently.' Karen's head has dropped; her chin begins to quiver and she makes a dash for the Ladies. Slowly Sharkey puts the page into his pocket and beams to the revellers: 'You see, even while he's partying, the CEO has to attend to business.' He wishes them a Happy Christmas, asks to be excused and walks heavily up the stairs.

For the previous few months, Sharkey has had dark thoughts about this moment, and when he picks up the phone to return the call from the Fraud Squad, he can hear the loud music from the downstairs party rooms.

The Garda-on-duty tells him in a brusque manner that the detectives are on their way.

'I know you have to do your job.' Sharkey pauses. 'Just one request.'

'What's that?'

'Please don't come in – all I ask. Please. I'll meet you at the basement door to the side.'

'Fine.'

But the Garda had also become a 'player' by taking out loans many times his salary to buy houses in his native Ballina, so not only did he forget to pass on the message, he tipped off a journalist with whom he has a pint now and again.

Within ten minutes two patrol cars with flashing blue lights are speeding down Dawson Street. The detectives are loud when they arrive. They swing onto the footpath in front of Icarus Hall; the lead detective and five others rush up the steps and ask a group of bankers having a smoke where they might find Mr Aengus Sharkey.

In the upstairs room, where the first Minister for Finance of the Free State, Michael Collins, had often hidden from the British forces during the War of Independence, the tall detective formally announces in front of the others, and Karen, that he is arresting Sharkey, and he will now be taken to the station for questioning.

As the Gardaí are bustling down the steps with Sharkey in the middle, passers-by, some carrying Christmas shopping bags, stop to gawk. A swarm of press photographers strain to get a good shot, but the Gardaí spirit Sharkey into one of the patrol cars, bang shut the doors and speed off with the blue lights flashing and a siren screaming.

After his lawyer has left the station, Sharkey is questioned by different teams of detectives, each covering the same ground. To each and every question he pleads ignorance, or makes a show of innocence or surprise at the allegations the detectives are making.

Afterwards, the Garda who had become a *player* orders Prisoner Sharkey to place his belt, shoelaces and watch on a worn plastic tray. He then accompanies him to a cell, gives him tea and biscuits, and locks the door. The prisoner is now alone beneath a glaring light that will remain on until morning when the questioning will resume.

With his back to a wall, Sharkey surveys his surroundings, and traces the strong smell of Jeyes Fluid to a galvanized hole in the bare floor; nearby is a roll of toilet paper. Somewhere in the distance people are shouting and breaking into 'Have Yourself a Merry Little Christmas' and for the first time since he stood at the graveside when his mother's coffin was being lowered into the earth, he sobs like a child, as he slides down the wall to hunker on the concrete.

The following morning, while he is being questioned, St John Dunleavy and the board of directors of Nat Am are at the executive suite appointing his successor, and rehearsing their imminent press conference.

25

A FEW DAYS before Christmas, when he is driving home from work, Philip runs his eye along the swags of amber lights that line the coast out as far as Sutton Strand. The Promenade des Anglais at Nice comes floating back to him – strolling hand-in-hand with Sam one sultry evening the previous spring – a short break to celebrate the purchase of La Salle, and an effort to delay the ebbing tide of what they once shared. Heedless of the young men in torn jeans streaking by on skates, they stand and embrace, and promise each other: from now on it will be different. We've learnt our lesson.

As soon as he switches off the headlights in front of La Salle, and steps out of his car, Philip is assailed by the thumping sound of his son's music system; the curtains are drawn back and the windows are open. He stands. Dylan and his friends are jigging around in the room; one of them is air-playing a guitar to hoots of laughter. *Better have them there: goodness knows what they might be up to somewhere else* was Sam's opinion when Dylan's interest in rock music began. Philip was in full agreement.

And yet one evening when he returned from work, he caught the cloying smell that sets off alarm bells in every parent's head. 'No, Dad. None of us goes near that stuff. Never. Cross my heart,' Dylan had told him when they went for a burger the following Saturday afternoon in the village.

He had tossed it around with Sam. 'Go easy with him,' she advised. They were unusually at one in searching out the best way to approach their son. 'Try not to lose his trust. And nowadays, kids are likely… well, we both know, I mean, what they're doing to themselves.'

'Only too well.'

A low burning light is on in the hallway. The forlorn Christmas tree stands half-naked beneath the broad curve of the elegant stairway: tinsel and glittering baubles lie beside it – a crushing reminder of their intention to trim it together. They were making progress the night before, when there was a phone call from Sharkey's successor about another developer in trouble. Half the houses in an estate he built outside Enfield are still empty, kids breaking windows and throwing stones at the security men.

'Don't go away,' he had said, leaving Sam and the kids in the hallway, and taking the call in the kitchen. 'I'll only be a minute.' When he returned, they had gone: Zara to the home cinema, Dylan sprawled on the couch, both thumbs busy on his mobile. Sam to the living room.

'Well,' he stood at the door of the den, 'are we going to finish it?'

'Later, Dad.' Both of them kept watching *X Factor*. 'Yeah, later, Dad.'

In the living room, the weather woman was showing the isobars, and Sam was flicking through the pages of *Hello!*: 'Tomorrow night. I'm jaded.'

Before she had gone for her Pilates, Sam had left out a salad and a stew on the draining board. The coffee maker is half-full. He pops the stew in the microwave and eats hurriedly, then rushes upstairs for his training kit. A trail of jeans, shirts and towels leads to the overloaded laundry basket on the wide landing.

When he pulls the front door behind him, the fall of the brass knocker echoes in the frosty air. A full moon shows in the clear sky; amidst the twinkling stars a plane is rising. He stands for a minute and, despite the beauty of the night, a wave of sadness threatens to engulf him, so that he is tempted to go back into the house again, pour a whiskey and slump before the television, but, with a determined effort, he throws his kitbag into the boot and activates the remote control for the electronic gates.

The car park of the Athenian Gym and Leisure Centre is almost full. Powerful lights from the all-weather pitch pick up the shining chrome on the bumpers and trim on the SUVs and Mercs sprinkled among Toyotas and Volvos. *More Mercs per capita than Munich during the recent boom* he had read in the dentist's waiting room.

A game of tag rugby is in full swing. Steam is rising from the players as they dodge and side-step and call to one another. At the gate, Poitr, the security man, is in seasonal mood; his wife has got a full-time job cleaning in the local community school. He raises one hand and splays out his fingers: 'Five day, but the landlord – no good. Rent is much money. *Much money.*' He brightens again and puts the torch between his teeth while he rummages in his inside pocket. 'There,' grinning broadly, he hands Philip a crumpled note that says: 'I luv ire land. To my Dad and Mumma is my gud friends'.

'My son learn English in school. Good,' Poitr says.

'Very good, Poitr,' Philip has a twenty Euro note ready, which he slips him in a handshake. He eases the BMW into drive. 'Happy Christmas to you and your family.'

The red glow from the tail lights picks up the high-visibility strips on Poitr's jacket, and the smile that still lingers on his face as he carefully places the twenty Euro and his son's note in his inside pocket.

Philip is hit by a blast of heat and sonic boom when the automatic doors of the Athenian part. Around the reception desk, young men and blonde-haired women with figures and flashing smiles out of an American soap opera are preening each other. Beyond the fogged-up glass wall, swimmers, looking like sea creatures in goggles and glazed caps, are streaking up and down in the choppy surface of the pool. More loud music is coming through the speakers as Philip changes in the locker room.

He nods and makes small talk with those he has come across since joining the Athenian. Some are getting ready to go upstairs, others are packing their kitbags. The thumping ceases for the ads, special deals for New Year sun holidays: 'Whopping great bargains for two at a West of Ireland hotel in January. Book now to avoid disappointment.'

The chat show host is winding up an interview with an American who works for Intel in Leixlip. Radio Man wants to know what it's like for an American to spend the holiday season away from home. The interview is glib and Christmassy. 'And something I always wanted to know about baseball: what's the difference, Brad, between hard balls and soft balls? Tell me.' He laughs at his own quip.

Upstairs in the gym, the mindless chatter gives way to the crank of pulleys, the thump of footsteps on the treadmill, and the fall of iron when middle-aged men rest the barbells on the trestle.

Dark patches show on the backs and armpits of serious tread-mill walkers, joggers and cyclists. Strands of hair are matted to the necks of resolute women, their ponytails bob with *attitude* as they strain to keep up to the speed of the cross-trainers. The smell of perspiring bodies and rubber mingles in the warm air.

Philip follows his usual routine: a warm-up on the bicycle, then the treadmill, the rowing machine; and he finishes with weights. The monitor on his treadmill is advertising *a holiday with a difference*. A woman smiles out at him, 'a holiday to die for, deep in the heart of Africa'. The video shows lovable cats lazing in the shade; others are draped over tree branches at the Serengeti National Park. In the vast expanse of savannah grasses, acacia trees stand out against a blue sky. Happy families are having a great time chugging along in jeeps.

Philip finishes off with a few lengths of the pool, and then goes back to the locker room. Radio Man is still on: now he's in serious mood listening to a caller explaining how she has lost three and a half stone in six weeks. She is about to go into more details but Radio Man makes sounds of impatience. 'Fantastic,' he cuts her short. 'Brill.' He hopes they will have an opportunity in the near future to talk again. But she's not quite finished, and begins to tell the nation how sad and depressing it can be when you're overweight – how at one time she thought of killing herself. Right now, he tells her, he is going to play one of the great Christmas records – 'Fairytale of New York'.

'D'you like Shane McGowan?'

'Yes.' But, again, she is off on her lonely life. Radio Man has had enough; he hopes this record he is about to play will cheer her up. She is cut off.

26

WHEN CHRISTMAS has well and truly spent itself, the first signs of spring show in the evening light. Garden centres are waking up, and Valentine cards are appearing in the shops. This spring is different: European Central Bank officials are making frequent visits to Dublin, throwing shifty glances and smiling when they appear on television. Through the windows of the Merrion Hotel and the Four Seasons, American and German investment bankers can be seen poring over papers while they dine alone. Some have come to see if they can salvage anything for their bosses; others, like birds of prey, are in search of fire-sale bargains.

In early February, Doc Clifford is stepping out of the village delicatessen one morning when he runs into one of his neighbours, a retired schoolteacher.

'Have you heard?' she wants to know.

'What's that?'

She glances up and down the street. 'La Salle will be on the market again. They're splitting up.'

'What a shame.' He checks his watch. 'Afraid I'm running late.'

She tags along beside him. 'He's going to live in an apartment in Donnybrook. The son is going with him, and madame is taking the daughter to London; she got another promotion recently. It couldn't last, I always told myself. Both in the fast lane. He's up to his neck in debt. Millions invested in that bank.'

Clifford presses the key fob of his Volvo. 'Such nice people,' he says, putting his groceries on the back seat. 'So sorry to hear that.' He does a clucking sound with his tongue. 'Although, I wouldn't place much store by rumours. Someone sees a fly at the top of O'Connell Street and it's an elephant by the time it reaches the GPO.'

She isn't listening. 'He's got a job as a branch manager.'

'Anyway, I'm sure they'll be fine. Good day to you.'

Later that day, as he is leaving the village clinic, his mobile goes off. He reads the text: 'Shoot the breeze over coffee when u got a minute? Philip'.

The following Saturday morning, Doc Clifford arrives early to shoot the breeze with Philip, and spends the time walking up and down the harbour. The sky is clear, but a cold breeze is blowing in from The Sleeping Giant and whipping up newspapers and empty chip bags along the front. A planned extension to one of the café bars is now a deserted building site: steel scaffolding and wooden planks as they were when the Polish workers were given their final pay packet. The head rusting, a hammer lies on one of the wooden planks. Shoots of grass are showing on a bag of topsoil.

'Dylan will be nearer to college, at least that's one plus,' Philip tells Clifford when they meet for coffee in the only café bar open after the financial collapse. 'Heavy loss on La Salle, but that's only part of the story. We'll be lucky if we get half the purchasing price. And as for Nat Am shares – well, I could throw them in the fire. Not worth the paper they're written on.'

'Don't I know.'

'I feel so bad about that. I was the one who gave you the wrong advice.'

'I went into it with my eyes open. I'll survive, Philip.'

'Sam has a place on the Baldoyle Road for herself and Zara,' Philip continues, stirring his coffee. 'And Zara won't have to change school. Thank goodness.' Beneath the stubble, his face looks pinched. 'Doesn't mean *we're* finished though.'

'No?'

'We may get back on track. We've talked it over, but we're agreed we need breathing space.' He attempts a smile, while doing a referee's T sign. 'Nothing definite.'

'A sabbatical, you might call it. I'm glad.'

In a monotone, Philip talks while he stares the rows of bottles across the counter, or follows the movements of the staff and customers, but his gaze is inwards, and he scarcely notices any of these. 'We were reaching for something that isn't there, chasing an illusion.'

He smiles at a memory. The time he and Sam took the children to New York to see the Christmas Show at Radio City Music Hall. Then, everyone was going to New York for their Christmas shopping, and boasting about the great bargains in Saks or Macy's. 'When we had more money than cop-on.'

They had joined the long queue of people who had lined one side of Sixth Avenue. Children wrapped in scarves and woolly hats were stamping along the footpath with excitement, and to keep warm; steam was rising from manholes, and the air was filled with the great Christmas smell of roasting nuts from the street vendor across the way.

'A Hollywood version of Christmas and we were now *in* the picture – the main actors, you could say. In the foyer, we were given 3D glasses to be used when Santa came on the stage, and after the Royalettes had done their "Little Drummer Boy" piece, he arrived. We put on our glasses. He was right there in front of us, floating in his sleigh, tossing out gifts, and *Ho Ho Ho*. The effect of the 3D glasses was so funny. People – not just children – were stretching out their hands, because you'd swear you could grasp the gifts.'

Philip took off his 3D specs to see the audience snatching the air, clutching at appearances. Everyone took it in good part; they laughed and then clapped like children at the futility of their attempts.

The rueful smile fades. 'That was OK, it was fun – part of the Christmas spirit. Trouble is – we bought into the real life version: grab what was going; we were stretching for a mirage. And we couldn't see because we had the 3D glasses on. And we had

Heinrich's credit card and PIN number in our pockets – Germany was our bestie!'

He holds the cup between his hands, and grows silent. 'Do you remember that odd padre we had at the house-warming? McKeever.'

Doc Clifford laughs. 'Said we should all be digging our gardens and talking to trees: back to nature.'

'That's an act. He might seem off his trolley – far from it. And lately, especially with everything going pear-shaped – Kevin's death, the banking collapse, I wake in the night and that line of poetry he kept quoting: 'What then?' sang Plato's ghost. 'What then?' Can't get the damn thing out of my head.'

'Yeats. I looked it up.'

'We had it all. Hah, the boxes ticked …' he shakes his head. 'And it seemed to slip through … I don't know. But we may still have a chance.' He looks directly at Clifford, 'One thing I know for sure: even though Sam and I have torn strips off each other over the years, I'm not letting her go without a fight. Here's something you may find strange. I strolled around La Salle one evening; the house was silent.'

'Right.'

'I was mulling over a few things – Sam and myself, the shenanigans at Nat Am, and Kevin's dead face in the coffin. And for some reason – don't understand it – I came to realize that when I'm about to pop my clogs, it's not golf at bloody Quinta do Lago, or the Beemer, or Guilbaud lunches that will count. It's – did I ever love anyone in my whole life? Did I notice the flowers in the spring, who our children are, or what was it like to give away Zara on her wedding day?'

'A salutary reminder.'

'I'll be getting a fraction of my salary in the branch job, but I'll have time for other things – like the Tanzania project.'

Clifford pushes the cup aside. 'I admire your courage. Not many – '

'The fault lines in here were crashing against each other, Ned. And I think my heart attack,' he does inverted commas with his index fingers, 'was a smoke signal. In a way I'm lucky; it was a wake-up call.' A half-smile shows: 'Had to confront the Queen Bee also.'

'Who?'

'Sam's put-down name for the mother. The Mam got on her high horse when she heard about my decision to take the branch manager's job, and give more time to others things I want to do. This time, I had to tell her to back off.' He grinned. 'We were not amused.'

That is their last conversation, apart from the morning Clifford goes to say goodbye when Philip and Sam are keeping an eye on the removals men: one truck is bound for Philip's apartment in Donnybrook, the other for Sam's bungalow on the Baldoyle Road.

The grim sight of the two trucks destined for separate stopping places casts a gloom over Clifford's day. By mutual agreement Philip and Sam had already apportioned the contents of the house, such as furniture, pictures, silverware, cut glass and china they had used for dinner parties. Philip would take the barbecue with the extra wide grill and the small fridge at one side, so that the alcove that contained the shrine to the Sacred Heart would be empty once more. They divide the bubble-packed Knuttels, Rooneys and others they had bought at the Stephen's Green gallery. They had come to a polite agreement also about plasma screens, the Bose, the gilded mirrors and the silver-framed photos of themselves as a family.

On the surface the arrangement seems courteous and very grown-up; that is, until the act breaks down when Sam goes searching for their wedding day photos.

Surrounded by boxes in the dining room, she asks Philip.

He looks at her. 'You mean you've forgotten!'

In an instant, she remembers that dreadful night in Raheny, when Philip confessed his affair with Ellen and, in a fit of rage, she ran out and flung their wedding photos into the bin: one taken in front of University Church and another on the steps of Newman House. Her eyes fill up, she rushes out of the room and

Clifford can hear her footsteps resounding on the curved stairs.

All their precious belongings are strapped to the inside of the trucks, or packed in straw and placed in boxes. The lights from Copenhagen, Sam's 'must have', are straw-packed also and fitted into secure niches.

While the removals men are checking the straps that hold the pictures in place, a couple of Sam's school friends arrive. Resting their coffee cups on the basalt stone top of the island, the women say little and, when they speak, their voices sound hollow and strange like at a wake. Their brave efforts to be upbeat have the same effect as sympathizers at a funeral who reassure the mourners that 'she wouldn't want to linger, anyway, or be a burden; your mother was that kind of independent woman'.

By the time the Lalors leave, the last of the hard hats and high-visibility jackets have disappeared from Auburn. Estate agents' men arrive in a van and hammer a 'For Sale' sign into the hedge at the entrance to La Salle.

Polish carpenters and painters drive to Dublin Airport, abandon their nineteen-year-old cars in the long-term parking lot, and take the next flight out to Krakow. Roofless shells of houses, pallets and mounds of sand and gravel lie deserted on sites that 'provide panoramic views of Dublin Bay' and which have cost a fortune. Blue sheets of insulation that have come loose from the walls howl in the wind.

Most of those who moved in during the boom manage to hold on to their trophies, but they are anxious about the future. Some are popping Xanax to help them get a good night's sleep. They hear the economists disagreeing about the country's prospects: some are saying that the recession will be over in four or five years, others are claiming that there's worse on the way. In any case, the party is well and truly over: the coloured balloons have drooped and fallen to the ground.

After they have gone, Philip and Sam live on in Clifford's head. Their fractured dream marked by the removal of bag and baggage in separate trucks bound for different stopping places comes back to him at odd times – and it compounds the still sad music that plays faintly in his head since the death of his wife. Before he draws the curtains at night, he finds himself staring at the outline of the sad bulk across the fence, and when he closes the curtains, he paces the room, hearing in his head his wife's reprimand, when, as a young doctor, he was getting too involved in people's problems. In a half-joking way, she had once remarked to her friend: 'Off again tonight after surgery to try and fix up a marriage, and his own in shreds.'

Usually Clifford's two sons and their families visit him over the weekend, but whenever they are away or have something else on, he bring flowers to his wife's grave and goes for Sunday lunch in the Marine, where he glances through the papers.

On one such Sunday, he drives to the hotel and finds his favourite table that provides a wide view of Dublin Bay. Beyond the palm trees, a lagoon, divided from the sea by a ridge of sand, runs parallel to the back of the hotel; the blue hills of Dalkey compose a restful backdrop.

In the lounge are mostly families: mothers and fathers whose children are playing out on the lawn. Taken out for the day, feeble grandparents at the table are bent over soup; one or two metal crutches are resting against the sides of chairs. The grandparents look up from time to time with the dread in their eyes that often comes with old age.

After lunch, Clifford returns to his house, and takes the dogs for their walk around the Head. Close to the top of Cooper's Hill are three unfinished houses on plots that had been bought during the gold rush. All are in a similar state: wire meshing and plastic insulation to save on heating bills.

Though sunny, the previous night's frost still lingers in the clear air. About to go through the turnstile, he is surprised by early snowdrops: little white speckles that have pushed through dead ferns. Other clusters are scattered all over a grassy bank: their tiny heads are full of spirit in the light breeze. He takes a closer look to admire their delicate beauty, before continuing around the Head. His step becomes jaunty.

On the way back, his dogs are in a hurry. Smoke is rising from chimneys. Sunday Auburn is in repose: glancing through the newspapers or resting its eyes on The Sleeping Giant and the sloping green sward running towards the village. In his head, Clifford is already preparing his garden for spring bulbs, which he will plant before St Patrick's Day. After that – in early April – it will be time to look in on his bees for any diseases, and begin to feed them syrup. That Sunday afternoon, however, he will read, and later meet his golfing friends in Robin Hill for a nightcap.